THE WOOD

Rachel McLean writes thrillers that make your pulse race and your brain tick. Originally a self-publishing sensation, she has sold millions of copies digitally, with massive success in the UK, and a growing reach internationally. She is the author of the Dorset Crime novels and the spin-off McBride & Tanner series and Cumbria Crime series. In 2021, she won the Kindle Storyteller Award with *The Corfe Castle Murders* and her books regularly hit No 1 in the Bookstat ebook chart on launch.

Joel Hames is a Lancashire-based writer of crime fiction, and the editor of million-selling books across multiple genres. Joel's own works include the Dead North series featuring lawyer Sam Williams, and the psychological thriller *The Lies I Tell*. Most recently, he has been working with titan of crime fiction Rachel McLean on the hugely successful Cumbria Crime series.

RACHEL McLEAN

JOEL HAMES

CUMBRIA CRIME BOOK 6

THE WOOD

ACKROYD PUBLISHING

Ackroyd Publishing

ackroydpublishing.com

Printed and bound in the UK by CPI Group (Uk) Ltd, Croydon CR0 4YY

THE STORY SO FAR

Warning: this contains major spoilers for the first five books in the Cumbria Crime series. If you haven't read those, we suggest stopping right now, reading those first, and then coming back to this book.

Happy reading,
Rachel McLean and Joel Hames

The Bobby Silver Case

DS Aaron Keyes's friend Bobby Silver has been revealed as the head of the blackmail and drugs network that has been exploiting local crime boss Myron Carter's operation at the Port of Workington. But Bobby was shot dead in her home, moments before PC Harriett Barnes and DC Tom Willis arrived to arrest her, with the killers escaping in a Jeep.

The only person who could have given Carter the information that led to Bobby's death is DI Ralph Streeting. Our protagonist, DI Zoe Finch, has long suspected him of corruption, but he has powerful connections within Cumbria Police.

Meanwhile, Bobby's network lies in ruins, with co-conspirators Huz and Josh McKenzie both dead, and police officers Carrie Wright and Tel Cummings in custody, Cummings also being questioned in connection with the death of drug addict Victoria Speares.

The Ryan Tobin Connection

Tobin is an environmental activist and former employee of Jenson & Marley, one of Myron Carter's businesses. He claims to have information but has been unwilling to provide it. Lately he's been contacting Zoe, asking for her help finding his missing friend Kevin Downes.

Elena and the Warehouse

Elena, who was smuggled into Cumbria through Carter's people-trafficking network, has been staying with DC Nina Kapoor, hiding from Carter's people and trying to remember where she was held. After smelling ammonia, Elena remembered she was kept in a warehouse somewhere close to Workington's paper mill.

Other Threads

Zoe's former boss, corrupt one-time detective superintendent, David Randle, continues to phone her with unsolicited advice, showing increasing interest in Myron Carter's operations and the whereabouts of Olivia Bagsby, who went on the run after reporting that she'd seen women being brought into the port.

Zoe hasn't told her partner DI Carl Whaley about her contact with Randle; he's a professional standards officer and might not be forgiving.

Zoe continues to investigate Carter's finances, with the help of local lawyer Alistair Freeburn and forensic accountant Zhang Chen.

Harriett's role as an undercover PSD officer has finally been revealed, to Tom's horror. Nina is considering taking the sergeants' exam and applying for promotion. Kay Holinshed, the civilian worker who was sacked after accessing police information for personal reasons, has been cleared of the more significant accusation of working with organised crime. Aaron's mental health is improving following his crisis at the climax of the fourth book in the series, *The Barn*, with regular appointments with police psychiatrist Dr Filey.

And to make Zoe's life even more complicated, the Independent Office for Police Conduct is planning a full investigation into the Hub, due to multiple incidents of corrupt officers and deaths following police contact.

THE WOOD

CHAPTER ONE

"Where's the little shit gone now?" Hettie Bradshaw muttered. "Persephone! Where are you, my darling?"

Two years, she'd had the dog. Two years of puppy training and all the care a special little girl could ask for, and she still didn't understand her own damn name.

Maybe it was too complicated for a spaniel. But Hettie had had eight King Charles Cavaliers, all named after overlooked figures from Greek mythology, and Persephone was the first to struggle with recall.

Mind you, Polyhymnia had been a handful.

"Perseph—" she began, then stopped. It was raining again, but over its patter, there was another sound. Paws on the soggy remains of leaves.

The sound stopped. Hettie peered between the trunks of the bare oaks, spotting a gap in the slate wall to her right. Baysbrown Wood was full of little walls like this. Difficult for a dog to get too far when it was hemmed in.

The sound had come from that direction.

"Persephone!" she called again.

Nothing. She shook her head and approached the wall. Hundreds of years old, but now a chunk of it had fallen in, and there was nothing between her dog and the tunnel entrances to the old slate mines.

Maybe naming her after the Queen of the Underworld hadn't been one of Hettie's brightest ideas.

But if the stupid thing had gone in there, she could bloody well get herself out again.

Hettie stepped through the gap, angling her feet to avoid slipping on the wet rock, and bent to catch her breath.

She was too old for this. Too old to go running around after stupid spaniels who didn't know their own names. Light-headed, she closed her eyes, reaching out for support and finding the cold but reassuring wall beside her.

She breathed. In for two, out for four. In for two, out for four. Six times.

When she opened her eyes, Persephone was standing there, looking up at her like she was waiting for something. Hettie narrowed her eyes and frowned, but she couldn't keep it up for long. And it wasn't like the dog even noticed.

"Who's a beautiful girl, then?"

The dog seemed to grin at her, tongue lolling long, yellow, and green from her mouth. Hettie reached for a stick and began to straighten, then stopped.

Yellow and green?

She bent again and checked the dog's mouth.

Not a tongue. A strip of fabric.

"What have you got there, girl?" She could have sworn the dog nodded at her. Hettie reached for it, but the dog turned and trotted away.

"Where are you—" What was the point? Sighing, she

walked after the dog, gently downhill and along the wall. That was good. They weren't heading towards the slate tunnels, and she could grab the wall if she felt she was about to fall.

The dog kept going, stopping every few seconds, and looking back to make sure she was following. Behind her, mounds of slate from the old quarry poked above the bare branches. Beyond, the hills rose red-brown behind Chapel Stile and the Church of the Holy Trinity, dressed in that same dark slate.

And the dog pressed on.

"Bloody thing," Hettie muttered. If this continued much longer, she'd need her more serious arsenal of curses. But for all her faults, Persephone was a gorgeous girl.

Hettie paused. The ground ahead was disturbed. Churned up. For weeks, it had been either snowing or raining, but this looked like the work of something different.

"Bloody animals," she muttered, and continued.

After another minute the dog stopped, a few yards ahead, still close to the wall. They were deep into the heart of the wood now, a fair distance from the paths. Even the quarry was out of sight.

The dog was looking down at something on the ground, then back up at Hettie.

"I'm coming," Hettie grumbled, and walked over. There was something there. Something long and blue, and then – was that snow? Surely the snow had all disappeared by now? Whatever it was, there was a gap in it, a patch of darkness, and on that those same shades of yellow and green she'd seen in Persephone's mouth. Yellow and green, and red and blue, as well.

A rainbow. It was a rainbow.

"What is it, then?" she asked, stepping closer, the words almost sticking in her mouth.

She knew what it was.

She took another step, to be sure, and stopped.

Long and blue. That was a leg. A pair of them, in jeans. What she had thought was snow was an expensive-looking coat. The black thing was a t-shirt, with a design she thought she'd seen before. All of it was torn and muddy.

And all of it around the body of a man lying on his back, her dog's tongue slurping at his equally torn and muddy face.

Backing away, one arm on the wall, Hettie reached into her coat pocket and pulled out her phone.

CHAPTER TWO

"Ta-da." Stella Berry stepped aside. Where she'd been standing, there was a hole in the wall.

"That wasn't there before," DI Zoe Finch observed.

"Not much gets past you." The crime scene manager's smile showed under her mask. "False section in the wall. You wouldn't notice it at all, or if you did, you'd think it was just an old chimney breast or something. Unless..."

"Unless what?"

"Unless you were a grade-A genius." She gave Zoe a *like me* look. "Now look at this."

Zoe leaned forward as Stella reached into the hole. Inside were two metal plates that slid apart, revealing a safe. Stella reached in again and fiddled with something, and the door to the safe sprang open.

"Bloody hell," Zoe said, peering inside. "How much?"

"Hundred and forty grand. Not a bad gig, working at the port."

"Tell that to the dead woman."

Stella nodded.

The dead woman was Bobby Silver. She'd worked at the Port of Workington, but that probably wasn't where she'd picked up a hundred and forty thousand pounds in cash. Zoe couldn't prove any of it, but she was certain the money had come from Bobby's other operation. The one where she found out which dealers were taking the drugs she unloaded at the port, told her friends in the police, got those dealers busted, and resold the drugs elsewhere.

"Wipe your feet," said a voice from behind them.

It was the parrot. The same parrot that had been instructing Zoe to wipe her feet, or bugger off, since she'd entered the house. Stella's team had confined the bird to its cage, but now it just sat there, insulting people.

There had been a dog, too, but that had already been taken in by a local kennel. Someone on Stella's team was trying to sort out accommodation for the parrot.

"Anything else?" Zoe asked.

"Nothing much," Stella replied. "Handful of burners, but it doesn't look like they've been used yet. We're taking everything away to be looked at."

"Good." Zoe nodded. She might have reminded Stella how urgent all this was, how everything had to be offsite and analysed for forensic evidence as soon as possible. But Stella knew all that.

Bobby had died because someone in the police had found out who she was, and got to her mere minutes before Zoe's team arrived to pick her up. Someone in the police, but working for the man running the biggest organised crime operation in Cumbria, right under their noses at the Port of Workington.

That man was Myron Carter, and the copper in his pocket was DI Ralph Streeting, whose remit, conveniently for him, included organised crime. Right now, this was Zoe's murder investigation. But Ralph Streeting had more influence than she was comfortable with. He could interfere.

Hence the urgency.

Get the evidence away. Somewhere safe. Somewhere Streeting couldn't get to it.

"For fuck's sake," Zoe heard. She turned to see two figures in forensic suits manoeuvring a chest of drawers through the bend in the stairs. "Watch where you shove that bloody thing."

Keisha was here, then. Zoe had seen Caroline Deane upstairs. And a whole bunch more of them. Everyone Stella trusted, all her team and more, gathering evidence. There were two vans outside, already half-loaded with furniture, clothing, laptops, door handles. Cars were coming and going, between the lab, the house, the little operations centre they'd set up in Mrs Gillespie's shop a couple of miles away, and wherever the evidence was being taken. Even now, another one was arriving, a little Nissan pulling up alongside the yellow Honda that had once belonged to Bobby Silver.

If the killers had left anything behind, Stella would find it. And Zoe would be ready to move.

She watched as Keisha and her colleague carried the chest of drawers through the huge doorway to one of the vans.

"Bloody freezing," Stella observed.

Zoe couldn't disagree. It had only just stopped snowing, and the wind was the kind she still wasn't used to. But there was too much stuff to shift. If they kept opening and closing the doors, they'd damage evidence. And it would take too long.

"Who the hell are you?" said a voice, and Zoe turned. A

woman had emerged from the Nissan and was staring at the vans, at Keisha and her colleague, at all the chaos.

Not a member of Stella's team, then. A civilian.

Shit.

Zoe ran outside, ignoring the cold seeping through her paper-thin suit. She reached the woman before Keisha could reply.

Keisha wasn't known for being diplomatic.

Ten minutes later, Zoe was sitting with the woman in the back room of Mrs Gillespie's shop. The woman was Stacey, a name Aaron had mentioned. DS Aaron Keyes had been a friend of Bobby Silver's, without knowing a thing about her little side gig.

"Here's your tea," said Mrs Gillespie, shoving a cup down on the table beside Stacey. She hadn't offered Zoe anything, and from the look of the grey liquid sloshing around, Zoe was grateful.

Stacey stared at the cup for a moment before lifting it to her lips, sipping, and putting it down again.

"I don't understand," she said for the fourth time. Either she was a very good actor, or she was genuinely shocked by Bobby's death. "I only popped round because she hadn't come in for her shift. But why would anyone kill Bobby?"

Stacey had worked with Bobby at the port, but that didn't mean anything. Most of the people working at the port spent their time unloading timber or helping with the maintenance of offshore wind farms, the legitimate business that masked all the drugs and weapons and people-smuggling Myron Carter made his real money from.

"I'm so sorry," said Zoe again, watching the woman carefully.

Were those tears? They looked like tears.

Stacey frowned. "What's happened to Taylor?"

"Who's Taylor?" Zoe replied. There hadn't been anyone else in the house. No sign of anyone else living there, either.

"The dog," Stacey explained. "Long-haired dachshund. And there's Freddie. The parrot."

"Oh yes," Zoe said. "We know all about the parrot."

CHAPTER THREE

"Tonight?" DC Nina Kapoor asked.

"This evening," said the man at the end of the phone. "Seven. Not late. We like our beauty sleep at the NCA."

"You need it."

He chuckled.

Nina had spent most of the day on the phone with Ellis Wood from the National Crime Agency's Modern Slavery and Human Trafficking Unit. Two days earlier, she'd arrested a killer at the Bassenthwaite Manor Hotel, and now there was another murder investigation: the Bobby Silver case. She was itching to get back to some proper police work.

But this was important. This was something Nina had been working towards for too long. She owed it to Elena to be there, after the long months the two of them had spent trying to figure out where Elena had been held after she'd been trafficked to the UK. Finally, they'd got it.

The smell of ammonia. A paper mill. A map. They'd identified a likely warehouse and watched it. They were as convinced as they could be that this was the place. There had been other women, too. Other women who'd been trafficked, before and since.

DI Finch had photos of them being unloaded. They could be there even now.

And tonight, that warehouse would be raided by the Ops team from Cumbria Police, supported by CID and the NCA's specialists.

If this worked out...

Nina grinned, then turned and caught the eye of Harriett Barnes, who looked away.

Harriett Barnes. Tom was on his way back from Bobby Silver's house, and Aaron was in the boss's office sorting out paperwork from the McKenzie case. So it was just Nina and Harriett.

Not PC Harriett Barnes, as she'd claimed to be, but DC Harriett Barnes of the Professional Standards Division. DC Harriett Barnes, who'd lied to them about who she was. Who'd sniffed around and pretended to care about her colleagues when all the time she was just looking for more dirty cops.

"What are you looking at?" Nina asked.

Harriett ignored her.

Nina understood the need for PSD. Hell, the boss's partner, DI Whaley, was PSD. He was Harriett's boss, in fact. But Nina had worked with Harriett. She'd trusted Harriett.

The phone rang again. Border Force wanted to get involved now. People trafficking was part of their remit.

Fine. The more the merrier. If this worked out, they wouldn't just be freeing these women. They might finally put Myron Carter and Ralph Streeting away.

Nina could hear Harriett Barnes talking in the background, on the phone herself. She raised her own voice.

"What's that?" she asked.

"Accommodation," said the woman from Border Force. "If we do find anyone, where are they going to stay?"

"It's sorted." Nina had been onto the local authority first thing. Ops, NCA, Border Force, Local Authority. Translators, too. So many moving parts. Any other time, the admin of it all would have killed her.

But this was important.

She ended her call, glared at Harriett, and picked up the phone again.

DI Finch answered on the first ring.

"What's Harriett Barnes doing here, boss?" Nina said.

"Eh?"

There were voices in the background. Nina recognised Keisha, complaining. Stella, too. Tearing a strip off somebody.

"Harriett Barnes, boss. She's still here. In our team room. Sitting at Kay's desk. She's PSD. Why isn't she back with them?"

"Listen." DI Finch sighed. "You need to focus on your own work. Is this raid happening?"

"Tonight."

"Good. Listen, if you're going to sit the sergeants' exam, if you're going to prove you can be a DS, you need to be a bit more understanding, Nina."

Understanding? Nina bit back a retort.

"Harriett's helping us with the Bobby Silver case."

"We don't need her help—"

"And you need to cut her some slack, Nina. I know you don't like it, but Harriett was doing her job."

"Yeah, fine. Sorry to bother you, boss."

Nina hung up, muttering to herself.

Harriett finally turned to face her. "What was that you just said?"

Nina eyed her. "Just following orders."

Harriett looked like she'd been slapped.

Nina felt the thrill of victory. But only for a moment. After that, all she felt was guilt.

She turned back to her phone and dialled the number for the translators.

CHAPTER FOUR

Zoe headed for her office, dialling a familiar number.

Usually, she'd stop by the team room. Pass on what she'd found out, learn what everyone else had. But there would be time for that. And the atmosphere in that room... she'd felt it down the phone. She'd have to resolve it, which didn't start with Nina, but with Carl.

"DI Whaley," he said. "Oh, it's you."

She raised an eyebrow. "Not the most romantic of greetings."

"Sorry. I'm a bit..."

"Yeah. Busy. Tell me about it."

"Well, we've got a couple—"

"Christ, Carl, I didn't mean literally. And not now, either. Neither of us have time for that. Listen, I need to talk to you about Harriett."

There was a pause. She could imagine his shoulders tensing, the same way she'd known Nina's jaw was set when they'd spoken earlier. She'd asked him time and time again if he had anyone undercover at the Hub. He'd refused to answer.

Now she knew.

"It's OK," she said. "I'm not calling to shout at you."

"Good," he replied, his voice tense.

"Harriett is in our team room now. She's part of your team, she's been working here, and her cover's blown."

"You want her out?"

She took a moment. It would make things easier, wouldn't it?

But Harriett Barnes was a good copper. She couldn't let her go that easily.

"It was Harriett who found Bobby Silver's body," she said. "Harriett chased the killer's Jeep through the snow. Harriett searched the house."

"With DC Willis," Carl reminded her.

"With Tom, yes. But the point is, Harriett's already working this case. For whatever reason, it seems to have just happened. And I..."

She waited.

"You want to keep her there?" Carl asked, surprise in his voice.

"I could do with her help, yes."

"Fine," Carl replied after a moment. "I'll need her back eventually. But for the time being, she's yours. I'll clear it with Branthwaite."

"Thanks, Carl."

Zoe was about to head over to the team room when her phone rang.

"Zoe? You downstairs?"

"Hi, Fiona," she replied. "Yes."

"I need you to pop up."

Superintendent Fiona Kendrick was in one of her impatient moods. No sign of Luke, her ash-pale assistant. No offer of coffee. Even the invitation to sit was just a gesture towards a chair.

"They're coming in soon. Maybe tomorrow. I don't know."

Fiona was standing, facing the window. Looking out at dark clouds and traffic.

"Who?" Zoe asked, although she thought she knew.

"Who do you think?"

Fiona turned and sat down opposite Zoe. There were dark rings around the super's eyes, and a helplessness in her expression Zoe hadn't seen before.

"IOPC," Zoe replied. "That's quick."

"They're worried, Zoe. And so am I."

The Independent Office for Police Conduct had initially been called in to investigate the death of Victoria Speares, a drug addict who'd seriously assaulted a police officer before being found by another officer. She'd choked to death on her own vomit. The contact with the police was enough to warrant an investigation, but there was more to it than just "contact."

It had been PC Cummings who'd found Victoria Speares. Tel Cummings, who, it turned out, had been part of Bobby Silver's drugs operation. And, he'd subsequently admitted, he'd "helped the junkie along." Turned her onto her back and watched her choke.

Tel Cummings being a nasty piece of work had come as no surprise. Tel Cummings being corrupt shouldn't have made any jaws drop.

But letting someone die like that?

The whole station would be getting looked into. The people. The culture. The leadership.

No wonder Fiona was looking rough.

"They'll be wanting to talk to you," Fiona said. "And your team. And it wouldn't surprise me if the investigation broadened out."

Zoe frowned. "Broadened out where?"

"Huz."

Huz. Hussein Mahmoud. Part of Stella's team, and another link in Bobby Silver's operation. He'd been questioned, then released and murdered by one of the dealers Cummings and Bobby Silver were ripping off.

Another death following police contact. Zoe was surprised Fiona didn't look even worse than she did.

"You can count on me," she said, unsure what she meant.

"I can count on you to tell the truth, Zoe. I don't want anything else. That, and, if you don't mind, catching the bugger who killed your Bobby Silver. If it's not too much to ask."

"I—" Zoe began, but Fiona held up a hand.

"It's all linked. Her murder, Vicky Speares, Huz. Even your McKenzie. And there's another link, too. I don't like unsolved murders. The IOPC doesn't like unsolved murders. You sort this one out, you'll make everyone happy. Understood?"

CHAPTER FIVE

"Is something wrong?" Aaron asked.

Nina was muttering again. When he'd entered the room, she'd been hammering away on her keyboard as if it had insulted Elvis. And while Nina being angry was nothing new, normally he knew why.

"It's nothing." She went back to her keyboard.

He glanced at Harriett Barnes, who was sitting at Kay's desk – the spare desk, he reminded himself. Harriett wouldn't meet his eyes.

Fine. He had more than enough to do without worrying about Nina's moods.

Most of all, he had to get to grips with Bobby Silver.

It had been two days. Two days since he'd learned that someone he knew – not well, but well enough to have a drink with – was a drug dealer. Was the mastermind behind an operation involving at least two corrupt police officers and a CSI. He'd only come across Bobby as a friend of Victor Parlick, another Port employee who'd been murdered by Carter and Streeting, not that Aaron could prove it. Bobby and Aaron had toasted him, with Stacey and Miles, more of Victor's friends.

Were they all bent? Was being honest the exception rather than the rule?

If this had happened a few months ago, at the height of Aaron's struggles with his guilt, his mental health, the crisis in his relationship with Serge, it might have been too much. But for this Aaron, for the new Aaron, it was all in a day's work. He hoped.

Bobby was dead. The more he learned about her, the better chance they had of finding her killer.

But Bobby Silver was a closed box. She'd cast barely a ripple on the internet and social media. She didn't appear on the PNC. She paid her taxes, her utility bills, her TV license.

He dialled the boss, who answered immediately.

"Aaron? I'm on my way downstairs. Need to get prepped for this raid."

"You're going?"

"I owe it to Elena. Nina wants to be there too. And Tom. You sure we can't tempt you?"

"You need me?"

"They don't *need* any of us. I'm worried we'll get in the way. But if you want to come..."

"It's OK, boss. But I was wondering about Carrie Wright."

"Carrie Wright? Sorry, Aaron, you're not going to get any joy there."

"I thought she might have known Bobby."

Carrie Wright was a corrupt former officer, now on remand on the other side of the country. Aaron had never heard of any connection between her and Bobby, but it was worth a punt.

"Sorry, Aaron," the boss said. "I don't think she knew Bobby. Don't think she knew anyone except Huz and McKenzie. But even if she did, she's not talking."

"Why not?"

"She's heard about Bobby's death. Figured it was safer to stay silent."

Aaron couldn't blame her. It was bad enough being a bent cop who'd been caught, even worse that most of her fellow inmates knew it.

No sooner had he ended his call and told Nina to go and meet the boss downstairs than his phone rang. An unknown number.

"DS Keyes."

"Aaron? That you?"

The voice was familiar. "Who's this?"

"It's Miles."

Aaron felt his shoulders slump. "I'm sorry," he said. Not much, for someone whose friend had just been murdered, but it was all he could think of.

"So it's true?" Miles asked. "I didn't know if maybe Stacey had lost the plot."

"It's true. And for what it's worth, I really am—"

"Save it," Miles said. "Dangerous being friends with you, Aaron Keyes."

Victor Parlick. Bobby Silver. Aaron couldn't argue with that.

"I've spoken to Stacey," Miles said. "We're taking Freddie and Taylor in."

"Freddie and Taylor?"

"Christ, you really didn't know her at all, did you? The bird and the dog. Bobby's pets. She wouldn't have wanted them going to strangers. I don't much fancy the bird, mind, but I reckon I can talk Stacey round on that one."

"Er, thank you," Aaron replied, at a loss for words.

"Be seeing you," said Miles, and ended the call.

Aaron stared at the phone. When he looked up, Harriett Barnes was watching him, concern on her face.

She knew. They all knew. Aaron Keyes and his nervous breakdown.

But that was the old Aaron.

The new Aaron? No problem.

Although it wouldn't hurt to schedule an appointment with the police psychiatrist. Dr Filey had insisted he could see her whenever he wanted. He didn't need to see her. But it was the sensible thing to do.

Later. In the meantime, he had work to do.

Bobby Silver. Her past. Her secrets. No one could run that sort of operation and stay completely under the radar.

He'd find something, sooner or later. And then he'd set up an appointment with Dr Filey.

But it looked like staying completely under the radar was precisely what Bobby Silver had done. There was nothing. When Aaron's phone rang twenty minutes later, he snatched it up like a hungry man reaching for the last chip.

"Aaron?"

"Oh." He was surprised. "DS Gaskill. How are you?"

"Call me Denise, will you?"

Would he? Denise Gaskill had always made Aaron uncomfortable. Part of that was her being PSD. But part of it was her being Denise Gaskill. Something hard and unapproachable.

But then, they'd worked together.

What did she want now?

"Listen," she said. "Do you mind popping upstairs?"

"Upstairs?"

"Sixth floor. You know the spot."

He certainly did, and not in a good way.

"The custody suite? Where you question the bent cops?"

She laughed, but it didn't ease the knot that had formed in his stomach.

"Just a quiet chat, Aaron. Nothing to worry about. Any time in the next couple of hours. OK?"

"OK," he said, but she'd already hung up.

CHAPTER SIX

JESUS CHRIST.

Tom looked around the room. He tried to make it look casual.

Who were all these people?

He knew Nina and the boss, but even they were different. It wasn't just the gear, the black, the protective vests. They took it all in their stride. Like they'd done this before.

Maybe the boss *had* done all this before, but Nina hadn't. She'd have said. She'd have boasted about it.

Weapons. Order of entry. Radio silence. Codes. All of them through his head and out the other side before he had the chance to say a word.

He recognised one of the women from ops, Sharon something. He'd seen her in the canteen looking normal, chatting with her colleagues, drinking Coke and eating crisps. Now she looked like she'd stepped out of a sci-fi movie, moving like the equipment was part of her, talking in a language he could barely understand. She had three colleagues with her. He'd been introduced, but he couldn't remember their names.

Two men and a woman from the NCA stood in a corner, talking quietly. They'd nodded along to the briefing. He couldn't remember their names either, but he'd probably never see them again. Border Force had an observer, a woman so tall she made the five-foot-eight DI Finch look short. She'd joked about her own height and role: "I'll just stand in the car park and report back what I see." There was one translator and someone from the local authority, a woman in her forties who looked bored by the whole thing.

"You ready?" the boss asked.

Tom nodded. He wasn't ready. He was Tom Willis, for God's sake.

They all stood and moved towards the door. What had he missed? Nothing important, he hoped.

Now they were through the door, making for the rear exit. Dedicated vehicles. Would he be expected to drive?

No. Dedicated vehicles with their own dedicated drivers. Everything taken care of.

"You OK?" asked Nina, eyeing him.

He tried to smile. "No," he said. "Not really."

She returned the smile. They'd stopped now. Waiting to load up.

"Nor me," she said.

"Really? Could have fooled me."

She raised an eyebrow. "It's an act. And remember what Silver Command told us at the start?"

Tom frowned. Silver was a man in his forties, dark hair, green eyes, a face that looked like it had seen more trouble than some whole countries. He'd singled them out, him, Nina, and the boss.

What had he said?

"You three," Nina said, in a passable imitation of the

man's voice. "I don't want you screwing things up. You do nothing. You say nothing. You act like you're not there. That's it.' Reckon you can manage that, Tom?"

He nodded. He could do that.

They got in one of three minibuses, darkened windows, moving smoothly onto the road.

Heading north.

A thrill of excitement shot through him, and he remembered why he'd volunteered for this.

Bring it on, he thought. *Bring the bastards on.*

CHAPTER SEVEN

"THIS IS A BIG STEP UP. You're aware of that, yes?"

DI Woolley stared at DC Lynn Hedley until Lynn nodded.

The DI grunted. "Isaac. What have you got for us?"

Lynn turned to see DS Isaac Bateman climb to his feet. He'd turned up late that morning, had a late breakfast of a bacon roll and two bags of bacon-flavoured crisps, and even now, hours later, she could smell the alcohol radiating from his pores.

"Looks like a murder, Guv. Looks like a murder, smells like a murder, sounds like a murder."

Bateman sat back down, grunting.

"Very good, Isaac," said DI Woolley.

Lynn blinked.

Very good? He hadn't told them anything. Was this the sarge's idea of a briefing?

"DC Hedley," said the boss. "What can you tell us?"

Lynn hadn't expected to be doing this, but since no one else was...

"Body found in the woods this morning, Ma'am." She hadn't got used to "Guv." Didn't feel it worked with DI Woolley. "Dog walker, name of Hettie Bradshaw."

"The body?" asked DI Woolley.

Lynn blinked. "The woman who found the body, Ma'am. Walking her dog."

The DI nodded. "Go on."

"Uniform attended, found the body of a man thought to be in his twenties or early thirties."

"Any sign of foul play?"

"Still being looked at, Ma'am. Body should be at the West Cumberland Hospital now."

"Right," said DI Woolley. "Why there?"

"Carlisle said they were too busy. A pathologist..." Lynn glanced down at her notes. "Dr Robertson said he could look at it in Whitehaven."

"Right," said the DI. "What else?"

"No obvious cause of death, but the body's been through the mill. Signs of disturbance by animals, Ma'am."

"What sort of signs?"

"Damage to the face." Lynn had seen it herself. She'd attended the site when PC Henniker had called it in. The sarge hadn't been in yet, and DI Woolley had insisted she was busy, so Lynn had attended the crime scene herself, where she'd taken a statement from the dog walker and arranged for the body to be taken away as soon as Forensics released it.

"Do we know who the dead man is?" asked DI Woolley.

Lynn opened her mouth to speak.

"Not a clue," said DS Bateman. "No ID on the body."

What?

DS Aaron Keyes had been in a week or so back. From

Whitehaven. He'd asked about a missing protestor. Kevin Downes. The sarge had dismissed it all then, but Lynn had told DS Keyes she'd keep an eye out.

It was true that there was no ID on the body. Maybe the sarge had already looked up Aaron's missing man. Maybe their corpse wasn't Kevin Downes. But she'd take a look herself, as soon as she got a chance. There was a photo somewhere.

"Right," said DI Woolley. "You both know what to do, yes?" She turned and walked into her office, leaving Lynn staring after her.

She was still staring when the DI reappeared a moment later.

"The scene. Who's looking at the scene?"

The sarge turned to look at her, like it was her responsibility. She stood up.

"I've had it cordoned off," she said. "Uniform have been keeping an eye, but CSI should be there by now."

"Right," said DI Woolley. "I... Hold on."

She walked away, back to her office, and was back again before Lynn had the chance to sit down.

The DI eyed them. "I've got... The procedure. The processes. We need to make sure we do everything by the book. You're unsure about anything, you ask me. OK?"

"OK," said the sarge.

DI Woolley walked away again.

Unsure about anything? Was there anything they weren't unsure about? Lynn didn't know when DI Woolley had last investigated a murder. Things had probably changed since then.

DI Woolley was right about one thing. This was a big

step up. And none of them seemed to have the faintest idea what to do.

None of them except Lynn. She knew there was a photo of the missing protestor. DS Keyes had mentioned it last time they'd spoken. He hadn't got around to sending it over – caught up in two different murder investigations that side of the county, last she'd heard. Best give him a ring.

She reached for her phone and sensed the presence behind her before the shadow fell over her desk.

"What you doing?" asked DS Bateman.

"Just making a call," she replied, as casually as she could.

"Who?"

Sod it. He'd find out eventually.

Lynn turned. "DS Keyes. At the Hub. I wanted to check whether—"

"I don't think so," said Bateman.

"But I think—"

"Last time I checked, I was your senior officer, so what I think is more important than what you think, Lynn."

"I just—"

"Do we need to have another conversation about exceeding your authority and why that's a bad idea?" he asked. There was menace in his voice, but the last time they'd had one of those conversations, the problem had been boredom more than anything else.

She swallowed.

"Do we?" he said.

"No."

"Good. Get on to CSI, find out what the fuck's going on. I want the body removed and the scene cleaner than a nun's knickers."

"OK," she said, and returned to her screen. She'd already been on to CSI three times. She had the feeling they were starting to get sick of her.

But at least they didn't have to deal with Bateman.

CHAPTER EIGHT

NINA FOUND herself holding her breath as they parked, a hundred yards from the target, lights off, engines dead, sliding into the darkness.

They weren't even allowed to close the doors. That would be done later, when it was all over. They assembled in the prearranged order. Ops. NCA. Then the boss, Nina, and Tom. Local authority and the translator hanging back.

Radio silence.

Complete silence.

The building was dark as they approached. Had they got it all wrong?

Then she heard the shriek of an engine, somewhere distant. No. Somewhere close by, for a few seconds, then further away, then distant.

Shit.

There was brief chaos. Shouts: "Police!" "Step away from the doors! Police!"

Then the doors were open, Nina was following the NCA

people in, and the shouting had subsided to a murmur. That was it.

Too late. They were too late.

No, they weren't.

Four women were at the far end of a cavernous space, all of them blinking in the torchlight, hands out shielding their eyes.

"Who are you?" barked the woman from Ops, Sharon. But Nina knew who they were. They all knew. One of the NCA men whispered in Sharon's ear, and she nodded.

"Stand down," said Silver Command.

It was all over. No arrests. Four women there, but no arrests.

Four women had been saved. Was it wrong that Nina felt disappointed?

There was an odd noise behind her. She whirled around, but it was just Tom, his hands on his knees, panting.

"You OK?" she asked.

"Yeah. Will be. Just... It was all a bit much."

It was difficult to believe this was the same man who'd been taken hostage at gunpoint a year ago and then gone down a mineshaft to arrest the woman who'd done it.

The NCA people were speaking into their radios, and the translator and the woman from the local authority appeared. The women seemed to have separated, clinging together in two groups of two. There were two women in their late twenties, both blonde, pretty, terrified. The other pair consisted of another young blonde woman and an older one, with hair dyed red and a toughness in her face and body that said she'd been through worse than this, with a look more of resignation than fear.

The translator was trying to speak with them. Her words

were met with shrugs from all four. She turned to the boss, who hadn't said a word so far.

"I've tried Polish and Hungarian."

DI Finch nodded. "Got anything else up your sleeve?"

"You bet." She turned back to the group.

This time, the older woman stepped forward, her eyes widening a little as she heard the words.

Then she smiled and said something back to the translator. Her voice was hoarse, and the words came slowly, but the translator nodded as she heard them, and for a few moments there were the beginnings of an actual conversation.

The translator turned back to DI Finch.

"We're speaking Ukrainian, but she's from Belarus. My Belarusian isn't that hot, but I can switch to Russian. Reckon we'll have more luck there."

"What did she say?" asked Nina.

"'Thank you,'" she replied. "She said, 'Thank you.'"

CHAPTER NINE

"THERE'S NO ONE WATCHING, is there?" Aaron asked as he and Denise Gaskill sat down, glancing at the camera.

She laughed. "There isn't."

He hadn't been joking.

But it was fine because Aaron had nothing to hide. Denise – yes, he was getting used to calling her Denise – just wanted to run through his relationship with Bobby Silver. How they'd met. How often. What she'd told him. What he'd told her.

That wasn't easy, given that he'd told her all about Josh McKenzie's death, sitting in the pub with her and her friends, unaware that McKenzie was on Bobby's payroll.

"And you didn't know this at the time?" Denise asked.

He shook his head. "Absolutely not. I... Look, as far as I was concerned, Bobby was clean."

"Even though she worked at the Port?"

"Even though she worked at the Port."

"And you knew her through Victor Parlick, is that right?"

He nodded and closed his eyes for a moment. "Yes."

"And Victor Parlick was someone you were cultivating as a potential source?"

"Yes." Aaron pulled at the collar of his shirt.

"So you believed Victor to be involved in criminal activity?"

"Well..." He frowned. "It's not that simple. I don't think Victor was dodgy. I just think he knew where a few bodies were buried." He saw the look on DS Gaskill's face and added, "Not literally."

"Understood. So if he was involved, it would have been very much on the periphery."

Was that what he'd meant? It was close enough. He nodded.

"And Bobby Silver, then. She was his friend. She could have been on the periphery, too."

"I suppose so." He hadn't imagined her being involved in any way. It just hadn't seemed likely. "I didn't think so at the time. But yes. It would have been a reasonable assumption."

They went on for a few more minutes before she nodded, smiled, and told him they were done.

"Done?"

"Look, Aaron, this is all very unfortunate. Of course it is. But looking through everything you've told me, I don't see how you could have known or even suspected Bobby Silver was involved in serious crime, much less the mastermind behind the whole thing. I'm going to recommend we leave this here, on file, no charges to answer, no questions about conduct or competence."

Aaron gave a long, low sigh. He wasn't an idiot. This was how good interviewers worked. Relax you. Then pounce.

Denise Gaskill hadn't pounced.

"Thank you," he said. "You've made this much easier than I expected."

Her smile didn't shift. "Look, I'm not blind, Aaron. I know you've been through a lot. In fact, it's my job to know."

"How so?"

"Officers with mental health issues might be more susceptible to... Well, it doesn't matter. It doesn't apply to you."

He nodded, then stopped.

"Hang on. Is that why you've gone easy on me? Because I'm through that. I don't need any special treatment."

"If I thought you were bent, you'd have had no special treatment from me, DS Keyes."

He believed her. He stood up to leave.

She spoke again. "But I'm glad you're through it."

He sat back down. "What do you want to know?"

She was frowning now. "What do you mean?"

"Are you just being nosy, or is this a professional matter?"

She laughed, and he found himself laughing with her.

"Neither, as it happens. I think you're clean, and I don't think your mental health is my business. But I've worked with you enough to think of you as..."

He waited, spotting her discomfort.

"As a good person, Aaron. A good cop, and a good person."

"Really?" He stared at her.

She nodded. "Really. So, yeah, I care about your mental health. But not in a nosy way. I'm not—"

He held out a hand to stop her.

"Things were hard," he said. "It impacted my personal life, and my ability to do the job. But I got help – I'm OK now."

"I'm so pleased," she said as he finally stood.

"Thank you."

"There's just one more thing." She gestured to him to sit back down.

And then she pounced.

"Certain information has come to light."

"What information?"

Her smile had dropped. "Information that you accepted a free meal from a potential witness during the Kate Bellamy investigation."

"The Kate Bellamy investigation?" He frowned.

She consulted her notes. "Yes. That's right. At the King George's Dining Rooms."

"Oh."

She raised one eyebrow. "Oh?"

"I can explain everything."

He told her what had happened. How he'd been trying to speak to Theodora Harding, the chef there, for days. How she'd refused. How Serge had taken him to the restaurant for their anniversary dinner, something he'd had no knowledge of at all.

"It was a surprise," he explained. "But she thought I was there to give her more grief. She told me I was harassing her. When I pointed to Serge and said it was my anniversary, she was mortified. I think the free meal thing was an apology. I certainly wasn't expecting it."

Denise nodded. "I get it. But you can see where you went wrong, can't you?"

He could, now. It had been an oversight. Too much drink. Too much fun.

"It was a mistake. I shouldn't have accepted it. She might

have ended up being a material witness. It wouldn't have looked right."

"Good." Denise nodded. "You can go."

"Is that it?"

"You want me to write you up?"

"Er..."

"Want me to tell my boss, DI Whaley, who'll no doubt tell his partner, your boss, DI Finch?"

"Er, no?"

"Thought not. A mistake, as you say. Lessons learned. No need to follow it up."

Not so much a pounce, then. More a friendly mauling.

He switched his phone back on as he waited for the lift. Two missed calls. From Lynn Hedley, over at Elterwater. He was about to call her back when a message came through.

A message from Lynn. With a photo attached.

We've found a body in the woods near the quarry. Wondering if it's the man you've been looking for. I can't send a proper photo, for obvious reasons, but does this ring a bell?

It was a close-up, but it was enough.

Ryan Tobin had sent the boss a photo of his missing friend, Kevin Downes, and the boss had passed it on to Aaron. In that photo, Kevin Downes had been wearing some pretty distinctive clothing.

Aaron peered at the image on his phone. It showed the central section of what he assumed was the body of the dead man.

The blue jeans could be anyone's. But the white Canada Goose parka, that was more unusual.

And paired with the Dark Side of the Moon t-shirt , it was looking very much like Kevin Downes had finally turned up.

CHAPTER TEN

"IS SOMETHING WRONG?"

Zoe approached the translator, who stood back. The Ops team were outside the building, keeping an eye on things. The NCA had gone home, disappointed.

Nina seemed disappointed too. Tom was shell-shocked. But Zoe was pleased.

It would have been good to catch one of the traffickers. It had probably been them leaving as the raiding team arrived. And there'd been more than four women in the building.

But four was better than nothing. For these four, it might be everything.

Only now, one of them was shouting.

It was the younger one, the blonde who'd seemed close to the older redhead. She was shouting at that woman. Zoe couldn't tell if it was anger or fear.

"What's she saying?" she asked.

The translator shrugged. "Beats me. Belarusian, I think. It has features in common with—"

"It's OK. If you can figure any of it out, let me know."

Zoe stepped away, outside the building and past the Ops team. The woman from the local authority took the last few drags on a menthol cigarette.

"Can you look after them?" Zoe asked.

The woman shrugged. "I can put a roof over their heads. For the next few nights, at least. But I can't guarantee they'll stay there."

"You think they'll run?"

The woman dropped her cigarette, ground it out with her heel, and looked up at Zoe. "Not gonna arrest me for that, are you?"

Zoe shook her head.

"Look, fact is, they came here for a reason, didn't they? They were lied to, didn't get what they wanted, but now they're here, and they're free. It'll take them a couple of days to figure out where they are, what they can do. After that... Some of them stay. But most of them..."

She turned and walked back into the building.

Zoe pulled her phone from her pocket.

"What do you want now?" said Stella, picking up almost immediately.

"Wondering if you could take a look at another scene for me," Zoe said. "We've just raided a warehouse where—"

"Anyone dead?"

"Not that I can—"

"Listen, Zoe, I'm sorry, but you've asked me to put everyone on the Bobby Silver thing, and I've had to send Keisha out to another murder we heard about this morning, so if your case doesn't have a corpse in it, I don't think—"

"Another murder?" asked Zoe.

"Yeah. Not local, though. Further east."

Zoe's phone was beeping. Another call coming through.

"East where?" She checked the screen. "Forget it, Stella. I've got to take this."

She ended the call and answered the new one.

"Boss," said Aaron. "Looks like they've found him."

"Found who?" Zoe asked.

"Kevin Downes. Ryan's mate. Body's just turned up in Elterwater."

CHAPTER ELEVEN

"Cheers," said Harriett.

Tom touched his glass to hers and threw on a smile. He took a long drink, looking away from her. When he looked back, she was still watching him, her face etched with concern.

"What's wrong?" she asked.

"Wrong?"

"Yeah. You're avoiding eye contact. That means something's wrong."

Bloody hell. She was good.

Or was that just something they taught you in PSD?

"Nothing's wrong," he replied. "The raid was a success. We didn't make any arrests, but we—"

"I know all that. But fine. If you don't want to talk about it, that's fine."

He nodded and returned to his drink. For the next minute or two, they drank in silence, looking around the room, catching one another's eyes and smiling, then looking away again.

He found himself frowning as he scanned the other drinkers.

If you don't want to talk about it, that's fine.

That was one of those sentences that meant the opposite of what it sounded like, wasn't it?

"OK," he said. "It was a shitshow."

He felt something on his hand and looked down to see hers over it. It made him feel better already.

"How was it a shitshow?"

"I was terrified. I was... I hung back a bit, and by the time we got in, I was breathing so hard I could barely see."

"Did you run away?"

"No, it wasn't—"

"Could you see them? The women?"

"Yes, but—"

"Did you need medical assistance?"

He shook his head. "Look, I can see where you're going with this, but I was a wreck, Harriett. I don't know if it was a panic attack or what, but I felt like..."

He couldn't say the word. He could see it in his head, but as soon as he tried it out in his mouth, it dried up.

"Like what?"

"I can't—"

"It's a word, Tom. You can say it."

"Fine," he said. "I felt like a coward. You happy?"

She shook her head.

"You're not a coward, Tom. I've seen you walk into places where you didn't know what would be waiting for you. Places a lot more dangerous than a warehouse with half the Cumbria police there to back you up. You're many things, Tom Willis, and some of them drive me up the bloody wall, but one thing you're not is a coward."

He returned her gaze, neither of them smiling, her hand still on his. He shook his head.

She smiled, and he found himself smiling too. Only this time, it was real.

It wasn't just something she'd learned in PSD. She really was good. Too good for him.

Two more drinks down, and they were sharing their days. He had a few stories about Keisha that made her laugh. Harriett had little more than the team room. Nina and the sarge.

"Could have done with being out at Bobby Silver's with you," she said.

This time it was her smile that looked out of place, not his.

"What's wrong?" he asked.

"It's nothing," she said, then corrected herself. "It's Nina."

"What about her?"

"She really bloody hates me." Her smile was lopsided. And Harriett didn't swear.

"I don't think so," he told her. "She hasn't said anything to me."

"She wouldn't, would she?"

"Listen," he said. "I'll have a word. I know she's still pissed off about the whole undercover thing, but that was just you doing your job."

"That was what she said. Only she put it differently."

He frowned.

"Don't talk to her," Harriett said. She gave his hand a gentle squeeze. "I think it'll just make things worse."

He nodded. "Look, Nina's... She's quite straightforward, really."

"You can talk."

He shrugged. Was that so bad?

"But the point is," he continued, "this whole PSD thing, it might take her a while to get to grips with it. But she's a good person. And you're a good person. And she knows it."

"So?"

"So give it time. She'll come around."

"And if she doesn't?"

"If she doesn't..." Tom said, thinking hard about what he could do, and then landing on it. "If she doesn't, I'll have a panic attack on her."

She laughed, a small laugh, but a real one, and then she pointed to the bar.

"Your round," she said. "I intend to get really quite drunk tonight."

CHAPTER TWELVE

ZOE SAT BACK on the sofa and exhaled.

It had been a good day. They hadn't got the bad guys, but they'd found four women. Stella's team had made progress at Bobby Silver's house. Either they'd find something there, or the women would identify the people who'd held them. She believed it.

She had to believe it.

Carl came in, a steaming bowl in each hand. She'd smelled it as soon as she walked in and had been waiting.

"Beef stew," he said.

Zoe took a mouthful. She raised her eyebrows.

"Why haven't you cooked this before?"

He looked at her. "You like it?"

"Why?"

"It takes most of the bloody day."

She nodded. "Thanks. It was worth the effort."

"I thought you deserved it."

She paused, fork halfway to her mouth. "Don't I usually deserve it?"

He opened his mouth to protest, then saw her half-smile.

"Anyway, congratulations," he said, after a few minutes of eating, broken only by Zoe's grunts of appreciation.

"For what?" she asked through a mouthful of stew.

"Your raid, of course."

She swallowed and turned to him. "We'd never have found the place without you. In fact, it was you who found it."

Elena had remembered a warehouse and the smell of ammonia. It was Carl who'd made the link between ammonia and the nearby paper mill, Carl who'd located every nearby warehouse.

"After months of patient work from you and Nina getting Elena to open up."

Zoe shrugged. "We can all share the credit." Yoda jumped onto the sofa beside her and began miaowing. "What do you want? As if I don't know."

"I've saved a bit for her," Carl said.

"We've broken up a people-smuggling operation and freed human slaves," she said. "What's the cat done to deserve this?"

"Cats don't earn things. It's a sort of divine right. What's yours is theirs, and what's theirs is their own."

Zoe looked around as they finished the meal. They hadn't been in the house long, and there were things they needed to do. This room could do with a fresh paint job, for a start. They hadn't agreed on a colour yet.

Not a problem. They had all the time in the world.

"Heard from Lesley?" Carl asked.

Zoe frowned. Not for a while. She was used to calling her old boss whenever things looked like they were spiralling out of control, but she'd handled the last couple of weeks

without falling back on her. Maybe she was finally growing up.

She missed Lesley. And there would be news from
Dorset. Lesley had two teams reporting to her now and was
struggling with the amount of time she spent behind a desk.

She'd just stood to take the dirty bowls into the kitchen
when her phone rang. Carl spotted the image on the screen
before she'd registered Nicholas's face.

"Mum!"

He always sounded so excited to speak to her. Surprised,
almost. As if, being hundreds of miles away and across the
Anglo-Scottish border, there was some doubt as to whether
she was real.

"You're looking well," she told him. He'd put on weight,
in a good way. There was a solidity about his face.

He was growing up. Not a child anymore. Hadn't been
for years.

"I've been working out," he told her.

"Really?"

"Yep. That and decorating my room."

He ducked, revealing the room behind him. It was
covered in pictures of...

"Hang on," she said. "Is that... Is that Oasis?"

"Yes." He turned around and nodded at the images.
There were dozens of them. Hundreds. Ranging from small
photographs clipped from newspapers to double-page poster
prints.

Zoe thought back. Had she missed something? "I didn't
think you were a fan of Oasis. Or at least, so obsessed with
them."

He laughed. "Don't worry. I'm not. But when I come
down to stay next week... I can still come, right?"

"Of course." She smiled. "Been looking forward to it for weeks."

That was a lie. She'd been looking forward to it for months.

"When I come down, Bella's gonna crash in my room. She's fallen out with her boyfriend and she's sofa surfing till she gets her own place."

"Right." Zoe was still unsure what this had to do with Oasis.

"And Bella's a massive Blur fan. She's obsessed with them. Her last place? Posters all over the wall. Kind of like this, but in reverse."

He grinned.

"So this is, what, a practical joke?" she asked.

He nodded. "Funny, right?"

She couldn't reply. But she couldn't help smiling, either. Maybe he wasn't grown up yet.

CHAPTER THIRTEEN

"AARON, GOT A MINUTE?"

Aaron followed the boss from the team room to her office. He was the only one in so far. He'd need to have a word with Nina about her punctuality.

"This Elterwater case," she said, closing the door. She turned and pointed to the chair.

He sat down. "Sorry, boss. Elterwater?"

"I'm not sure we can handle two murder investigations at the same time."

He frowned. "But we need to be handling them. Both of them."

DI Finch nodded. "I can't trust anyone else to run the Bobby Silver case. And if we don't find out what happened to Kevin Downes..."

"Then his mate Ryan Tobin won't give us whatever he's got on Carter. Got it, boss. Did you tell Tobin?"

She nodded. "Last night. He didn't seem surprised. I explained that we couldn't be sure it was his friend, but he's convinced."

Aaron thought about the photos. The parka. The t-shirt. He nodded.

"Ryan's determined to get to the bottom of it," the boss said. "He's got this idea that the police don't care when it's people like Kevin."

His cheek twitched. "He's not wrong, is he?"

"No. And if Jasmine Woolley ends up running the case, he'll be even righter."

"Has she ever run a murder investigation?"

The boss smiled. "Not for a while. But the moment I go to the super and tell her this, she'll agree, remind me that I've got Bobby Silver to crack, and hand Kevin Downes over to Alan Markin."

Aaron repressed a shudder. DI Markin had run murder investigations before. But not well. Markin wouldn't be much improvement on Jasmine Woolley.

"And we can't have that, can we?" she asked.

Aaron frowned.

"Thing is, Aaron, it's your old stamping ground, Elterwater. Right?"

The boss knew he'd been brought up there. They'd even been there together a few months back.

"I know you're technically not a DI..." she said, eyeing him.

"But I was running the team before you turned up. I've run murder investigations."

She nodded. "Successfully, too. Unlike Alan Markin. You know the area, you're an experienced detective, and when it comes to manpower, DI Whaley's agreed that Harriett can stay with us while we're working on Bobby Silver."

"So you wouldn't miss me."

She grinned. "Of course we'd miss you, Aaron. But we'd survive. In the meantime, though, you'll have manpower problems of your own."

"Unless I can get DI Woolley's people onside."

He shuddered. Lynn Hedley was a decent person, and a good copper. But DS Isaac Bateman was neither of those things.

But still. Running a murder investigation. Taking a lead...

"I'll do it, boss. If we can get the case off DI Woolley, I'll run it from Elterwater. I'll manage it. One way or another."

"We'll get you made up to Acting DI and give you whatever resources we can from here, Aaron," DI Finch said. "But Bobby Silver—"

"Has to take priority. I know. I just need to cancel an appointment, and then I'll be available for whatever comes next."

Dr Filey didn't sound happy when he called her from the still-empty team room a few minutes later.

"Are you sure, Aaron?" she said. "Your mental health is your most important asset. Without it, you're no use to anyone."

"I know." He'd seen how useless he could be, how much damage he could cause to his own life and the lives of others, when he wasn't in the right frame of mind. "But really, I'm OK. I made the appointment because I wanted to talk over a few things, but it can wait."

"Bobby Silver?" she said.

Aaron frowned. How did she know?

"It's out there now, Aaron," she said. "The press knows she's dead. And you'd mentioned her before. A friend of Victor's, right?"

"Right," he said.

"This isn't bringing all the old feelings back, is it?"

"No." It was true. "It's not my fault. I mean, Victor wasn't my fault, I know that now, but Bobby Silver really isn't my fault. It's sad, and it's a bit weird, and I wanted to talk it over. But really, it can wait."

"As long as you're sure," she replied, as the door opened and Nina walked in, followed by Harriett and Tom.

"I'm sure," he said.

CHAPTER FOURTEEN

NINA HEARD footsteps and glanced behind her. Harriett Barnes. Late, by her standards, her eyes narrowed against the weak overhead light.

Was Harriett hungover?

Nina pushed open the team room door, toyed with the idea of letting it shut in Harriett's face, and decided against it. A good decision: Tom walked in half a pace behind Harriett, and the sarge was already in the team room.

No point making yourself the bad guy. Not in front of witnesses, anyway.

She caught sight of Tom's face. He looked worse than Harriett. "State of you."

"Yeah." He groaned.

So they'd been out, then. Out celebrating, while she was stuck in her little living room studying for the exam, or at least, scrolling on her phone while trying to persuade herself to study for the exam. Why should Tom get to...

She stopped herself. It was her choice, going for sergeant. And yes, she didn't like Harriett Barnes. But couples would do their coupley things. She'd been there herself, often enough.

"Congratulations on the raid," said the sarge.

Nina turned to him. "You've heard?"

He nodded.

She fought back disappointment. She'd wanted to tell him about it herself.

But reports would have been filed already. And the sarge was diligent. He'd probably known what had happened only minutes after she did.

"Wish we'd caught one of the bastards," she said.

Her phone rang. She snatched it up.

"DC Kapoor? It's Ellis Wood. NCA."

She knew the voice. The bloke from the Modern Slavery and Human Trafficking Unit.

"How can I help you, Ellis?"

"You hear about the two women?"

"What?" Nina felt something unpleasant in the pit of her stomach.

"They've gone."

She clutched the phone tighter. "Which women? Where?"

"The ones we found yesterday. The one who spoke. You know who I mean?"

"Belarusian woman, red hair?"

"That's the one. Her and the one she was arguing with. You remember?"

"It was last night, Ellis. I'm hardly likely to have forgotten already."

"Yes, of course. Sorry. I didn't mean to imply anything."

"Right." Nina walked out of the team room into the corridor. She hadn't even sat down yet, and she'd already managed to ignore Harriett, criticise Tom's appearance, and snap at the NCA. "No," she said. "I'm sorry. You didn't deserve that. What's happened to them?"

"That's it, DC Kapoor. They're gone. I'm sorry. They disappeared. Sometime between midnight and four."

"No one checking on them? No security?"

"It's not that sort of place."

She shut her eyes and thought back, to her conversations with the woman from the local authority, and what the boss had told her later. "They called it a safe house. Not exactly safe, was it?"

"From what we can gather, they left of their own accord. Out through a side door, then a gate you can only open from the inside. Seems like there was a car waiting for them."

"CCTV?"

"Yes, but the image is shit and the plates were cloned anyway. Given the way these operations work—"

"They were part of it, weren't they? The older one, at least. She wasn't a victim. She was one of the traffickers."

"It looks likely. I'm sorry, Nina."

"The other two," she said. "The other two women. Are they still there?"

"Yes, I think so."

"So if you're right, the people who brought them into the country know exactly where they are."

"Yes, but like I say, they shouldn't be able to get at them. You can get out, but getting in—"

"I'm sorry, Ellis, but I can't risk that. I'm going to find them somewhere else to stay, and then I'll be in touch to sort it out."

"But—"

Nina had already hung up and was dialling another number.

"Nina," said Kay Holinshed, when she answered a moment later. "How are things?"

"No time for that," replied Nina. "I've got a proposition for you, Kay."

CHAPTER FIFTEEN

ENTERING THE CORRIDOR UPSTAIRS, Zoe saw a figure walking slowly towards her.

Luke. Fiona's assistant.

"Looking well," she said.

"Thank you." He rolled his eyes.

He looked as pale as ever. If he'd come out of Fiona's office through a wall instead of the door, she wouldn't have been surprised.

"What can I expect?" she asked.

Luke tilted his head, his smile pained.

"Bad as that?"

"She's been worse." He walked away.

Zoe steeled herself and tapped on the super's door.

"Come in."

Zoe opened the door. For once, the super was sitting behind her desk, head down, scanning a sheet of paper. She continued to peruse it for a moment before looking up and beckoning Zoe to sit.

"You'll excuse me if we skip the usual niceties, Zoe," she said. "I'm rather pushed for time."

That suited Zoe. Given what she was about to say – and what she'd already done – it would work better if the super didn't have time to think about it.

"That's fine," Zoe began.

Fiona raised a hand. "I wanted to see you to go through your workload."

Zoe nodded, unsurprised.

"This new case, the body over in Elterwater. I don't see how you can handle that on top of the Bobby Silver investigation and your insistence that you remain involved in the follow-up from the raid last night."

Zoe had put in requests on Elterwater and the raid, but she hadn't expected Fiona to be on top of it all.

"I've already discussed it with Aaron Keyes," she said. "He's from Elterwater. He knows the people there, the land. He's run murder investigations before, and he was in charge of my team before I arrived. He's happy to take point on that."

"Good."

Zoe, who'd been braced for an argument, who'd already sent Aaron to Elterwater and was expecting to fight for her decision, blinked in surprise.

"I want your team to run this case," Fiona said. "I've already made some calls to that effect, and I think putting Aaron in charge is an excellent decision. He can be made Acting DI for the duration of the investigation. I expect him to justify your faith in him."

"I'm sure he—"

"I haven't finished."

Zoe set her jaw.

"I've just got off the phone with the ACC's people," Fiona said.

"People?"

Fiona waved a hand. "Policy? Admin? Politics? Media? I don't remember which one. Legal, maybe. Sometimes I think Joe Carghillie has more people working for him than the Prime Minister. The point is, they're interested in Bobby Silver."

Zoe's sense of foreboding grew.

"More pertinently, they don't think *you* should be interested in Bobby Silver. Too much of a connection with your team. Aaron's friendship. Huz's death. It's all too close."

"With respect, Fiona—" Zoe began.

Fiona silenced her with a glare. "On top of that, they've made the not unreasonable assertion that the case has links to organised crime."

Zoe felt sick. "You're saying Ralph Streeting's taking the Bobby Silver case off us, aren't you?" she asked.

Fiona nodded.

"I can't—"

Fiona stopped her. "I don't like it any more than you do, Zoe."

Unlikely. Zoe had told Fiona what she knew about Streeting, but she wasn't sure the super believed her. Fiona might nod and make the right noises, but deep down, she wouldn't accept that Streeting was almost certainly the man behind Bobby Silver's murder. The man who'd learned that Silver was ripping off his paymaster, Myron Carter. The man who'd ordered her death.

"But there's nothing we can do about it," Fiona continued. "It's organised crime. It's his case. His remit. His team have the authority to investigate everything up to and including murder. You've got another murder and a people-smuggling operation to get to grips with. I wish it wasn't the case. But it is."

Zoe blinked, lost for words.

They couldn't do this.

But if they did, she'd make them regret it.

CHAPTER SIXTEEN

THE DRIVE HAD BEEN pleasant enough. A little rain, no snow, the clouds parting now and then to reveal the tips of the larger fells. Aaron had driven down one side of Bassenthwaite and the other side of Thirlmere, the light skimming off the water and vanishing. And then the village, all the old slate and stone, and the sense of travelling back a hundred years.

There was something new, though. The signs. The ones for the quarry had always been there, but now there were signs for construction traffic, marked with a familiar name and logo.

Conway Developments.

There were more signs. One just down the road from the Langdale police station, where he found a spot to park. Signs for what would eventually become a theme park.

Sinead Conway's theme park, which Kevin Downes had been protesting when he disappeared.

No. Before he died.

Aaron stared at the sign, took a few breaths, and got out of the car.

"Looks like the binmen forgot something," he heard.

He turned to see Isaac Bateman, as big and red-faced as ever, sneering and pointing at the Volvo. If the village felt like something from a different century, DS Bateman felt like a different species. The missing link.

Aaron grinned to himself, then turned the grin on Bateman.

"Hello, Isaac. Life treating you well?"

Bateman frowned. "Er, fine. Yeah. Lunch break."

He walked away, something like uncertainty in his gait. Aaron glanced at his watch.

It was half past eleven, and Isaac Bateman was supposed to be working a murder case.

Aaron walked on to the station. The main door was closed, and when he knocked, nothing happened. After a minute, he gave it a push and walked in.

Nothing. No one. A small reception area, but no one behind the desk. There were two doors leading off, and he went right, where he knew he'd find the team room. Isaac Bateman wouldn't be in it.

It hadn't changed much since the last time he was there, Bateman's absence aside. The same mug on the big man's desk, emblazoned with the words "I'D LIKE TO TAKE DOWN YOUR PARTICULARS." The same empty desk. At the third desk, where there had previously been just a mysterious orange scarf, sat Lynn Hedley, staring at her monitor and biting her lower lip.

"Hello, Lynn," he said.

She whirled round, her eyes wide, and made to stand up, but her swivel chair had continued its rotation and she ended up lurching towards Aaron, veering off at the last moment to the unoccupied desk, which she fended off with an outstretched hand before coming to a breathless halt.

"DS Keyes," she said. "It's great to see you."

"You too," he replied. "But 'Sarge' will do."

He'd considered asking her to call him Aaron, but she'd be reporting to him while he ran the investigation.

"That might be a little complicated." She smiled sheepishly. "DS Bateman has me calling him 'Sarge' too."

Aaron nodded. "OK. DS Keyes, for now." He eyed the empty desk, before approaching it and sitting down.

The chair was fine. Clearly the worst of the three in the room, or it would have been snapped up by now. But he wasn't going to be here long.

"I'm about to report to DI Woolley," he said. "She in?"

Lynn glanced over his shoulder and nodded. "In her office. Is it true, then? You're taking over the case?"

"Yes, but I'll need your help, Lynn. You'll still be working it." He watched her face light up. "What can you tell me about Kevin Downes, then?" he asked.

He noticed Lynn's gaze flick over his shoulder again, and turned.

DI Jasmine Woolley was standing at the entrance to the room, a thin smile on her face as she watched him. He stood.

"DI Woolley," he said. "Good to see you."

He approached her, hand outstretched. She made no move to take it.

The case was his – the boss had texted, just before he'd reached Elterwater, to confirm it. But if Jasmine Woolley decided to make things difficult, he'd never get to the bottom of what had happened to Kevin Downes.

He stood there, hand still out. With a painfully deliberate slowness, she reached out and shook it, briefly, before letting it drop like it was a stone.

"Aaron," she said. "DS Keyes. I understand you're SIO for the Downes case. Acting DI." Her lip curled. "Temporarily," she added.

"That's right, Ma'am," he replied.

She nodded. "Fine. I've been told to give you the manpower you need, so you can have DC Hedley."

He nodded, his expression neutral.

"Thank you, Ma'am. I appreciate it."

"But it's a murder investigation," she went on, "and one DC probably won't be enough. Not when the SIO's really just a DS himself."

Aaron had solved murder cases before. And he had no doubt DI Woolley knew it.

"Ma'am?" he said.

She pursed her lips, eyeing him. "I'll be assigning DS Bateman to help you along."

Shit.

"Thank you, Ma'am," he said. "I appreciate it."

But he knew he was lying, and he imagined she knew, too.

CHAPTER SEVENTEEN

"Zoe?"

The confusion receded, and she could hear the super's voice.

"Zoe? Did you get all that?"

She nodded. She'd got it. She couldn't let them do it.

"You know about Ralph Streeting," she said.

"I know what you told me, Zoe. It's... It's an interesting story."

Zoe swallowed. "You don't believe it."

"It doesn't matter what I believe. There's no evidence. You yourself told me that."

"Yes. And if there is any evidence, chances are it's at Bobby Silver's house. That's why he wants to take over. The evidence is there, Fiona. And if we can just..."

She stopped, frowning.

Bobby Silver wasn't Streeting's only crime. And if there was anything left in Bobby's house, it wouldn't be the only evidence.

"Look," she said. "Here."

She pulled out her phone and opened the photos app.

"I don't have time for this, Zoe," Fiona told her. "The IOPC—"

"It won't take long. Here."

Zoe held the phone up and talked the super through what it displayed.

"Long-range shots of the Port of Workington. You see those women?"

Fiona nodded.

"Victims of human trafficking."

"The ones you picked up yesterday?"

"I don't know," Zoe admitted. When the dust had settled, she was hoping the women would be able to point themselves out.

If they were even in the photos.

"Well, what use is that, Zoe? You've got a bunch of women walking across a bridge—"

"Being herded across a bridge. In the middle of the night, in the Port of Workington, with a bunch of men watching their every move. One man in particular."

Zoe swiped across, and watched recognition dawn on the super's face. Streeting had been in the earlier shots, but facing away from the camera. It wasn't until this shot that he turned and became identifiable.

"Oh," said the super.

Zoe nodded.

The super looked at her. "Without the women—"

"I know, Fiona. I know we need them. But it's not a jury I'm trying to convince here. It's you."

The super nodded. "You want me to stop Streeting taking over the Bobby Silver case. I get it."

"It's not just—"

"I'll do what I can. But if I succeed, that leaves you managing the trafficking case and two murders. How do you propose to handle that?"

Zoe drew in a breath.

"We'll cross that bridge when we come to it," she said, hoping they would.

CHAPTER EIGHTEEN

IT WAS DIFFERENT, coming back.

Aaron drove through Chapel Stile like a stranger. He'd been raised here. Knew every corner, every slate in every wall, every stile and gate. The village sat on Great Langdale Beck, just west of the better-known Elterwater. Lang How and Silver How hung above them, so close it was like he could touch their peaks.

It was beautiful, but it was all so closed in. The Langdale Pikes were breathtaking, but after a while, they felt like a gigantic wall. Aaron was glad he didn't live here anymore.

His parents did, though. His dad's look of surprise, followed by a delighted smile, reminded Aaron that he hadn't told them he was coming. Barry ushered him inside, where he was ordered to stay for a brew. Yes, he was busy, yes, there was a murder investigation to run and a killer to catch, but some orders couldn't be ignored.

His mum, Gloria, always made an excellent cup of tea.

"You'll stay here, then," she said. His dad nodded encouragingly.

Aaron hadn't thought about it. Driving back and forth between here and Whitehaven every day... It would be a lot.

"Give me a moment." He stepped into the tiny box room his dad called his 'study.' He pulled out his phone and was pleased to see three bars of 4G.

"Hello, gorgeous," said Serge.

Aaron felt his heart quicken, then sink when he remembered why he was calling. "Back at you. Listen, I've got bad news."

Serge took it well. He could shift some work around, delegate. The little drone business he'd set up less than a year ago had actual employees now. He could look after Annabel outside preschool hours. He understood, he told Aaron.

"It might be a few days," Aaron pointed out.

"That's OK. Work has to come first."

"No," Aaron shot back. "It doesn't. You and Annabel come first. But this is—"

"It's important," Serge finished for him.

Aaron had just put down the phone, still smiling, when it rang again. He answered with the traditional, "Hello, gorgeous," assuming it was Serge.

"A little casual, Aaron," said a female voice. Aaron's eyes widened in horror before he heard a chuckle and recognised it.

"DS Gaskill. I'm sorry. I—"

"No need to apologise. I have that effect. And it's Denise, remember."

"Of course. What can I do for you?"

"Just wondering how you were doing."

His eyes narrowed. What was all this about? Had he made a mistake?

"What do you mean?"

"Just that. Wondering how you were doing."

"Checking up on me?"

"If you want. But only in a friendly way."

"I don't need..." He closed his eyes.

Paranoia. That was all this was. And hardly surprising, given what he'd been through. And what Denise Gaskill's job was.

"Thank you," he said. "Not bad. I'm drinking tea at my parents' house in Chapel Stile and feeling like I'm a teenager again, but otherwise, all fine."

"Sounds intriguing. I've... Oh. Bugger. Call coming through. Stay out of trouble."

She was gone. She hadn't been checking up on him. Or if she had, only in the way a friend would.

Nothing to do with her job. Nothing to do with PSD.

Back in the kitchen, enveloped by the smell of scones in the oven and the memories of decades past, Aaron found himself answering questions about the past few months without having to fend them off. When he couldn't tell them something, or didn't want to, he simply shrugged and said, "I can't really talk about that," and instead of tensing up and fighting their way around the subject to come at it from a different direction, they just spoke about something else.

It was good. It was... relaxing. If someone had asked him a few months back how he'd feel about staying in his old bedroom in his parents' house, he'd have shaken his head and shuddered. But now, he was looking forward to it.

"Seen Sara?" his mum asked.

"Sara?"

"You know. Sara Miller."

"She's still here?"

"Aye," his dad chipped in. "Moved away for a bit, then... Well, she's back, anyway."

"Where?"

"Where she always was, silly," replied Gloria.

"Her parents' place?"

She nodded.

Sara Miller had been a friend of his. A close friend, which was something for him, in that place. He wasn't sure how they'd lost touch, but he'd assumed she'd wound up in a city somewhere hundreds of miles away, like most of the brighter kids. Carlisle, at a push. Last he'd heard, she'd hooked up with that Marc Langham. Hadn't they got engaged?

He'd imagined her in a London mansion surrounded by servants and fine art. Perhaps a country estate in the Cotswolds.

But not back home, with her parents, in the ancient Elterwater cottage where she'd been raised.

"You should drop in," his mum told him. "Sure she'd be pleased to see you."

He had work to do first. But when he got the chance, he'd do just that.

CHAPTER NINETEEN

KAY HOLINSHED's house was a small, nondescript end-of-terrace in Moresby Parks. Out of the way, but not in the middle of nowhere.

Nina sat in the living room drinking tea. She tried not to intervene as Kay and Elena made awkward conversation. Elena, she'd learned, took time to trust people. Given what she'd been through, that was no surprise. Kay assumed it was her right to know everyone else's business. Since she'd left the police force – been kicked out, more like – that side of her hadn't softened. Nina had things she wanted to ask Kay, but the woman didn't leave a gap, firing questions at Elena with the regularity of a metronome.

"It's OK," Kay said after a short silence following a particularly intrusive question about Elena's time in captivity. "You don't have to tell me."

Elena nodded, grateful.

A car drew up outside and the three women stood and went to the front door. Kay opened it, and they stared at a blue Peugeot. Nina found herself questioning whether it had been there all along.

The driver's door opened and the woman from the local authority emerged, lighting a menthol cigarette. Behind her, in the back, Nina saw two shapes, faces turned towards the window but not recognisable.

"Alright?" said the woman.

Nina stepped forward, reintroduced herself, and introduced Elena and Kay.

"They can stay here a fortnight, probably longer," Kay said. "My daughter's away."

Abigail was travelling, out of the country. Exploring Europe with Davey Grant, her boyfriend. Whenever Nina switched on the news she half expected to hear about a pair of British tourists who'd got themselves into some unusual trouble, but so far there'd been nothing. Davey insisted he was a changed man. Maybe it was true.

"What'll happen after that?" Nina asked.

The woman from the local authority stared at her like she was speaking Japanese. "If they haven't sorted themselves out in two weeks, they're not gonna sort themselves out in a year, love. These two, they're quiet, but they'll perk up. Just keep 'em safe, right?"

"We will," Nina assured her.

"I mean it," the woman said. "It's my job on the line."

Nina grunted. If she'd shown the same concern the previous night, there might be four women here instead of two. But there was no point in antagonising her. Besides, Abigail's room wasn't that big.

The woman ground out her cigarette and opened the car door behind her. A moment later the two women were out.

In daylight, they looked younger, still scared and confused, but less so.

One of them stepped forward and spoke. It might have been her name. Might have been whatever passed for hello. Nina couldn't pick out the sound.

But Elena could. She stepped past Nina and Kay and spoke back with the same distinctive up-and-down lilt.

Both of the newcomers began to speak, at the same time, their faces full of expression, their eyes bright. Elena smiled, spoke back to them, listened, replied.

"What's going on?" Nina asked.

"They're talking," replied the woman from the local authority, fishing another cigarette from her pack.

"I can see that, but—"

Elena turned. "They are Romanian."

"That's good, isn't it?" Nina replied.

"It is excellent. They are from Barlad."

Nina's mouth fell open. Elena was from Barlad.

"I even know the sister of one of them." Elena was beaming, and the two women looked more alive than Nina could have imagined.

Nina turned to the woman from the local authority, now halfway through her second cigarette. "I think we're going to be just fine here."

"I bloody hope so," the woman replied. "Because it's—"

"Yeah," Nina interrupted. "I know. It's your job on the line."

"Actually," the woman said, "I wasn't going to say that."

"No?"

"No. What I was going to say was that I've never seen new ones open up like this. You've got a real opportunity here. Make them feel more like themselves, and see if they can help you find the others."

"And the bastards who brought them in," added Nina.

"Yes," agreed the woman, grinding out her cigarette with a relish that Nina found alarming. "Wouldn't mind getting my hands on them."

CHAPTER TWENTY

SARA MILLER COULD WAIT. Kevin Downes couldn't. That much should have been obvious.

But Isaac Bateman seemed to have a different opinion.

"Yeah, yeah, I know. We've got a dead man and your dosser's missing. Doesn't mean it's the same person." He sat back in his chair and spoke between mouthfuls of bacon crisps that lent the room a dark, meaty flavour.

"What about DNA?" Aaron asked.

"What about it?"

Aaron peered down at Bateman. He'd chosen to give this briefing standing, so Bateman wouldn't be half a foot taller than him.

"The victim's DNA," Aaron said, slowly. "When will we get it back? Are the victim's prints salvageable? Come to think of it, what's the situation with the PM?"

"Forensics released the body earlier," said Lynn Hedley. "It was taken to West Cumberland."

Aaron silently thanked a god he didn't believe in for providing him with at least one half-competent officer.

"Good," he said. "That means the pathologist will be Chris Robertson." Aaron turned to Bateman. "When's it happening?"

Bateman put his hands out. "How the fuck am I supposed to know?"

"Christ," Aaron muttered.

Bateman rose to his feet, walked over to Aaron, and said, "What was that?"

Aaron took a step back.

Bateman had been waiting for the chance to put that height difference to use. To remind Aaron that he, Isaac Bateman, was the local man. DI Woolley's favourite. The big man, in every way.

And really, Aaron didn't care. He'd left this place a long time ago. It was his past.

But backing down would mean not finding out what had happened to Kevin Downes.

"I said," he said, his voice level, "'Christ,' and I said it because the DS on a murder investigation is supposed to know when the PM's going to be."

Bateman opened his mouth.

"I don't care what you might have gotten away with in the past," Aaron said, "and I don't care what you think your rank entitles you to. This is a murder investigation, I'm the SIO, and what I say goes. If you've got a problem with that, you can take it up directly with Detective Superintendent Kendrick. Or you can sit down and do what I say. Got it?"

Bateman took a step back and stared at Aaron, his lips working soundlessly. Another step, and he came up against his chair and dropped heavily into it.

"Got it?" Aaron repeated.

Bateman nodded. Aaron glanced to his left and saw Lynn Hedley wipe a smile from her face.

"Kevin Downes, then. Until we get DNA, we'll assume it's him." He turned to the screen he'd screwed into the wall a few minutes earlier. He'd picked it up from Stores on the way out of the Hub, having assured the pencil-chewing guardian of the place that he'd return it in good condition. "Last known photo, here he is wearing a Pink Floyd t-shirt and a white Canada Goose parka. Just like the victim."

The image was on the screen now, the man's face half-turned towards the camera, his smile easy and natural. He was thirty-two years old, with brown wavy hair and just enough stubble to be deliberate. A good-looking man. The sort who got themselves into all kinds of trouble.

They didn't usually end up dead, though. Not quite so young.

Aaron continued.

"Last seen on the twenty-seventh of November at the protest camp near Langdale Cemetery, where he was coordinating local efforts to stop the Conway Developments theme park project at Elterwater Quarry."

"Useless fucking dossers," Bateman said. Aaron ignored it.

"He has a record," Aaron said, pointing to the bullet points below the photograph and the mugshots beside them. "All small stuff. Low-level dealing. Criminal damage, associated with his protest activities. What else can you tell me about him, DS Bateman?"

Bateman shrugged.

"About him? Syndrome?"

"What?" Aaron asked.

"Syndrome," Bateman replied. "Kevin Downes. Syndrome. That's his nickname, isn't it?"

"Is it?" Aaron asked. DC Hedley shook her head with narrowed eyes.

"Dunno," Bateman said. "If it isn't, it should be. Anyway, we've got their prints and DNA."

"Whose prints and DNA?"

"The dossers. All of them."

"Oh. Right. That's good. I didn't realise you'd made that much progress."

Bateman laughed and shook his head.

"Nothing to do with all this." He waved at the photo of Kevin Downes. "This was months ago. DI Woolley didn't like the look of them. Suggested they submit to having their prints and DNA taken. To make life easier."

"And they agreed?"

"Oh, they agreed alright."

Aaron shook his head. Whatever Bateman had done to get hold of those prints and DNA, it wouldn't be legal. And he wouldn't have made any friends down at the camp.

Which would make Aaron's life harder. But then, making Aaron's life harder was the only thing Isaac Bateman was good at.

CHAPTER TWENTY-ONE

"DS KEYES?"

Aaron looked up. With Lynn's help, he'd finally linked into the Langdale system and was reading through the notes DS Bateman and others had taken on the protest camp. Bateman himself was out, chasing news on the PM, he claimed.

"What can I do for you?" he asked.

"I've been trying to put together an idea of Kevin's last known movements. But it's difficult."

"Why's that?"

"Well, for a start, no one seems to have a phone number for him."

"Hang on." Aaron pulled up another file and scrolled down, running his finger along the screen.

"No," he said finally. "No sign of one in the notes we got from his friend. I'll chase that."

"What notes are these?" Lynn asked.

Aaron hesitated. *Thank God Bateman isn't here.* "We have a sort of relationship with a friend of Kevin's."

"Relationship?"

He shrugged. "We pulled him in over a murder last year."

Lynn's eyes widened.

"He didn't do it," Aaron continued. "Ended up being quite helpful. He's... Let's just say, it's in our interests to keep him happy. He told us Kevin was missing. Gave us the photo and a little more information."

In our interests. She nodded.

"Right," Lynn said. "Well, that's probably more than we've got. No phone, and no clear record of when he was last seen."

"There must be people who saw him. You just work backward and forward until you've got the last sighting."

"There's a possible sighting of him leaving the camp. On the twenty-seventh, like you say. Just walked off. But no real detail on that. We can't even tell who saw him."

"No record?"

She shook her head. "And it's possible people saw him after that. But it's all jumbled up."

He sighed. "Don't tell me. DS Bateman's notes don't make any sense."

She gave a small smile, but shook her head. "If only it was just that, DS Keyes. But it's not just DS Bateman's notes. PC Henniker spoke to them too, and Sergeant Fraser, and they're both..."

"They're both what?"

She paused, looked directly at him, and answered carefully. "They're not DS Bateman. Neither of them."

"What's the problem, then?"

"It's the protestors, sir. We spoke to them when he was

just missing, of course. No one knew he was dead. But they weren't very helpful."

"Why not?" Aaron glanced at his desk, at the report he'd been reading.

Shit on ground. Shit tents. Shit attitude.

Shit bloody cops.

She was twisting a ring around her finger. "The... er, the policing of the protest may have been a little heavy-handed," she said.

"How so?"

"There've been..."

She stopped, chewed her lip for a moment, and looked away. The ring stopped moving. "There've been incidents. We were called a couple of times, when they got too close to the site."

"By who?"

"The developers," she replied.

He nodded. "So, heavy-handed, you say," he prompted, and she returned the nod.

"And the fact that some of my colleagues made no pretence of the fact that they didn't really care about another missing crusty."

"Crusty?"

"It's that or 'dosser,' DS Keyes. It's a limited vocabulary."

Aaron glanced over at the report he'd been reading. *Shit on ground. Shit tents. Shit attitude.* A limited vocabulary? He wasn't arguing with that.

CHAPTER TWENTY-TWO

It was quiet in the team room, but Harriett didn't mind. Just her and Tom, staring at their screens, focusing on Bobby Silver's life. Her business. Her money. Her friends.

Even her pets.

"Think we could bring the parrot in for questioning?" Tom asked. "Seemed to have a lot to say about Cummings."

Harriett laughed. "'Bugger off, Cummings.'"

Tom returned the laugh. "'Wipe your feet.'"

No doubt it had picked up some of Bobby's favourite expressions, and the fact that she'd expressed her contempt of Tel Cummings that often was interesting.

But not interesting enough to waste time on.

The animals had been taken in by two friends of the dead woman. Miles and Stacey. DI Finch had already spoken to Stacey, and before he'd gone to Elterwater, DS Keyes had told them he'd had a chat with Miles. Neither of them were serious suspects, but then, nobody had thought Bobby Silver was the mastermind behind a drugs and blackmail gang.

They'd be calling them in. Miles and Stacey. They'd been Bobby's friends. They'd worked with her. That work being at the Port of Workington only made things more interesting.

Tom's phone rang. He picked it up and listened for a moment before speaking.

"Hang on, boss. It's just me and Harriett here, but I'll put it on speaker."

Tom stabbed at the display, and DI Finch's voice emerged.

"Listen, I'm stuck in my office with some calls to make, but I need to brief you about the meeting I've just had with the super."

Tom nodded. "Fire away, boss."

Harriett suppressed a grin. There was an eager boyishness to Tom when he was talking to DI Finch. So desperate to impress. Some women would have hated it. But she found it charming.

"It's bad news, I'm afraid. Fiona's going to fight in our corner, but it looks like Streeting's taking over the Bobby Silver investigation."

Harriett blinked. "I'm sorry," she said. "Can you repeat that?"

"It's as bad as it sounds, Harriett. Streeting's trying to take over Bobby Silver's case, and it looks like he's done it."

"Shit," said Tom. Harriett looked up, meeting his gaze, the same thought in both their minds.

Shit. Streeting investigating a murder he'd probably ordered.

"That's crazy, boss," Tom said.

"I know," DI Finch replied. "And I'll give you more details when I get the chance. In the meantime, we need to protect all the evidence we've got. If he gets hold of this case, he'll do everything he can to make a mess of it. The longer we can keep him away from it..."

There was a short silence, Tom mouthing more four-letter words while the consequences of the news raced through Harriett's mind.

"Okay," Harriett said. "I'm on it."

The line went dead. Before Tom could turn and discuss it with her, she had her own phone out, her hand up to fore-stall any questions, the number already ringing.

"Stella Berry. Who's this?"

"It's Harriett Barnes. There's been a development in the Bobby Silver case."

Stella remained uncharacteristically quiet while Harriett outlined the news.

"Fuck," said Stella, loudly enough for Tom to hear. Harriett glanced over to see him nodding.

"You need to get the evidence out of there."

"Nearly done," Stella replied.

"Where are you keeping it?"

"Well, the plan was to store it at our main off-site premises. The park in Workington."

Harriett knew the place. Which meant Streeting would, too.

"You can't—"

"I know, I know. It's OK. I'll find another site. Some-where no one knows about."

"And make sure—"

"There's a proper chain of custody. Jesus, woman, who do you think you're talking to?"

"I'm sorry."

"Yeah," Stella replied, slightly mollified. "Well, leave it

with me. We'll have to turn it all over eventually. But we'll push that day back as far as we can, right?"

"Right." Harriett exchanged a grim smile with Tom.

Stella was going to have to fight back against Streeting, and the more desperate Streeting got, the harder that would be. But if anyone could do it, Stella Berry could.

CHAPTER TWENTY-THREE

BATEMAN WAS BACK, but he had no news on the post-mortem.

"Who did you ask?" Aaron said.

Bateman shrugged. Alongside the aroma of bacon crisps, there were undertones of something else. Lager, maybe.

Aaron picked up his phone, dialled the number, and found his call diverted to a nursing station. Why would you need a nurse in a mortuary? Then he remembered that Dr Robertson occasionally still worked with the living as well as the dead.

"Dr Robertson?" said the woman. "Yes. He's just seeing a... Oh, he's here. Hold on a moment."

A few seconds later, Aaron was greeted by the familiar tones of Chris Robertson.

"Aaron Keyes? We did Bobby Silver the other day, didn't we? Don't think I've got one of yours here."

"Body recovered from Baysbrown Wood. Found yesterday, I believe."

"You on that? Bit out of your way, Elterwater."

Aaron glanced to his right. Bateman was leaning back in his chair and rubbing his stomach.

"I'm helping out," he said.

"Well, I'm glad you've called, because all I've had from Langdale is some garbled message from someone called Bateman, who insisted it was a rush job but didn't bother answering when I called him back."

"Figures," Aaron muttered.

"Well, the bad news for you is, you've missed the post-mortem."

"Shame. You know how entertaining I find them."

Dr Robertson gave a little laugh. "Anyway, here's the headline. Your man was murdered."

"Not a huge surprise, but good to have it confirmed. Any idea how?"

"He was strangled. Hang on. Let me send you some photos, and I'll talk you through it. Can I call you back in five?"

"Perfect." Aaron put down his phone and turned to see Bateman standing up and pulling on his jacket.

"Going somewhere, DS Bateman?"

"Pub," Bateman replied, looking pointedly at his watch.

Aaron glanced at his phone. It was barely five.

"Haven't you just got back from the pub?"

Bateman shook his head, fervently but unconvincingly. "Not for hours, Aaron. Not for hours."

"I want to visit the scene."

"Be my guest," Bateman replied. "It'll be dark there and a fucking mess, but you do what you want, DS Keyes."

Aaron turned to Lynn Hedley, who nodded. At least he wouldn't be alone.

"I'm waiting for a call from the pathologist," he said. "Five minutes. Then you can show me. That OK, Lynn?"

"Yes, DS Keyes."

"Fucking hell," Bateman grumbled.

"What is it?" Aaron asked.

"Well, if you go, I'll have to."

"Why?"

"I'm supposed to be..."

He stopped and looked down.

"Supposed to be what, DS Bateman?"

Nothing.

"Supposed to be keeping an eye on me?"

Bateman shrugged.

Aaron's phone pinged.

One photo. Two, three. Ten.

Dr Robertson called, explaining what he'd sent. Aaron wondered what would have happened if the pathologist's finger had slipped and he'd sent nearly a dozen photos of a mutilated corpse to a random phone number.

"In the fourth image. If you zoom in on the top right, got that?"

"Got it." Aaron had the phone on speaker so he could examine the image more closely. He sensed a figure behind him.

He turned. It was only Lynn. Bateman was still sitting down, looking aggrieved.

"What am I looking for?" he asked.

"Marks. You see them?"

Aaron zoomed in a little further, and then a finger darted into his field of vision and touched the screen.

"There," whispered Lynn.

He saw it. Them. Why hadn't he seen them before?

"Young eyes," he whispered back to Lynn, who swallowed a laugh.

"You see the contusions?" Dr Robertson asked. "He was strangled. The tongue and the eyes might have made it even clearer, but they've been taken."

"Taken?" asked Aaron.

"Wild animals, by the looks of it. Body's been badly disturbed. It's lucky we got what we did."

"So, what, these marks were made by someone's hands?"

"No," the pathologist replied. "That's the thing. These marks couldn't have come from anyone's hands. Too even. Something else was used to strangle your man."

"Any idea what?"

"Sorry, Aaron. Something smooth. You find it, I'll see if I can match it."

Aaron nodded. "Thanks, Chris. What about DNA?"

"The victim's? Stella's team have it. Still being analysed, I'd imagine. You need an ID?"

"We're fairly confident, but it would help. In the absence of prints."

"Yeah, you're not getting anything off this guy's hands. Sorry. As for the killer's DNA, that's a no too, I'm afraid. Too long, too much exposure, too much damage to the body. We might find something, but I wouldn't count on it."

"No more than I was expecting. Thanks."

"Speak soon," replied Dr Robertson, and ended the call.

"Right," said Aaron, standing. "Who's coming to see where Kevin Downes was killed?"

Lynn was already wrapping her orange scarf around her neck.

Bateman rose slowly to his feet. "I could kill for a pint."

Aaron ignored him.

CHAPTER TWENTY-FOUR

It was just past five, but looking out of the window from Zoe's office, it could have been midnight. Three in the morning, even. Just dark, without enough cars on the road below to tell her she was in the middle of what counted for rush hour up here.

Up here. She had to get out of that frame of mind. It had been more than a year now that she'd lived in Cumbria. It was her home.

She stood by the window looking out on the darkness and hoping she'd done the right thing. Fiona had already known what she suspected about Streeting. But showing her the photos was different. It was evidence. Hardly cast-iron, throw-away-the-key evidence, but still evidence.

She could trust Fiona, couldn't she?

Her phone rang and she snapped it up, desperate for anything to save her from her thoughts.

"Have you locked him up yet?" said a voice she'd been hearing, on and off, for most of that year, without seeing the person behind it.

"Olivia."

"Who else?"

Olivia Bagsby was an artist. She was in hiding, on the run since Zoe had met her, in her first week in Cumbria. And the reason she was in hiding was that she was the one who'd taken the photos Zoe had just shown Fiona.

She hadn't meant to take them. Hadn't meant to capture evidence of organised crime and police corruption. All she was hoping for was a sense of the Port of Workington in darkness, something she could paint later.

She'd got a lot more than she'd bargained for.

"I'm sorry," Zoe said.

"This can't go on," Olivia replied. "I've had to move on again."

"Why?"

"Because Carter's people caught up with me. I won't end up like Ahmed Iqbal, Zoe."

Zoe didn't ask how Carter had found her. Olivia wouldn't tell her. Olivia wouldn't tell her where she was, or what she was doing. She couldn't risk exposing herself until Carter was locked up. Zoe had tried to explain that locking Carter up would be a lot easier if Olivia was there to testify that she'd taken the photos, but that was a step too far, and Zoe couldn't blame her.

They'd both seen what Carter could do. His reach. He'd managed to track down a witness from a case Zoe had worked years back in Birmingham. Tracked him down, handed over his location, and the man, Ahmed Iqbal, had been tortured and murdered as a result.

Ahmed Iqbal had been in the Protected Persons Program. There were clever people all over the country dedicated to keeping him safe and hidden. And still, Carter had found him.

It was amazing that Olivia had lasted as long as she had.

"Olivia," Zoe began, ready to repeat the same useless reassurances she'd made so many times before, but the line was already dead. She stared at the phone, frustrated.

She had to speak to someone about this. And there was only one person who might understand.

"Good to hear from you," said David Randle, answering the phone like a regular guy, like two friends.

David Randle was a lot of things. *Regular guy* wasn't one of them.

"We need to talk," Zoe replied. "There've been developments."

To give him credit, Randle managed to stay silent, while Zoe told him everything. Not just what Olivia had just said, but the news about the Bobby Silver case. For Randle, a man who loved the sound of his own voice even more than he loved money, that was quite the achievement.

He'd been her boss back in Birmingham. She'd never liked him, but there were plenty of senior officers she hadn't liked. The difference was that Randle was bent, and when he'd finally been caught, and turned on the organised crime gang that had paid him, he'd entered the Protected Persons Program himself. Just like Ahmed Iqbal.

And like Ahmed Iqbal, he was a target. There were people out there who'd very much like to get their hands on David Randle, and if those people wanted to find him, the first person they'd go to was Myron Carter.

Which was why, to her amazement, Zoe had found herself working with David Randle.

Not that Carl knew.

"If Streeting takes over that case," Randle told her, "you can kiss any chance of finding Bobby Silver's killer goodbye."

"Thanks, David. I hadn't thought of that."

He sighed. "If my memory isn't failing me, you were the one who called me, Zoe."

She closed her eyes, leaned back, and counted silently to ten.

"OK. Sorry. I just wanted to unload. See if you have any brilliant ideas. I need to keep Streeting off the Bobby Silver case, keep Carter away from Olivia, find Olivia, if I can, see if I can get anything out of the women we picked up, and all that while IOPC are tearing the place—"

"Women?" Randle said. "What women?"

She thought she'd told him. Clearly not. "We raided a warehouse. Found four women who'd been kept there, but none of Carter's people. And two of the women have disappeared already. The other two... well, who knows?"

"Right." There was another short silence. "OK. Maybe they'll give you what you need. But you have to assume they won't. So let's work with what we've got. Take me through the money side again."

Zoe spent the next ten minutes explaining the flow of cash from Myron Carter's customers and through his businesses. The product, for the most part, was human: the women he imported and sold to people like Dean Somerville, who was currently in the hospital wing of Wakefield Prison, recovering from an assault that had almost killed him. The money went through a series of Carter's companies, starting with Mills Allen Begbie Alliance, to Dagon, River Samuels, to Jenson & Marley Offshore Services, the company Ryan Tobin had once worked for. From there, Carter siphoned it off.

A forensic accountant had verified it all. But they couldn't prove Carter knew a thing about it.

"OK," said Randle. She could hear the tap of a keyboard in the background.

He was making notes.

"Anything useful for me?" she asked.

"Not yet. But the more I know, the more chance I have of finding his weak spot."

Reluctant as Zoe was to admit it, this was true. Randle hadn't been a brilliant detective superintendent, but he had a better grasp of how organised crime worked than anyone else she knew. From both sides.

"Now, your artist woman. Olivia. Tell me what you've done to find her."

"Not a lot, lately. She's gone quiet."

"Not good enough, Zoe. You need to keep looking."

Another silent count to ten.

"What do you want to know?" she asked.

"Everything," he said, and Zoe obliged. Olivia's social media aliases, or the ones she'd used before they'd been identified. Her previous locations. The sort of art she sold: coastal, bold, full of colour.

"Right," he said, finally. "I've got to go. I'll be in touch."

The line went dead.

CHAPTER TWENTY-FIVE

"OVER HERE!"

Lynn gestured to DS Bateman and DS Keyes and headed towards the voice, through a gap in a slate wall.

She'd been to the scene, but finding it at night was different. She stumbled on rocks that had come away from the walls. People liked to talk about how those walls had lasted centuries, but their slates had been lost and replaced so often that you couldn't say if they were the same thing they'd been at the start.

And the rains had done damage. It wasn't just wild animals that had wreaked havoc on Kevin Downes's body.

They'd passed PC Henniker before the woman had shouted for them. Now Sergeant Fraser appeared out of the darkness, pointing.

DS Bateman stepped back into a morass of leaves and mud that covered both his shoes.

"Fucking hell." He pulled one foot out, then the other. "Don't just lurch out like that," he shouted at Fraser, who shrugged and pointed again.

"She's waiting for you."

"Who is?" Lynn asked.

Fraser stared at Keyes. "Do I know you, sir?"

"Aaron Keyes. DS Keyes now. And I remember you, Ben. When I started working here, you were still dodging bus fares and stealing cigarettes from the shop."

Fraser stepped back. "Bloody hell, Aaron. Good to see you."

There was a handshake and a few seconds of reminiscing, accompanied by Bateman's sighs and another shout from the woman.

"I haven't got all day!"

"Got to do what the lady says." Keyes grinned.

They found her a minute later, close to another of those ancient walls, staring at something on the ground in the centre of a beam of torchlight. She turned. "No farther."

"Hello, Keisha." Keyes gestured to his colleagues. "Keisha Middleton, DC Lynn Hedley, DS Isaac Bateman."

Even in her mask and forensic suit, the woman had a presence. She weighed them up one at a time, then returned to whatever she'd been looking at.

"Hi," said Lynn.

The woman nodded.

"Hello," said Bateman, in a plummy, mid-twentieth-century lothario voice.

The woman shook her head and made a noise with her throat that expressed disgust.

"Look, Aaron, I'm gonna stick around a bit longer, but there's not much here. What with the animals and the weather..."

DS Keyes nodded. "Fair enough, Keisha. Do what you can."

"Told you it was a waste of time," the sarge said.

"Not entirely." Keisha looked up at Bateman. "The way the earth sits, I don't think the animals and the weather are a coincidence."

"No?" DS Keyes asked.

"No." She shook her head. "If I had to guess, I'd say he'd been buried. Not too deep, but deep enough that no one would have noticed him. But all this..." She waved around. "Brought him back to the surface."

"Mind if I take a look around?" Lynn asked.

"No problem." Keisha pointed at a narrow makeshift cordon she'd set up. "Stay outside of that."

Lynn pointed her torch at the ground and stepped onward, away from the direction Hettie Bradshaw had taken the previous morning. She walked slowly, sweeping the beam of light from side to side, trying to ignore the way the rain in the torchlight gave the impression of movement. After a minute, she thought she'd found something, but it was only a leaf catching the light.

"Did you ask me if you could wander off?" DS Bateman called.

"I don't..." She sighed and drew the torch back along the ground.

She stopped.

What was that?

She took a step towards it and bent down, careful of her balance. Lynn edged closer.

The edge of something long and narrow, caught on the end of a leaf. Lynn reached into her pocket, and then remembered she was already wearing gloves. DS Bateman had refused to do so on the basis that it wasn't his job to handle evidence.

She leaned forward and picked it up.

"What are you doing?" the sarge asked.

She ignored him.

It was a strap. Leather, although she couldn't be sure. Holding it in her left hand, she reached into her pocket with her right and pulled out an evidence bag. She slid the strap in.

"What have you got there?" DS Bateman asked.

She stood and walked past him.

"I asked you what you've got there," he called after her.

"I don't know."

Keisha seemed excited by what Lynn had found. DS Keyes kept saying, "Well done."

"It's probably nothing," Lynn pointed out.

"Maybe," Keisha agreed, holding up the bag and examining its contents in the torchlight. "But maybe not. I'll take it back to the lab."

Keyes held out a hand to stop her. "Let's get a photo first."

She held it up a moment longer while he photographed it from half a dozen angles.

"Good. I'll get this off to the pathologist. See if it's a candidate for whatever the killer used to strangle Kevin Downes."

There was a deep, rumbling noise, and it took Lynn a moment to place it. She swung her torch around to see Bateman, lumbering back, breathing as if he'd just climbed a dozen Wainwrights.

"What've you found?" he called out. Before anyone could answer, he gave a startled yelp and disappeared.

"Fuck," she heard. "Fucking hell. Fuck's sake. Fuck."

No one moved. A moment later, Bateman reappeared,

his head first, then the rest of him. All of it covered in a thick, dark slurry of mud.

Lynn turned to see Keisha, bent double and laughing so hard she could barely breathe.

She smiled, careful to hide her face from the sarge.

CHAPTER TWENTY-SIX

TEN MINUTES in the team room was enough for Zoe to see that problems were brewing.

Nina had dropped into her office just as she'd finished talking to Randle, full of excitement over what she'd achieved with the two women who hadn't run. A new safe location, with someone they could trust, and someone who could translate for them and make them feel at home.

It was more than a start; it was excellent news. Zoe didn't have the heart to remind Nina how long it had taken Elena to open up. The women they'd found, the ones who'd stayed, who knew what they'd been through? But at least they were both still alive.

Zoe followed her to the team room so she could share the news with the others, but Aaron was over in Elterwater. Tom was focused on his screen, and Zoe hoped he'd found something she could use to keep the Bobby Silver investigation away from Streeting. Harriett was putting down her phone when they walked in. She looked up, glared at Nina, and looked away.

Problems brewing. Nina had made no secret of her dislike. Zoe would have to do something about it, sooner rather than later. She'd just opened her mouth to kick off what would no doubt be a memorably unpleasant conversation when her phone rang.

Ignore. She glanced down, ready to tap the red button, saw the name above it, and tapped green.

"Zoe? Upstairs, now."

She sighed. "Super wants to see me. Sorry." She turned and walked straight upstairs. If Fiona had news about Bobby Silver, then Nina and Harriett would have to wait.

There was no sign of Luke. Zoe tapped the super's door and walked in without waiting. She was surprised to see others there ahead of her.

She'd only seen Alan Markin a few days earlier, but he seemed to have aged years. He'd never been tall, but he looked shrunken as he stood leaning against the wall.

In the middle of the room stood Morris Keane. If Markin had shrunk, then Inspector Keane had grown, but generally outwards. It suited him, in a way that nothing would suit Markin. While Markin gave the tiniest of nods, Keane at least offered her a smile.

Fiona, standing, as ever, by the window, was the only one to speak.

"Good," she said. "I'm pleased you're all here. The IOPC are in."

Morris Keane nodded, calm and thoughtful. But Markin's eyes were wide, his body stiff. If he'd had hair, it would have been standing on end.

Fiona just looked weary.

"You know what to do, OK?" she said.

Glances were exchanged.

"I'm sorry, Fiona, but I'm not sure what you mean," Zoe said.

"For crying out loud, do I need to spell everything out to you people? Just keep things steady. Even hand on the tiller. No fuck-ups. Don't do anything stupid."

Zoe's eyes met Morris Keane's. She was certain he was having the same thought she was.

How was Alan Markin going to manage that?

"What do they want?" said Markin. "Who are they going to speak to?"

There was a tremble in his voice that almost had Zoe feeling sorry for him. Before she remembered his response to the death of Victoria Speares. He'd forgotten her name. And when Zoe reminded him, it had been nothing more than, "That one. Choked on her own vomit."

With the assistance, it had turned out, of former PC Tel Cummings.

Fiona turned to him. "They'll speak to everyone, Alan. You. Your team. Uniform."

Fiona's gaze moved over to Morris Keane, who nodded gravely at her but otherwise failed to react.

"Cummings was one of yours, Morris," she said.

"Yes."

"And as well as being a thoroughly unpleasant man, he was a corrupt officer."

"He was," agreed Keane.

"Aren't you concerned about the effect of having someone like that in your team? How the IOPC will see it? How it'll affect the rest of the uniformed officers here?"

He shrugged. "The rest of the team hated Cummings. As you say, a thoroughly unpleasant man. They're professional enough to get on with their jobs. As for the IOPC, they can ask whatever they want of whoever they want. I'll make every uniformed officer at this station available. We've got nothing to hide, Ma'am."

Zoe saw Fiona wince at that "ma'am," but Morris Keane wasn't one of hers. He didn't pop in to see her half a dozen times a day and listen to her insisting he call her "Fiona."

Zoe watched the super pacing between the window and desk.

It wasn't the "ma'am" Fiona was wincing at. It was the attitude. The calm. Morris Keane's relaxed approach had only served to make the super more nervous.

Zoe glanced at Markin, who looked back at her. There was desperation in his eyes. His hands were moving fast, the fingers tapping on an invisible keyboard.

Don't feel sorry for him, she reminded herself. The man was an arse. If he couldn't handle the IOPC, that was his problem, not hers.

Fiona, on the other hand, was everybody's problem.

CHAPTER TWENTY-SEVEN

AARON STOOD IN THE DRIZZLE, looking up at the cottage, at its familiar windows and walls, the stone bulging over the kitchen window, the dark stains from the fireplace incident back in their teens, the marks left by centuries of wind and rain.

He stepped up to the front door, reached out to the side, his eyes closed, and traced his fingers across the stonework.

He'd know this anywhere.

"Aaron? Aaron Keyes?"

He turned to see Mrs Miller gawping at him like he'd just landed from another planet.

"Mrs Miller. How are you?"

She shook her head, stepped forward, and wrapped him in her arms. "We'll have none of that 'Mrs Miller' nonsense. It's Val, same way it's always been. How have you been? It's so lovely to see you. What have you been doing?"

"This and that."

"I bet. Well, don't just stand there getting wet. Get in. I'll get the kettle on. Joe!" she shouted, so suddenly that Aaron, who'd just followed her through the front door, jumped.

"Joe! You won't believe who's here!" She turned to him, smiling. "Go on, get your shoes off, get your coat off, go and sit down. You know where. Nothing's changed. Sara's going to be so pleased..."

She strode off to the kitchen, leaving him alone in the little hallway.

Aaron removed his shoes and coat and entered the living room, where Joe Miller sat in the same armchair he'd sat in for the decade and more Aaron had been frequenting the place.

"Bloody hell," said Joe, pulling himself up and shaking his head. "Look what the cat dragged in."

Aaron smiled, walked over, and bent to shake the man's hand. Joe was a little under five foot tall, missing the bottom of each leg following a quarry accident when Aaron and Sara were...

Aaron had been six years old. Maybe seven. Sara had stayed at his for a fortnight, which had felt like a year, and it was probably that fortnight that had cemented their friendship.

Val returned with a tray laden with tea and biscuits, but Joe shook his head in disgust and pointed to the cabinet beside Aaron.

"Grab a couple of glasses and a bottle of Scotch, Aaron. Weather like this, tea just won't cut it."

"You've heard about Sara, then?" Val asked when all the drinks had been poured and the three of them were sitting. *Nothing's changed*, she'd said. She wasn't wrong. Aaron was perched awkwardly on the same lumpy cushion he'd half-flattened in his teens.

But where was Sara?

"Not really," he replied. "I just heard she was here." He looked around the room as if expecting to find her hiding behind a chair.

"Yes," said Joe. "Thanks to that shit."

Val gave him a look. "Now, Joe, we don't need any of that language."

"He bloody deserves it, Val. He—"

"Well, if anyone does, I suppose it's him. To throw her aside like that, without... Well, it's not right, Aaron. It's not what a decent person would do."

"Who?"

"Who? Marc bloody Langham, of course," replied Joe.

"What happened?" asked Aaron. It wasn't any of his business. But these people had been like family. If they wanted to tell him...

"Well, they were engaged," said Val. "Even set a date for the wedding. You knew that, didn't you?"

"Yes," he lied.

"He'd moved back here from that place, bought the big house outside town."

That place, Aaron knew, meant London. The big house outside town could be one of a number of buildings. Marc Langham had made money in something Aaron didn't really understand, but then, he and Marc had never been friends. Not enemies, either. They simply hadn't moved in the same circles.

Aaron hadn't really moved in any sort of circles. More a line, with Sara at one end and Aaron at the other.

"Well, she were living there with him," Val went on, a hint of disapproval in her voice. "Till she weren't."

"What happened?"

"He broke it off and kicked her out," said Joe, the venom in his voice startling Aaron so that he almost spilled his Scotch.

"What... Why would he do that? When..."

Aaron turned from Joe to Val and saw the same anger reflected on her face.

Val nodded. "Few weeks ago. And no, I don't know why. She won't tell me. Hardly talks, she does. Just stays in her room. That man. But now you're here." She brightened a little. "Maybe she'll come down."

She stood, and a moment later he heard the tread of her feet on the stairs.

"That Marc Langham," Joe said. "He gives all that 'man of the people' nonsense, pretends he's all nice and friendly even though he's a millionaire, but he's just like the rest of them."

"What d'you mean?"

Joe shrugged, took a sip of his whisky, and closed his eyes. "Selfish," he said.

Anything he might have added was interrupted by more footsteps on the stairs, and the return of Val Miller.

Sara walked in behind her, wrapped in an old, tattered dressing gown, her steps so measured they were almost robotic.

"Sara," Aaron said, standing and forcing a smile. He walked over, held out his arms, and she stepped into them, almost mechanically. He hugged her. Through the fabric of the gown, she felt hard. Cold.

She didn't hug him back. Instead, she waited a moment, then stepped away and nodded.

"Aaron," she said.

They both stood there, looking at each other. She was so

thin. She'd always been slight, but now she was barely there at all. And so pale.

"It's wonderful to see you," he said.

"Aye, well, it's nice to get out of the room, isn't it, pet?" said Joe.

"Joe!" hissed Val.

"Well, it's true, isn't it? Someone like Aaron, he knows. He knows what people are. Knows how to treat 'em. Not like objects. Not like just another thing you can buy and throw away when you're tired of it."

Aaron watched Sara. She'd seemed close to emotionless, but as her father spoke, she flinched.

"I can't do this," she said. "I'm sorry."

She turned and walked away, and Aaron found himself looking into the sad, weary eyes of her mother as they listened to her footsteps climbing the stairs.

CHAPTER TWENTY-EIGHT

IT WASN'T A KARAOKE NIGHT, but the Miner's Yard was still busy. If Nina got up and started singing, no one would object.

Maybe Tom, but he deserved it.

He returned to the table with her vodka and his lager. Hers was a double and his was a half.

"I'm sorry," he said. "But I'm still recovering from last night."

"Yeah. You and Harriett." She hadn't meant to say it.

"What does that mean?"

"Nothing," she lied. "Just, if you're going to get drunk, you should include me from time to time."

"I will. But if you're serious about these exams, you'll need to work."

She took a large swig from her glass and set it down. She could feel the evening slipping away, all the little niggles building up to something bigger.

"What do you mean?"

"It's not going to be easy." He seemed relaxed. He hadn't picked up on her tone.

"Are you suggesting I'm not clever enough, Tom?"

He leaned back, palms out, shaking his head. "No."

"No, I'm not clever enough?"

He rolled his eyes. "No, that's not what I'm saying. Shit, you'll be a better DS than I would. By a mile. But you've got to take the exams seriously."

"OK." That was fair.

"I was studying last night," she said. "While you were out, I had my head in a book."

"Good. But now you're here, drinking double vodkas like water. You need to be consistent."

Fuck's sake. First, the boss telling her she'd need to be more understanding, now, Tom telling her she had to work harder.

"I'll work tomorrow."

"You'll be drinking tomorrow."

"I'll work. Seriously."

"Bet?"

She narrowed her eyes. "Yeah. Usual stakes?"

He nodded. The antimacassar had been on his chair for a few days now, and she could see him picturing it on hers.

She'd have to make sure that didn't happen. Elena would help. She'd said she would.

They raised their glasses and drank. Tom opened his mouth, then shut it again.

She frowned. "What?"

"Harriett." He hesitated. "What's your problem with her?"

So that was what all this was about. Harriett Barnes.

"Look, it's not that—" She stopped as an arm landed on her shoulder and a face lurched towards hers.

"Moira," she said.

Moira's makeup had run, and her hair was a mess. She'd been at the pub since opening time. It was quite something that she was on her feet at all.

"Nina! Why didn't you say?"

Nina edged back. She didn't know what the other woman had been drinking, but it didn't smell great.

"Say what?"

"Say you were gay?"

Nina shook her head. Over Moira's shoulder, she could see Tom, looking amused but as bewildered as she was.

"I was what?"

"Gay! If I'd known, babes..."

"No," said Nina. "I don't think—"

"Shhhh." Moira put a finger over Nina's lips. "No point denying it now."

Moira leaned back. For a moment, Nina thought she was leaving, but then she shoved something in front of Nina's face.

A phone.

"Look," Moira said, triumph in her voice.

Nina looked. The display showed a Facebook feed. And there...

"Shit," said Nina.

"What is it?" asked Tom.

"Shit." Nina picked up the phone and read it again.

"What is it?" asked Tom again.

She passed him the phone.

She didn't need to read it a third time. She wouldn't forget it in a hurry.

It was her mother. Her mother's bloody Facebook. She'd posted an update.

Congratulations, it said. There were balloons and party poppers and all the extra stuff people put on their updates now.

Congratulations to my daughter Nina and her friend Elena. Nina and Elena are living together and very happy, and if anyone has a problem with that, they can take it up with me.

Tom looked at her. "Oh, hell."

CHAPTER TWENTY-NINE

It had been an awkward few minutes after Sara had gone back upstairs, but Aaron could hardly just get up and walk out. He had most of a glass of Scotch to finish, for a start. So he'd been forced to listen to Val berating Joe for his bluntness, and Joe defending himself and insisting they had to speak plainly or "the lass would never sort herself out."

"I'm so sorry about all this," Aaron said during a brief lull in hostilities. "Has she—"

"What you just saw, lad," Joe told him, "that's as good as it gets. Getting her out of the bedroom was a bloody improvement."

"I'm so sorry," he repeated. "And you don't know what caused this?"

"Marc bloody Langham caused it," said Joe.

"No," said Val. "I mean, yes, it's down to that bugger. But I don't understand why she's being like this. It's sad. It's awful. It's turned her life upside down. Ours, too. But this..."

She gazed at him, the sadness all too clear in her eyes.

And it was true. Aaron had seen breakups. Seen families torn apart. But Sara's behaviour, weeks later...

This wasn't the Sara he knew.

He made his apologies and left, heading back to his parents' house. It was just a mile away, but he'd chosen to drive, given the weather. Just the thirty-second walk from the cottage to the car had him shivering, and as he slid gratefully into the driver's seat and pulled the door closed, his phone rang.

Serge, he thought, but when he glanced at the number, he didn't recognise it.

"DS Aaron Keyes."

"DS Keyes," said a voice he'd heard, but not for more than a year. "I hear you're on the case."

Ryan Tobin. Their contact. He didn't trust Tobin, but Tobin wouldn't have minded that, because it was the small things he didn't trust Tobin over. The bigger picture?

Well, the boss trusted Tobin. That would have to be good enough for Aaron.

"Ryan. How did you get this number?" he asked. No way DI Finch would have given it away. Not without telling Aaron, anyway.

"I have my ways. Is it true, then? You're the man when it comes to finding out what's happened to Kevin?"

"Look, Ryan, I don't know what you expect me to say. I can't confirm or deny anything. There's no positive ID on the victim yet."

"But you reckon it's Kevin, yes?"

Aaron leaned back and closed his eyes. What was the point in holding back?

"Look, I'm sorry, but yes. No positive ID, but between you and me, it's him. It's Kevin. Your friend's dead, Ryan."

"Shit."

"I'm sorry."

There was a silence, and Aaron decided it was up to him to break it.

"I'll do what I can to find out who killed him."

"So it was a murder, then?"

"We think so, yes."

"Well, you know where to look, don't you? You know who..."

Ryan Tobin launched into an impassioned attack on "vested interests" and the "usual suspects" while Aaron listened wearily and watched the raindrops bouncing off his windscreen, picked out by the streetlights.

He gave it nearly two minutes before cutting in.

"Look," he said. "I appreciate Kevin was a friend. But I've been asked to run this investigation, Ryan, and the reason I've been asked to run it is that I know the area, I know some of the people, and believe it or not, I've solved murder cases before. If this one can be solved, I'll solve it. I have no doubt I'll be in touch to find out everything you know about Kevin. But until then—"

There was a pained laugh from down the line.

"Leave you alone? Understood, Detective Sergeant. I will await your call."

"Thanks, Ryan. And I am sorry. Oh, one more thing. We haven't found Kevin's phone. And we don't have any record of a current contact number for him."

"That figures." Another laugh. "He used to change his number all the time. Paranoid. And look where that got him."

Aaron's phone beeped. A text. He thanked Ryan, ended the call, and opened the message.

It was from the pathologist, replying to the photo Aaron

had sent earlier that evening. The strap, or whatever it was. The thing Lynn had found in the mud. Aaron had been expecting an easy *no*, something that would mean he could ignore the object, tell Keisha to focus her attention elsewhere and write off any chance of getting useful forensic evidence from the scene.

But Dr Robertson wasn't so sure.

I'd have to examine this strap of yours, he'd written. *I want to check its structure against pressure marks on the neck.*

But if you're asking whether this could be the murder weapon, then my first inclination is yes, it could.

CHAPTER THIRTY

CARL WAS in by the time Zoe got back, sitting in the living room with a beer and a visitor.

"Jake!" she cried.

Both men stood, Jake awaiting his turn to greet her. Jake Frimpton was a journalist at the local paper, the *Whitehaven Chronicle*, and a good friend.

"I hear they're in," he said, and Zoe tried a frown of confusion, but she knew what he meant, and he knew it.

"Today. Fiona's not happy." Zoe sniffed. "Do I smell chips?"

"Yes," Carl said. "But Jake's finished them. And your fish got cold, so..."

Zoe looked over to see Yoda stretched out on the floor by the electric fire. At least Jake had the grace to look sheepish.

"Bloody hell," she said.

Carl grinned at her. "Don't worry. I'll get you some in a minute. What did they have to say, though?"

"Not seen them yet." It was a strange conversation to be

having in front of a civilian, a journalist at that, but Jake was one of the few people up here she trusted.

"You think they'll want to talk about Huz?" he asked.

It had been Carl's team that had chosen to release Huz, before he was killed. Carl's boss, DCI Branthwaite had insisted on it and shouted down any objections. Branthwaite had apologised since. There'd been no real reason to suspect Huz was in danger. It was all just bad luck. Not really even a mistake.

That was what she'd told Carl. That was what she believed.

Hopefully, the IOPC would believe it, too.

"I'm afraid so," she told Carl. "But you've got nothing to hide there."

"I'll get your food. Jake, grab another beer while you're here."

They waited for Carl to leave for the chippy, and then Zoe followed Jake into the kitchen, where he helped himself to a bottle of lager. She and Carl hadn't been in the house long, but already Jake had spent enough time here to feel at home.

"How's your latest murder going?" he asked, grabbing the bottle opener from the cutlery drawer.

She almost said, "Which one?" but then, Elterwater wasn't his patch, or hers, for that matter.

"It's difficult," she said. "We don't know as much as we'd like to about the victim. And between you and me, there's a good chance it's linked to a broader investigation."

He raised an eyebrow. He'd know what that meant. What all of it meant. Off the record, not to be printed. Myron Carter.

"I hear she knew your DS. Aaron. That true?"

"You hear a lot, Jake. And yes, it is, again, between us. But I don't think that has any bearing on the investigation."

"Will he be able to get involved, though?"

"He's..." She chose her next words carefully. "He's working on other matters."

"Good." Jake took a swig of beer. "He's all better now, though?"

She nodded.

"Not good, though. First Victor Parlick, then Bobby Silver. Both friends of Aaron Keyes. If that got out..."

"Jake," she said, a warning tone in her voice.

"Don't worry. I'm just saying, tread carefully."

She nodded. If she could trust anyone, she could trust Jake Frimpton.

Sod it.

"We've got another murder investigation, as it happens," she said.

He put down his beer, surprise on his face. It was no wonder. She didn't know how his sources operated, but Jake tended to hear about dead bodies around the same time she did.

"Not local," she said. "Over near Elterwater."

"Why you, then?"

"They don't have the expertise," she replied. "And, well, let's just say that, again between you and me, there's a good chance this one's also linked to a broader investigation."

"Oh," he said, and then the front door opened, letting in a burst of cold air and the smell of vinegar.

Zoe's stomach rumbled. Yoda had appeared, perched on one of the stools by the kitchen island like an impatient diner at a restaurant.

"Not this time," she told the cat. "This one's all mine."

CHAPTER THIRTY-ONE

WHAT THE HELL WAS THIS?

Aaron had been driving for thirty seconds when a dark shape appeared in front of him. He slammed on the brakes. Another shape followed, heading in the same direction, from the pavement beside him to the other side of the road.

And there were voices. Shouts. He wound the window down, and things became clearer.

"Fucking piece of shit!"

"Selfish bastards, the lot of you!"

"Get out of our town!"

"How much are they paying you?"

He'd heard this before. Not here. In Whitehaven, during the near-riots after Daria's murder, a year and a half earlier. And elsewhere, in larger towns and cities when politics, emotion, and a personal stake ignited in a hot flame.

But not here. Never here.

He'd stopped in the middle of the road. He could manoeuvre the car somewhere less likely to cause an accident. Or he could put on his hazard lights and act like what he was.

A police officer.

He sighed and got out of the car. No one noticed him.

"Oi!" he shouted.

Nothing happened.

"Stop it!"

Still nothing. It was a blur. Lunges. Fists. Boots. Shouts. No one wailing or screaming. No one seriously hurt.

Yet.

He stepped back to the car, opened the door, and leaned on the horn. One second. Two. Three.

He kept the pressure on for ten seconds. When he took his hand away, the only sound was the rain.

He turned around. Seven men stood around the car, a frozen tableau of low-level violence. Even the snarls were still there, like someone had turned them all to stone. He carried on turning. Two more on the pavement. Another two, farther up.

"Aaron Keyes, Cumbria Police," he shouted.

There were a couple of murmurs of recognition.

"What the hell do you lot think you're playing at?" he said, loud enough to be heard against the drum of the rain.

That set them off. Eleven voices competing to be heard. Complaining about something the others had done, or said, or wanted to do or say.

He waited. The voices died down, and he approached the two on the pavement. He turned around and shouted, "The rest of you, don't you bloody move."

Sullen silence.

Fine.

Two minutes with the pair on the pavement, and things were falling into place.

Seven local lads, either out of work or in work they hated. Signed up for Sinead Conway's development and the jobs they hoped they'd get out of it. And four who weren't local, but weren't tourists, either. Four protestors, only one of them from Cumbria, but all angry about what Sinead Conway was doing to the heritage of the area, and its natural resources, and some other issues Aaron couldn't follow. Because the place wasn't exactly pure and untouched.

It was a quarry, wasn't it?

"You back for good, then, Keyesie?" said one voice. Aaron turned to see a face that looked familiar, but not familiar enough to put a name to. He frowned.

"Jed Starling," said the man.

"Niall Gallagher," said another. "So is that it, then? You back here permanently?"

Gallagher and Starling. They'd been a few years younger than him. Friends with Ben Fraser. But Fraser had moved on to better things.

"Not sure," he said, a lie. Hell would have to freeze over and then melt and boil and freeze all over again before he came back for good.

He just had a job to do.

"Well, reckon we've got all the cops we need here," said Starling.

The others were silent.

Aaron told the protestors to head back to the camp and watched while they walked away. Then he sent the rest back to their homes. He had no doubt they'd be at the pub instead within a few minutes, but he couldn't arrest them for that.

He had a job to do. That was all. Keeping these idiots from kicking seven shades of shit out of each other? That was just a bonus.

CHAPTER THIRTY-TWO

WALKING into Fiona's office had always been unpredictable, but these days it was like stepping into a minefield. This morning's summons had come by text, which meant there wasn't even a tone of voice Zoe could analyse.

Upstairs, Luke stood at the end of the corridor, his face inscrutable. When Zoe asked him if everything was OK, he shrugged and pointed towards the super's door.

Fine. If that was the way it had to be, that was the way it had to be.

"Sit down," said Fiona, sitting down herself. Zoe couldn't tell if that was good or bad news, but at least it was just the two of them. No Markin to drag everyone down. No Morris Keane to infuriate the super.

"What's up?" Zoe asked, taking a seat opposite Fiona.

"Streeting. He's got friends in high places."

Zoe felt her heart sink. "He's keeping the case?"

Fiona nodded.

"But after what I showed you—"

"You think I can send that up the chain?" Fiona asked. "You think that's enough? For you, maybe it's enough. For me, well, let's just say I wouldn't allow that man near any of my cases. But it's not enough for the CPS, and it's not going to be enough for Little Joe, either."

"So it was Joe Carghillie? The ACC? He intervened personally?"

"Personally? I don't know about that. I don't get to breathe air that pure. I heard from Becca Grey."

Zoe frowned.

"You don't know her? Stick around much longer, you will, especially if you're thinking about moving up the ranks. She's Joe's admin woman, or policy, or something. Not sure. These titles don't really mean much, do they?"

Zoe stared at Fiona. Was that a real question?

"Anyway, the long and the short of it is that Streeting's pulled out all the stops. He's keeping the case, and short of arresting him, there's nothing we can do about it. Got it?"

Zoe nodded, briefly tempted by that *arresting him*.

"OK. I appreciate that's where we are. And thanks for trying. But what can we do to limit the damage?"

Fiona smiled.

"Good. I like a woman who can move on fast. So, there I am, pleading with Becca Grey, which is a bit like begging from a rock, only with less chance of success, and it occurred to me that even if we didn't have good reason to keep Streeting away from the case, we'd have good reason to keep Streeting away from the case."

Zoe frowned again. "I beg your pardon?"

"His team. It's him and one DS. Morrigan, I think his name is."

"Mulligan," Zoe said.

"Whatever. It's not enough. I don't know if it's his morals or his fabulous personality, but DI Streeting can't keep a DS longer than a few months, and there's not a whisper of a DC asking to join his team. I'd be surprised if your man Mulligan was around much longer."

Zoe thought back to the DS. On first impression, he was another Streeting. Tall, dark, younger, better-looking. But she remembered something else. A warmth in his eyes. If he was a half-decent copper, he wouldn't stick around Streeting.

"So Streeting can't manage a case like this," Fiona said. "Not an important murder. Not with all the other organised crime and intel nonsense he claims he has to deal with."

Zoe blinked. Did that mean they *had* got the case back after all?

"No, Zoe," said the super, reading her. "He's keeping the case. But Becca agreed that he doesn't have the resources to do it as it stands. So he's taking one of your team with him."

What?

"Temporarily, of course. Just for the case."

"So I lose the case *and* I lose one of my team? Which one? Who does he want?"

"He doesn't want any of them, Zoe. It's up to you who you send. Think about it for a moment. This isn't as bad as it could be. In fact, it might be just what you need."

Zoe considered. Fiona was right.

She thanked the super and headed back down the corridor. It wasn't until she was back on her floor that she recalled Fiona's comment about moving up the ranks.

It had come up before, the idea of promotion. There was a gap in the hierarchy, something a DCI could fill quite nicely. And with Nina taking the sergeants' exam and Aaron acting up as DI...

Well, things couldn't stay the same forever. Maybe it was inevitable.

Whether it was what Zoe actually wanted, though, was something else entirely.

CHAPTER THIRTY-THREE

SOME THINGS NEVER CHANGED.

Like the noises the pipes made at night that kept Aaron awake as a child. The way his mum insisted on a coffee last thing at night, then spent half the morning wondering why she hadn't slept well. The view from his window, the woods, the fells, the ancient trees.

He'd forgotten about the heating. The radiator pumped it out all night, right next to the bed. *That* was why he never got a good night's sleep.

Aaron hadn't mentioned it, of course. Instead, he'd listened to his mum complaining about her night and his dad complaining about his mum, and reminded himself that this was just a hiatus. He'd be back soon. In his sensible bed with its sensible heating and his not-entirely-sensible husband and their perfect daughter.

Just the small matter of a murderer to catch.

He stood at the edge of the quarry pit, looking down, and trying not to feel dizzy, as he tried to picture how this was going to become a theme park. There was activity all around them, diggers coming and going, loaded with rock.

Pretty much the same as when it had been a quarry.

"Why the fuck did we have to come here?" asked Isaac Bateman. Lynn Hedley was a few yards away, turning a slow circle, trying to take everything in, but Bateman was standing next to Aaron, closer to the edge than he was. For a moment, Aaron saw himself reaching out and giving the man a gentle shove.

It wouldn't take much.

He shrugged.

"We don't know a lot about Kevin Downes," he replied. "First rule in murder investigation: get to know your victim. One of the things we do know is that he hated this place. I wanted to see it."

"Good." Bateman stepped away from the edge and shivered. It was cold, and Bateman was wearing a lightweight denim jacket instead of a proper coat. "You've seen it now. Let's go."

Aaron was about to agree, just to shut Bateman up, when he saw a figure approaching. He'd seen that figure before.

"Hang on," he said.

The woman walked carefully towards them from the far side of a long, metal-roofed building that looked like a good breeze might knock it down. There were signs all over the place, warning the unwary of the dangers, an incongruous mix of *Danger of Death* and *Children Playing*. Aaron had grown up here. The paths hadn't changed much, despite the best efforts of the woman now walking towards him.

"Hello?" she shouted, stopping about ten yards away. "Can I help you?"

Even from this distance, there was something striking

about her. Her height. Her presence. There was something almost serpentine about the mass of long dark hair that fell in waves past her shoulders.

Medusa, Aaron thought, as he stepped towards her.

"Ms Conway?" he said, close enough now not to have to shout. "I'm Detective Sergeant Aaron Keyes, from Cumbria Police. We've met before, but I'm sure you won't remember."

She frowned at him, then nodded. "Of course. DS Keyes. Is everything OK?"

"I'm sure you'll have heard about the body."

She shivered. "The one in the woods?"

"Yes."

"Have you identified him?"

"Not formally, but our initial findings suggest he was one of the protestors." He pointed behind her, in the direction of the cemetery and the camp beside it.

Her face was blank. Her eyebrows went up a little, a slight flicker of surprise. Then back down. Nothing.

"Well, I hope you can find out what happened to him, DS Keyes. And I'll make sure my people give you their full cooperation."

She stood there, looking first past him, then directly into his eyes. She was watching for his reaction, and he fought to keep his expression neutral.

"Thank you." He turned. "Come on," he called. "Let's get some work done."

He walked back alongside Lynn, Bateman a little way in front. "Have you met Sinead Conway before?"

"I've seen her," the DC told him. "But not met her in person. She's not usually here."

Aaron nodded. Now there was Conway Developments on top of Conway Homes. The woman was busy.

"What did you make of her?" he asked.

"I don't know." Lynn frowned. "She doesn't give a lot away."

He nodded again. Fair. You couldn't jump to conclusions.

"Where are we going now?" she asked.

"First rule in murder investigation."

"Get to know your victim." They'd reached the main road, and she stopped, frowning. After a moment her face cleared, and she turned to him. "The protest camp, then?"

He nodded, and cast a worried look in the direction of Bateman, who'd insisted on bringing his car again. Lynn must have seen the look because she walked over to Bateman and spoke quietly with him for a minute. Then Bateman got in his car, reversed hard and fast, without looking, and sped out of the car park.

"Why's he in such a hurry?" Aaron asked.

"I told him we were going back to the crime scene," Lynn explained. "He's gone home to get some wellies."

CHAPTER THIRTY-FOUR

By the time Zoe reached her office, thoughts of politics and promotion had been replaced by something more urgent.

Who would she put on Streeting's team?

It was obvious, really. Aaron was in Elterwater. Harriett wasn't hers to assign. Nina wouldn't keep her cool.

Zoe had seen Tom at the raid. Seen his panic attack. But she'd seen him react with a calm head when others hadn't.

He wasn't the ideal choice. But he was the only choice.

She only intended to sit at her desk for a moment, to gather her thoughts and check her messages. Her phone rang. She considered ignoring it, then saw the display. She sighed and answered.

"DI Finch," he said. "Glad I caught you."

"Mr Freeburn." She'd tried to turn their relationship into a "Zoe" and "Alistair" one, but it hadn't stuck. Alistair Freeburn, a corporate lawyer who acted for half the local crooks, was a close friend of the super's husband. He'd ended up providing Zoe with invaluable information about the finances of some of his clients. He was also the sort of man who thrived under formality.

"I hope everything's OK," she said.

"Well, I was hoping you could reassure me on that point, Detective Inspector. I've just heard about Dean Somerville."

Zoe closed her eyes, then opened them again.

Had she not told him about Dean? She thought back through her recent contact with Freeburn and realised there hadn't been any. He'd helped her trace the money Somerville had paid Carter for women to staff his so-called "salons." And she'd thanked him, and all but forgotten about him.

While Dean Somerville had been attacked and almost killed in Wakefield Prison.

"I'm sorry, Alistair. Mr Freeburn. I should have told you. But you don't need to—"

"Should I be concerned, DI Finch? I told you everything I knew about Somerville's financial arrangements. I spoke to your accounting man, Zhang. And now... Well, whoever got to Somerville in prison, they're not going to struggle if they want to get to me."

"You're fine, Mr Freeburn. There's a big difference between you and Dean Somerville. He had a firsthand relationship with the traffickers. You worked on a vaguely related business deal, and you've already told us everything."

"So I don't need to worry?"

She closed her eyes. Dean Somerville, injured. Olivia Bagsby, on the run. Bobby Silver and Victor Parlick, both dead.

"I'm sure you're fine. I can ask Uniform to run a regular sweep past your home and offices, if that helps."

"No, DI Finch. If you think everything's OK, I'll take your word for it. Thank you."

"Hold on. Are you familiar with the name Bobby Silver?"

"Yes," he replied.

She almost fell off her chair. "Yes?"

"Yes. She was a client. Why do you ask?"

She wasn't sure why she was surprised. Freeburn had made no secret of the fact that he acted for anyone and everyone.

As long as they could afford it.

"I'd like to discuss her affairs with you, if you don't mind. Can you—"

There was a knock on her door. A woman she'd never seen before stood there, a man behind her, waiting for her to admit them.

"I'm sorry, Mr Freeburn. I'll have to call you back."

She ended the call and waved the pair in.

"DI Finch?" said the woman.

"Yes."

"I'm Catherine Silverman. Senior Investigator, IOPC North West. This is my colleague, Ravi Sharma. Ravi's an investigator on my team. I hope we're not interrupting anything important."

A call with Alistair Freeburn? There were a lot more important things than that.

"No," Zoe said.

"Do you mind if we have a quick chat? We've been given an office on the fifth floor."

Lofty heights. Zoe hadn't spent much time on the fifth floor. She stood.

"Thank you," said Catherine Silverman. "Please follow me."

Zoe followed them both out of her office to the lifts. No walking up the stairway for the IOPC. It wasn't until they'd passed the fourth floor that she remembered there was something important she had to do, and it wasn't about Alistair Freeburn or Dean Somerville.

Bobby Silver. Ralph Streeting.

Tom.

CHAPTER THIRTY-FIVE

GETTING RID of DS Bateman had been a necessity.

Lynn had always thought of the sarge as annoying, and probably stupid, but she'd assumed he was a decent police officer. Then DS Keyes had turned up, and she'd seen how a competent detective sergeant was supposed to act. All Bateman had done was complain and fall in the mud.

The protestors at the camp weren't in favour of the police anyway, and Bateman had only made that worse. If they were going to get anything useful, Bateman couldn't be with them.

So yes, getting rid of him had been a necessity. She'd pay for it later, but it would be worth it.

She walked beside DS Keyes along the road, back towards Chapel Stile and past the Wainwrights' Inn, and then down the path to Thrang Burial Ground, with its ornate wrought-iron gate. She kept thinking she'd have to point the way, but he'd lived around here for years. Decades. He didn't need her directions.

They walked through the cemetery, picking their way

among the graves to a gap in the wall and the open fields beyond. The way the land curved here, you couldn't tell what you were going to see until you were right on top of it, and the camp appeared as if from nowhere as they crested a gentle rise.

They'd done that deliberately, she'd heard. Kept out of sight. Didn't want to ruin things for people visiting their dead relatives. Whatever you thought of them, at least they'd considered the feelings of the locals.

It wasn't much of a protest camp. Maybe a dozen tents and a handful of caravans. There'd been a lot more of them in the summer, but you had to really hate something to stick at it through a Cumbrian winter. These were the diehards.

"Have you spent much time here?" the DS asked as they entered the field and approached a few people standing around outside one of the caravans.

"Nope. Been along to check up on them a few times. There was a complaint about a burglary in town, but we decided it was probably malicious. There've been a few fights with the locals, like the one you saw last night, but no one got badly hurt."

"Tell that to Kevin Downes."

She turned to him in surprise. "You think that's what happened? A fight with a local that got out of hand?"

He shrugged. "Could be anything, couldn't it? What are these people like, then? Young? Old? Many kids?"

"No kids. Mostly in their twenties, a few in their thirties or forties. Men and women, but more men. They keep to themselves, for the most part, but that doesn't stop them attracting trouble."

DS Keyes had told her about the incident last night, and she'd not been surprised. Tensions were high, and as the deadline for the next stage of Conway Developments' planning application drew near, they were getting higher.

Lynn was on the fence. She didn't like the idea of her beloved Elterwater being overrun by tourists, but it was easy for her. She had a good job, a job she liked. Outside the police and farming and a few specialist products, tourism was all they had around here; most of the houses were second homes these days. And the place had been a working quarry. It wasn't like it was pristine, untouched territory.

She turned to face south, in the direction of the quarry, as if she could see it through the woods. If it weren't for the hum of distant machinery, you wouldn't know there was anything there at all.

"What the fuck you want?" said a voice.

She turned to see a man walking towards them. Mid-twenties, thick, dark hair. A jaw that seemed to cast its own shadow. Carefully groomed stubble. Good-looking in a way that suggested he knew it.

"DS Aaron Keyes. DC Lynn Hedley." DS Keyes flashed his ID card, and Lynn followed suit. "We'd like to talk to you about—"

"Got a warrant?"

"No," said DS Keyes. "But one of your friends has died, and I thought you'd want to—"

"Guess you thought wrong, then, didn't you?" There was something approaching a sneer on his face. "Now, if you haven't got a warrant, DS... What was it?"

"Keyes."

"If you haven't got a warrant, I'd be most grateful if you'd fuck off and not come—"

"Leave it out, Paddy," said a man who'd appeared at the doorway of one of the other caravans. "He's trying to help."

The man jumped down and walked towards them. From the way he moved, Lynn could tell he wasn't old, maybe in his thirties, but as he drew closer, she saw signs of age, or maybe just tiredness. Thin face, rings around the eyes.

"They just want..." began Paddy, but the newcomer shook his head, and Paddy fell silent.

DS Keyes watched as the man approached them and then held out his hand.

"Ryan," the DS said. "Good to see you."

"You too," replied the man, taking the offered hand and giving it a cursory shake. He turned to the others – there were more of them now, people drawn out of their tents by the voices, heads appearing in makeshift windows – and spoke loud and clear.

"This is DS Aaron Keyes. And this..." He turned to Lynn and spoke more quietly. "I'm sorry. I didn't catch your name."

"DC Lynn Hedley."

"This is DC Lynn Hedley. They might be cops, but they're trying to find out what happened to Kevin. I don't care what you thought of Kevin. He was one of us. So we're going to help these two get to the bottom of it. Right?"

There was a gentle murmur of sullen assent.

"Right?" he repeated. The murmur grew a little louder and split into individual voices. Lynn smiled to herself.

Sending Bateman away had definitely been the right call.

CHAPTER THIRTY-SIX

THE FIFTH FLOOR WAS A DISAPPOINTMENT. The rooms were bigger, but they still used the same carpet tiles and faux wood furniture as the rest of the building. Good to see money wasn't being wasted.

The two investigators led Zoe to a room not much bigger than her office. A round table with three chairs, positioned at what looked like a precise one hundred and twenty degrees. Zoe was invited to sit in whichever chair she wanted and chose the one facing the door, not wanting to be distracted by the views from the window. Then she glanced behind her and saw the usual cloud and rain. It wouldn't have been a problem.

The other two sat down, and Catherine set a briefcase on the desk, opened it, and pulled out a handful of papers. She was tall, slender, with mid-length grey hair and something feline in her movements. Her colleague was shorter, more solid, with what looked like a permanent grin. For a moment, Zoe had the sense she was about to be interviewed by a pair of cartoon characters. Then Catherine pulled a small recording device from the briefcase and spoke.

"Interview with DI Zoe Finch, conducted by Catherine Silverman, Senior Investigator, IOPC North West, and Ravi Sharma, Investigator, IOPC North West. This is not an interview under caution, and we are not at this stage investigating a misconduct allegation against you, DI Finch. Would you like legal or Police Federation representation?"

"No, thank you."

"DI Finch has waived her right to representation. DI Finch—"

"Can you call me Zoe?" Zoe asked.

"I'd rather not, if you don't mind. DI Finch, are you aware of the background behind our investigation?"

"I understand you're here in connection with the deaths of Hussein Mahmoud and Victoria Speares," Zoe replied.

"Very good." Catherine nodded, and Ravi Sharma's smile deepened. "Let's begin with Mr Mahmoud. What can you tell me about the decision to release him from custody?"

Zoe took a breath, looked at each of the investigators in turn, and began.

"Well, you're probably aware that it wasn't my team that had Huz in custody," she said.

"I'm sorry," interrupted Ravi Sharma. "Huz. That's Hussein Mahmoud, is it?"

"Yes. Sorry. It was PSD, but we were interviewing him. We'd established his role in a drugs operation. Do you need the full background on that?"

Catherine shook her head. "It's OK. We've read the files. I'll ask if there's anything unclear."

"Good. In that case, you'll know that Huz had already led us to the next individual in the chain, PS Carrie Wright, and that we'd had confirmation of her involvement from independent sources. Huz wasn't considered a risk to the public, or a flight risk, and I don't think anyone in the Hub would have challenged that assessment."

"Do you have a basis for that belief?"

Zoe shrugged. "We knew him. We'd worked with him. And the fact that he tried to go back to work the next day, begged to be let in, I think that justifies the general view that he wouldn't run."

"Very good," said Catherine.

"PSD made the decision to release Huz, and obviously with the benefit of hindsight that looks like a mistake, but you must understand that at the time, we had no reason to believe the drugs operation he was part of was being specifically targeted by the killer."

"Right," said Ravi. He held a sheet of paper up, frowned as he scanned it, then put it back down. "But I understand a member of your team, DC Nina Kapoor, challenged DCI Branthwaite on that decision. Why would she do that if she didn't think Mr Mahmoud was at risk?"

Zoe had known this would be coming. As far as she knew, it was the only weak point in PSD's defence. And she had it covered.

"DC Kapoor thought there was a possibility Mr Mahmoud might have had more useful information for us."

Huz might have named Bobby Silver, in an ideal world, and then they'd have got to her before Cummings and she wouldn't have died. Except Huz knew nothing of Bobby Silver. Even Carrie Wright knew nothing of Bobby Silver. The only people who did were Cummings, who was in prison, and Josh McKenzie, who was dead. And, it turned out, Alistair Freeburn. She'd have to talk to Alistair Freeburn when she got out of here.

"And did you agree with this?" he asked.

"I wasn't around at the time. But it was very much an edge decision and an operational matter, and Huz wasn't our prisoner."

"And if he had been?"

Zoe thought about it. "If he had been, I'd probably have kept him in. But only probably. And not out of concern for his safety."

"Very good," said Catherine, for a third time. "Now, turning to the matter of Victoria Speares, can you tell me what you know about her death?"

Zoe ran through her knowledge of what had happened, which was brief. She hadn't been involved in the operation to find Vicky Speares. All she knew was what she'd heard from Markin, and subsequently, from Cummings himself. She was asked to give her impressions of Tel Cummings, and she didn't hold back.

Catherine set down the papers she'd been holding and looked Zoe in the eye.

"Do you believe it's possible that more than one person was involved in Vicky Speares's death?"

"No," Zoe replied. "Look, I'm not naive. You'll be aware of my background. I've come across bent coppers before, and I know the Hub isn't squeaky clean. But I've got no reason to believe anyone else was involved in Vicky's death."

"Why not?"

"Well, if they had been, Cummings would have named them immediately. He's a man with no sense of loyalty whatsoever."

"Good. Thank you."

The investigators took her through a few more general questions before the shuffling of papers indicated things were coming to an end.

"Before we conclude, DI Finch," said Catherine, "what are your general impressions of the culture of this station?"

Zoe took a moment. She thought about her team. About Fiona. About Morris Keane, and PC Martinez, PC Collins, PC Chen, the man who'd been nearly killed by Vicky Speares.

And then she thought about Markin, and his DS, Tracy Giller-Jones.

"Look, it's not perfect," she said. "There's always room for improvement. But in my view, there's no real cause for concern, not when it comes to the culture of the place. The leadership is excellent, and the officers know their jobs and do them well."

She asked herself, as she made her way back downstairs, whether she really believed what she'd just said.

On balance, she thought, she did.

CHAPTER THIRTY-SEVEN

AARON TOOK his phone from his ear, stared at it, then put it back.

"Say that again, boss."

"Ralph Streeting's taken over the Bobby Silver case."

"You're kidding."

"I wish I was. Look, I've got to go. I'm doing all I can to minimise the damage. But whatever happens, I want you to stay where you are and sort out this Kevin Downes thing. OK?"

"OK." She'd already gone.

It didn't make sense. DI Ralph Streeting might not have shot Bobby Silver himself, but he'd given the order. He'd been involved. And now he was investigating himself.

But of course, it made perfect sense. The Ralph Streetings of the world had the contacts. It was politics, a cesspit where the scum always rose to the top.

Aaron turned back to the woman he'd been talking to.

"I'm sorry, Gal... What did you say your name was?"

"Galadriel," she said. "Like the elf. From—"

"Yes." The woman was maybe twenty years old, four foot tall and squat. Whatever he thought of her, it must have taken guts to come up with a name like that and stick with it. "Apologies for the interruption. So, you were saying, about Kevin."

"Yeah. Well, he dealt a bit, didn't he?"

Galadriel wasn't the first to mention this. Paddy had mentioned it, earning an angry look from Ryan, followed by something more like resignation when it was corroborated by half a dozen others. He'd been the go-to man for the camp, and there were rumours he'd supplied tourists and villagers, too, but no one seemed sure.

"The man liked his clothes," Paddy had said, and others since. "How else you gonna afford a jacket like that?"

Aaron had looked up the jacket online. Nearly fifteen hundred pounds.

"And I'll tell you something else," Galadriel continued. They were standing outside her caravan – she hadn't wanted him going in, which, he reckoned, meant she'd been one of Kevin's clients. But at least it had stopped raining.

"What?"

"That Conway woman, she didn't think much of him."

This was another popular theme. He'd spoken to four protestors and had a quick chat with Lynn before he got to Galadriel. They'd heard the same thing from everyone. Kevin might not have got the villagers on his side, but he'd struck a chord with people from elsewhere in Cumbria, and the wider environmental community across the north.

"You've heard her mention him?" he asked.

"Well, no, not personally," Galadriel admitted. "But I heard her bitching about the challenges and all that, and she must have known it were Kevin behind most of it."

"Did Kevin have any interactions with anyone else locally?"

"Well, you lot didn't like him, but you don't like any of us much, do you? Cops, I mean."

Another familiar theme. They'd all been forced to give prints and DNA, under threat of violence at the hands of Isaac Bateman. They still resented it.

Aaron resented it even more. Sometimes inadmissible evidence could be useful. But sometimes it was worse than no evidence at all. If it turned out one of this lot had killed Kevin Downes, their lawyers would have a field day with Isaac Bateman and his bloody threats.

"Apart from the police?" he prompted. "Girlfriend? Boyfriend?"

She shook her head. Again, the same from almost everyone. There was a man who'd insisted on being addressed as Saladin, who'd said there were rumours about a woman in the village, but no one else had heard a thing.

"And do you have a phone number?" he asked Galadriel.

"You asking me out, Detective?"

She pouted at him, and he fought back the urge to point out just how far from his type she was.

"I mean a number for Kevin. No one else seems to have one."

"Sorry, Detective." She looked disappointed. "If I wanted to talk to him, I'd check out his tent."

His tent had been thoroughly checked out. CSI would come and collect what was left behind, but anything of value would have disappeared in the last few weeks. No sign of a phone there, but again, that wasn't a surprise.

No one knew Kevin's number. Ryan had an old one, but Kevin had stopped using that even before he went missing.

Paranoid, as Ryan had put it. He hadn't even used a smart-phone. Just cycled between old, cheap models using pay-as-you-go to avoid having a contract.

Kevin Downes was a mystery. He wasn't enormously popular, even at the camp, and he seemed to have annoyed plenty of people outside it.

But whether he'd annoyed any of them enough to get himself killed was the biggest mystery of all.

CHAPTER THIRTY-EIGHT

"Here's your brew." Kay handed Nina a mug.

"Thanks." Nina forced a smile.

She liked Kay. She respected her. She might have broken the rules, but for a good reason. If a relative of Nina's had been dating Davey Grant, she'd have wanted to know more about him.

But everybody had their flaws, and Kay's, it seemed, was making a brew.

Nina couldn't figure it out. You dropped your teabag in your cup, you added sugar or sweetener, or nothing at all. You added hot water. You stirred, you added milk, you drank it. It was the kind of thing a child could do.

Unless you were Kay Holinshed.

"I think we're done," Elena announced, entering from the living room, where she'd been sitting with the other two women.

"That's a shame. I was looking forward to that brew." Nina winced. When would she learn to keep her mouth shut?

"Don't be silly," Kay said. "You don't have to rush off. Have your tea while Elena tells us what she's learned. Elena, do you want a cup?"

"No, thank you, Mrs Holinshed. I don't drink tea."

Nina raised her eyebrows. Elena had drunk plenty of the stuff at her house.

"It's Kay, remember? Not Mrs Holinshed." She pointed back into the living room, where the murmur of conversation could be heard. "Least they're talking. Not sure they said a word last night. You find anything out?"

Elena shrugged. "Not a lot. I know their names. Maria and Alexandra. Yesterday I thought they would tell me more, but now I think they've had time to change their minds. They thank you for letting them stay here, Kay. The other place... They didn't like it."

"What about the warehouse?" Nina asked. "Anything about the people who kept them there?"

"They said something about another woman. Belarusian. Kaciaryna, they called her."

"Red hair?" Nina asked.

"Yes. They said that too. She was with the smugglers, they said. One of *them*. Not one of *us*."

The same conclusion Nina had come to – she and Ellis Wood from the NCA.

"Anything else?" she asked.

"No. I asked them, and they looked at each other, and said nothing more. But maybe next time."

"You show them the photos?"

Nina had given Elena edited versions of Olivia Bagsby's long-range shots before she went in. The ones that showed the women, with Streeting looking on.

"I tried. They didn't want to see. Maybe next time," Elena repeated.

"Well, time's one thing we're not short of," Kay said. "Abigail finally deigned to call this morning. Said she's found work in a bar somewhere and she wants to stay out a bit longer. A month. Maybe more."

"Where is she?" Nina asked.

"Greece, I think. Or some island. Somewhere a lot bloody warmer than it is here, anyway."

In the car on the way back, Nina asked Elena about the tea. Elena fell silent.

"Come on. I know you drink tea."

"Sometimes," Elena said slowly, "it's better to lie than to hurt a person's feelings."

"You could have just drunk it and said it was fine."

"It's better to lie than to drink bad tea, Nina. And you, you're not always truthful yourself."

Nina shot her a wounded look. "What are you talking about?"

"You say you want to be a sergeant, to do the sergeant's exam, and you go out and drink and sing. If you really want to do it, you'd study."

"Yeah." Nina sighed. "It's not exactly a lie. I do want to do it. I even bet Tom I would study tonight. But it's hard work."

"How would you know? The book, it hasn't even been opened."

"That's..." Nina began, then stopped. "Yeah. Fair enough."

"I'll help you," Elena told her.

"What?"

"I'll help you study. I'll make you read the book. I'll test you. You'll get one hundred percent."

"I won't."

"With attitude like that, no. But if you work hard, Nina Kapoor, you can."

Nina wanted to argue with that. But there was something about Elena that made her want to prove the woman right.

CHAPTER THIRTY-NINE

DS Keyes had left her there.

He'd told Lynn he wanted to visit the quarry again, and he'd driven off and left her alone at the camp, surrounded by hostile protestors.

And she couldn't have been happier.

"Yeah, he was the man you could score off," Albert was telling her.

Albert was a tall, thin white man with dreadlocks who looked about fifteen but claimed he was twenty-five. She'd started off on the wrong side of him. She'd asked if his parents were around, and not given up the thread until he'd shown her his driver's license, which verified both his age and his equally implausible name.

Who called their son Albert in the twenty-first century?

"Do you know if he had any significant relationships, either here in the camp or outside it?" she asked.

Albert shrugged and closed his eyes. For a moment, she thought he might have fallen asleep.

"Don't think so," he murmured eventually.

The smell of weed was intense. Even outside, in the wind, she kept a few feet away from Albert. He'd clearly found someone else to score off since Kevin had disappeared.

She'd spoken to four more protestors since DS Keyes had left her. Or rather, had trusted her with the responsibility of questioning key witnesses, as she preferred to think of it.

None of them had a current phone number for Kevin. A woman who called herself Katniss had heard the same rumour Saladin had mentioned, about a woman in the village, but like Saladin, she couldn't remember who from. No one seemed fond of Kevin, but there wasn't any sense of hatred or the sort of strong emotion that might lead to someone getting killed.

Those were all the negatives. But there were positives, too.

There was a date, for example.

The man she'd spoken to before Katniss wasn't any older than Ryan, but had somehow acquired both a mane of silver hair and the sort of self-importance Lynn associated with cult leaders. Pete – a normal name, she thought, until he explained that it was short for Petrochemicals Will Kill Us All – was pretty sure Kevin had walked out of camp on the twenty-seventh of November, around seven pm. The time wasn't much more than a guess – "Darkness had fallen, I can tell you that much" – but the date was firm.

"His destination, of course, was the public house. To watch the big match."

"Big match?" she asked.

Pete eyed her as if she'd just asked him what colour the sky was. "The brave women of England against the German warriors, my child," he said, and she fought the urge to shiver. "The Lionesses, hoping to repeat their mighty Wembley triumph."

Pete gave Lynn the creeps, and she resolved to keep an eye on him. But what he'd said about Kevin leaving was backed up by both Katniss and, when he finally understood the question, Albert. She wasn't sure how reliable Albert's memory was, but he'd perked up when he remembered the football match.

There was only one pub Kevin might have gone to for the football, and that was Wainwrights' Inn. Katniss threw the name at Lynn almost before she asked. So maybe Kevin Downes had left the camp, headed for the pub, and somehow got himself killed on the way there.

Only, it didn't make sense. To get from the camp to the pub, Kevin would have walked northwest, and he'd have been there in a few minutes. But the spot in Baysbrown Wood where his body had been found was southwest of the camp, over the Langdale Beck, more than twenty minutes' walk away.

Closer to Sinead Conway's quarry than to anywhere else.

Lynn tried again, and things became even blurrier. Pete was convinced Kevin had walked out of camp that night and was certain he'd talked about going to watch the match.

But now that he thought about it again, he hadn't actually seen Kevin walking out of camp. Neither had Katniss. Albert was asleep, but even when he'd been awake, his answers had been less than certain.

Lynn was attempting to rouse him when she heard a familiar voice shouting from a distance. Every muscle in her body tensed up.

"'S'pose you thought that were funny, did you?"

She turned to see Isaac Bateman striding towards her, ignoring the hostile glares of the few protestors lingering outside.

"I'm sorry, Isaac." She forced a smile onto her face. "We were going to visit the crime scene. But we changed our minds."

She waited, certain he wouldn't believe her, but to her astonishment, he seemed to relax, his shoulders dropping, his jaw loosening.

"Could have called me, couldn't you?"

"I really am sorry." The protestors had lost interest and returned to whatever they'd been doing before Bateman had turned up. "DS Keyes was just too busy."

"I bet he was," he grumbled. "But what about you, eh? You could have called."

She nodded and threw on that smile again. "I suppose I could have done, Sarge. But I wouldn't want to exceed my authority."

She'd pay for that later. But for that brief moment, watching the annoyance and frustration on Bateman's face, it was worth it.

CHAPTER FORTY

"HELLO!" Aaron called.

The woman stopped and turned. She stood by her car, a long, low chunk of dark green metal and glass. Her shoulders slumped as she recognised him.

Aaron focused on her as he approached. Sinead Conway was giving nothing away, except maybe mild annoyance. And even Aaron had to admit that was a reasonable reaction to the police showing up.

He drew closer. His attention switched to the car.

"Blimey." He forgot himself for a moment. "I'm sorry. I shouldn't have said that."

She smiled. "You like it?"

"It's yours?"

"My pride and joy. Well, one of them. Doesn't take kindly to all the dust round here, but it's better than the salt in the air further west. I usually keep it garaged."

"Don't blame you. Do you mind?"

She nodded, and he walked around it. An E-Type Jaguar. He wasn't sure he'd ever seen one in the flesh.

"Racing green," he observed.

"Nineteen sixty-three, semi-lightweight," she replied. "Did you want to speak to me, DS Keyes?"

He stood, narrowly avoiding banging his head on the car. "The man who died. Was murdered. I understand he'd caused you and the development here quite a lot of trouble."

"Had he?" She glanced at her watch. "What was his name?"

"Kevin Downes."

There it was again. The briefest rise of her eyebrows.

"Yes. I'm familiar with the name," she said. "And I'm happy to talk with you, DS Keyes. But right now, I'm in something of a hurry."

"Oh?"

"I'm due back at the stables. Taking Jenkins out for a canter."

"Jenkins?"

"My horse. He'll have been prepared, and they're sensitive creatures, thoroughbreds. You don't want to keep them waiting. As I say, I'm happy to discuss this further. But not now."

"You knew the man, then?"

She opened the car door, climbed in, and looked back at him. "Not personally. He was one of the more persistent troublemakers, though. But really, DS Keyes, dealing with people like Kevin Downes is all in a day's work. Nothing unusual. Now, if you'll excuse me."

She reversed, then took off in a haze of dust. Aaron imagined the squadron of lackeys waiting for her with buckets and sponges, ready to clean her precious car. Then he pulled out his phone and called Lynn.

"Sarge," she said.

He felt a jolt of pleasure that she'd forgotten her earlier decision to reserve the word for Isaac Bateman. He related the conversation he'd just had, and waited for her reaction.

"'Dealing with people like Kevin Downes is all in a day's work'? That's what she said?"

"Those very words. What d'you think?"

"Well, Sarge, if she was a suspect, I'd be treating that like the sort of inadmissible confession I usually get from the toerags round here."

"What do you mean?"

"You know, there's a burglary, and Uniform picks up the little git who probably did it, and they sit there and say something like, 'Oh yeah, there's some nice stuff in that place, shame it got taken.' They're taunting you. You know they did it, but they know you can't prove it."

"Yes." He nodded. There'd been nothing like that in Sinead Conway's tone of voice. But the choice of words was interesting.

"And, Sarge," Lynn said. "There's something else."

"Yes?"

"I heard back from Whitehaven. The DNA's conclusive. The dead man's definitely Kevin Downes."

CHAPTER FORTY-ONE

"WHAT?" Tom said. "I mean, sorry, boss, but *what*?"

"I said," DI Finch repeated, "that DI Streeting has been granted strategic and operational control over the Bobby Silver investigation. He's SIO."

"But Streeting's... He's... "

Tom glanced at the spare desk for help, but Harriett wasn't there. She'd nipped out to get them both coffees and a snack. They'd played three rounds of rock paper scissors to decide which of them would have to go.

"Yes," said DI Finch. "I know. But there's more."

She was watching him with a look he hadn't seen since the Alice Winstanley incident. Something approaching concern.

"What?" he repeated. "What is it, boss?"

"You've been assigned to assist, Tom."

He blinked. "Sorry, can you repeat that?"

"They need more bodies. As things stand, it's just him and DS Mulligan."

"Kieran," Tom said without thinking. "I've met him. But hang on..."

His head was swimming.

Assigned to help Streeting?

"I don't understand," he said.

"No, neither did I, at first," she replied. "The super said I had to hand over one of my team, and I thought she'd lost her mind."

Tom frowned.

"Tom, you've got two assignments," she said. "On the surface, you're helping with the investigation into Bobby Silver's murder."

"Right. Yes. And?"

"The real assignment is to watch Streeting. Watch him like a hawk. Record everything he does. If you can record it to evidential standards, so much the better."

"Oh," said Tom. "Oh."

"Streeting wanted this case for a reason," the DI told him. "He's used every trick in the book to get it off us. If he's covering something up, I want to know what that is."

She looked him in the eye. "And you're going to find out."

CHAPTER FORTY-TWO

Lynn stared at DS Bateman, then forced herself to look away when he looked back at her.

"What?" His face was even redder than usual, but that wasn't what she'd been looking at.

"Nothing." She bent over her keyboard, biting her tongue. Digging her nails into her palms.

"What is it?" said Bateman.

She turned to him, looked him up and down, and shook her head. "I thought you were going to get a pair of wellies."

The upper half of DS Bateman was the same as usual. Big. Jacket and shirt. Shiny red face.

The lower half... There were trousers, certainly, but from the knee down, they were streaked with mud.

And as for his shoes...

"I thought it wouldn't be so bad in daylight," he grumbled. "I got a bit lost."

To fall over once in a muddy crime scene was unfortunate. To fall over twice, the second time in broad daylight, in a wood you'd walked through a hundred times just a stone's throw from the village you'd lived in all your life, that was something else. To do that wearing decent shoes and smart trousers, after you'd already decided that was a bad idea but then changed your mind?

Lynn shrugged and turned back to her screen.

Sinead Conway's name cropped up on the PNC, but Lynn already knew that. There was the Whitehaven case DS Keyes had worked on, but Conway hadn't really been involved there, or at least, not as far as anyone could see.

But a search of the force intelligence and incident databases brought up a couple of matters that weren't so clear.

Conway Homes (Ambleside) appeared just over a year ago, which meant Elterwater wasn't Sinead Conway's first venture this side of the county. A residential development. Nineteen houses, so nothing massive, but this was the Lake District. Nineteen houses could cause the kind of furore it would take half a city to kick up somewhere else.

This furore had resulted in someone's death. And not just a random "someone."

A protestor.

Gabriel Morales had been one of a number of people bussed up from London and elsewhere to protest against the development alongside local objectors. They'd gone to the site and, as the report had it, "made a nuisance of themselves."

And then Gabriel's involvement, and his life, had come to a premature end under a digger.

In the wake of the tragedy, the protests had melted away. The new houses had been built. People were already living in them. They probably had no idea about the man who'd died.

And Gabriel Morales wasn't the only one.

Conway Homes (Maryport) was less recent. Two years ago. This time, the protestor was a local woman.

Jan Calloway.

But Jan Calloway hadn't died. Or if she had, her body hadn't been found.

Jan Calloway had simply disappeared. Much like Kevin Downes might have disappeared, if heavy rain and snow, and the hunger pangs of wild animals, hadn't disturbed the earth that covered him.

Jan Calloway had disappeared. Gabriel Morales had been killed.

Kevin Downes had disappeared, and been killed.

It was time to do some more digging.

CHAPTER FORTY-THREE

"Well, I won't pretend I liked the woman," Mrs Gillespie was saying. "But I s'pose it's a shame. Who's going to buy all this now?"

Tom stood against the wall in the back room of the shop. There was a table and three chairs, but when he'd pulled one out, DI Streeting had shot him a look of such venom he'd pushed it back in again.

Streeting, who'd insisted on all three of them being present, was sitting down.

DS Mulligan leaned against the wall next to Tom, silent. He hadn't even tried to sit.

"Look at it all," continued the old woman. "What'd she need all this for?"

Mrs Gillespie was in the front room, the bit that served as a shop, with the connecting door open. She stood in front of a cupboard by the front door, pointing up at the top shelf, where Tom could see maybe a dozen little blue tins of Vaseline.

"Working at the Port," Tom said. "Dries your lips out."

Streeting turned to him. "Did I say you could talk?"

"No, sir—"

"Then don't."

He glanced to his left, saw Mulligan grimace in what he thought might be sympathy, then looked straight ahead.

At Streeting.

"And you never saw anything unusual, Mrs Gillespie?" Streeting asked. "I know you didn't like Bobby Silver or her dog. You've told us that. I'm interested in whether you noticed any of her visitors."

"Why would I see something like that?"

"I was just—"

"You city folk might spend all your time spying on your neighbours, but round here, we mind our own business." She pulled the cupboard door shut with more force than necessary.

Streeting turned to the other two. "We're done here. Back to Durranhill."

Streeting had driven himself out there. Tom had driven Mulligan, who'd spent most of the half-hour drive from Carlisle warning Tom that DI Streeting was in "an even worse mood than usual."

Tom was hoping it was his presence that accounted for that mood.

Outside the shop, Streeting stopped by his car. "We're not going to learn anything here, are we?" he said.

Tom opened his mouth to reply, then spotted Mulligan shaking his head.

"Bobby Silver was a dealer who ripped off other dealers," Streeting continued. "People like Tony Harris. One of them figured it out and killed her. When we get back to the nick, I want the two of you going through all the two-bit lowlifes who fit the bill. Then I want them rounded up and brought in."

It was something, at least. It was a waste of time, deliberately focusing attention in the wrong direction, but apart from following Streeting around and leaning silently against walls, it was the only task Tom had been given so far.

In the car, with Mulligan, he concentrated on keeping Streeting's BMW in view without making it obvious to the DS beside him what he was doing.

Mulligan seemed like a good guy, but then, Huz had seemed like a good guy, too. And Mulligan worked for Streeting.

You couldn't tell.

"What do you reckon?" asked Mulligan suddenly.

Reckon?

"What do you mean?"

"Boss's view. Some low-level dealer."

"I don't know." It wasn't entirely a lie. Tom couldn't be completely sure it was Carter's men who'd killed Bobby Silver. Just mostly sure.

But then...

"If he's right," Tom said, "then he'll have to hand over the case, won't he?"

"How do you figure that?"

"A spat between street dealers. It's hardly organised crime, is it?"

There was a long silence. After what seemed like an age, Mulligan finally spoke. "You could be right. But the boss wants this case. Anyone who wants to take it off him, they'll have to work hard."

Better get working, then, thought Tom. Because the

sooner this case was back where it belonged, the sooner he could get back to the Hub.

CHAPTER FORTY-FOUR

AARON FOLLOWED a trail of muddy footprints into the team room.

No sign of Bateman, just a pair of shoes under his desk. They might have been nice shoes, once. You'd think a man born and raised up here would have learned not to wear expensive shoes in the woods in winter.

The room wasn't empty, though. DC Hedley sat at her desk, speaking into her phone. She turned as he entered, smiled, and pointed at her ear. He frowned. Of course he'd noticed.

But she was used to working with Bateman.

He pulled off his coat and slung it over his chair, but his phone rang before he'd sat down. He answered and was greeted by a voice he was starting to recognise.

"Alright, Aaron?"

"Not bad, Keisha. Got anything for us?"

"Don't waste time on pleasantries, do you?" she said. "But yes. The strap DC Hedley found. I think we can get prints off it."

"Oh, good. I didn't expect that."

"Don't get excited. I can't guarantee it, and anything we do get will probably be so degraded it won't be conclusive anyway. But we've scraped it for DNA and sent it off to check."

"Good. Anything else?"

"Animal hair," she told him.

"What, from the... From whatever it was that disturbed the body?" Useful word, that. *Disturbed*. He didn't have to say *ate*.

"Not sure. Still looking into it."

"Thanks, Keisha."

She was being cooperative. Time to ask a favour. "Can you pass the strap on to Chris Robertson?"

"You're kidding, right?"

Be patient. Stay calm.

"He needs to check whether it's a match for the wound," Aaron said. "Whether it could have been used to strangle the victim. If it isn't, there's no point examining it any further."

"Fuck's sake, Aaron."

"And he's just next door." The lab Keisha was calling from was based in an industrial estate right beside the West Cumberland Hospital.

"Fine. I'll be in touch when I've heard about the DNA." She hung up.

As he pulled out his chair, he heard a throat being cleared behind him, and turned to see DI Woolley looking at him, her smile so inauthentic it wasn't fooling anyone.

But then, of course, she was used to working with Bateman, too.

Bateman stood behind her, looking at the ground.

"Good morning, Aaron," she said.

"DI Woolley." He ignored the fact it was afternoon.

"And how's my little murder team doing?"

"We're making progress. A number of—"

"Yes. Very good. I just wanted to remind you to keep Isaac here in the loop."

Aaron looked past her at Bateman, who was staring at the ground.

"Isaac's an experienced DS," she continued. "His insights could well prove invaluable."

She turned and walked away, and Isaac Bateman stomped over to his desk and sat down without once looking at Aaron.

At least he was wearing socks.

Aaron was about to sit down himself, finally, when his phone rang yet again. He answered it with a sigh.

"Yes?"

"Aaron. I was wondering how you were. Whether you had time for a chat."

"Dr Filey." He glanced at his watch, then around the room, and closed his eyes.

A chat with Dr Filey might be a good thing. Being back had stirred up all sorts of memories. There was Aaron Keyes, the man, comfortable with who he was and how he'd got there. But inside that man, there was still Aaron Keyes, the boy he'd been. The boy filled with neuroses, with worries about fitting in.

A chat with Dr Filey might help, but he couldn't have it here, with two people listening in. If it wasn't raining, a walk would be just the thing.

"Yes," he said, picking up his coat and slinging it over his shoulders. "That sounds like an excellent idea."

CHAPTER FORTY-FIVE

"Can't really chat, boss."

Zoe heard the tension in Tom's voice, along with engine noise; he was driving.

"It's OK, mate," she heard. "You chat away."

Another man's voice. So Tom wasn't alone.

Not Streeting, she thought. *Mulligan?*

She didn't want Tom overloaded with stress and blowing his assignment. Best to dial it down.

"Not to worry, Tom," she said. "Nothing important. If you get a chance, call me later. Otherwise, take care."

She ended the call and climbed out of the car into a dull, persistent drizzle. She'd just pulled up outside the offices of William Freeburn McNeil Todd, and the sea was so close she could have run in a straight line and been in it within a minute. But she couldn't see it through the thick fog and low cloud that had been hanging over Whitehaven all morning.

Inside Freeburn's office, she sat in a comfortable armchair sipping coffee while she waited for the man himself to arrive. The fact that she was in there alone spoke volumes about how their relationship had changed.

He'd been more than cagey when they'd first met. He'd been hostile. And, Zoe reminded herself, she could have been friendlier.

She stood as the door opened and he walked in, carrying a handful of files, and waved her down.

"DI Finch. Looking well." He gave her the sort of appraising look she'd have challenged from most men. But there was a naiveté to Alistair Freeburn that made the otherwise offensive, harmless.

"You, too," she lied. He'd added weight and lost hair. Aging before his time.

He grinned, patted his gut, and shook his head. "Very kind." He sat behind his desk and passed over the files. "But utterly untrue. Now, your Bobby Silver. I did act for her, briefly."

"Go on."

"First time was a few years ago. Details are in the file. She'd heard my name, wanted me to do a house purchase for her. I explained I wouldn't usually work on something so mundane for someone who wasn't a regular client, and passed on the name of a conveyancer. Harrison Murty. You know them?"

Zoe nodded. She and Carl had used them to buy the house they'd just moved into.

"Anything else?" she asked. If not, this was going to be the shortest meeting she and Freeburn had ever had.

He gave her a curt nod. "Eighteen months ago, she got in touch again. Told me she wanted to invest in some local businesses, but wasn't sure which ones or how to go about it. Now, as you know, that's much more my thing."

Zoe sat forward, intrigued.

"The first thing you do in these circumstances is see if they can afford it."

"And?"

"Oh, she could afford it, alright." Freeburn lifted an eyebrow, and Zoe felt she knew what was coming. "Next thing is, you see how they can afford it. So I went through her paperwork, and that's where things got a little murky."

"Proceeds of crime?"

Freeburn shrugged. "Maybe. Maybe not. I asked her where she'd got the money, and her answers weren't satisfactory, and in those circumstances, you have to assume the worst. I passed my concerns on to the NCA."

Zoe nodded. She'd seen the NCA report. Inconclusive, and Freeburn hadn't been mentioned by name, but she could have guessed it was him.

"You told her you couldn't act for her?" she asked.

There were rules about this. You had to be subtle. If you let the subject of a potential money-laundering investigation know they were being looked at, you could get into all kinds of trouble.

"Didn't have to. She changed her mind about the investment, and our brief professional relationship was over before it really started."

"She suspected?"

"Almost certainly. Realised she'd been too obvious about it all. I assumed she'd decided to pursue a more sensible strategy in future. Perhaps even a legitimate one."

She looked at him and sighed.

"Unfortunately," she said, "Bobby Silver didn't pursue a more sensible strategy after all."

CHAPTER FORTY-SIX

DURRANHILL NICK LOOKED MORE like a supermarket with a multistorey car park than a police station. The enormous multicoloured metal sheets outside the building were already fading.

But it was what was on the inside that counted.

Tom parked near the building, Mulligan guiding him to a spot he wouldn't have noticed. When the boss had called, Tom had frozen. He'd heard his heart pounding, felt bile rising into his throat, and prayed she wouldn't reveal the truth about why he'd been sent to Carlisle.

The call had ended, and after a few minutes of silence, it had been back to the usual casual banter. Mulligan had a handful of friends in the station but didn't have much to say about Streeting himself, or about DCI Carnegie, Streeting's boss.

"She seems OK, I think," Mulligan had told him. "But we never really see her."

Inside, the two of them followed Streeting up two sets of stairs and through a maze of corridors to a small office, one corner of which had been walled off to make something even smaller. Streeting's office. The DI pushed open a door and disappeared without a word.

Tom turned and looked around. There were two desks in the L-shaped room, one clearly Mulligan's, with a screen and a keyboard, a photo frame, and a pile of neatly stacked papers. The other was empty.

Not even a chair.

"Hang on," said Mulligan, and walked out.

Tom examined the room again. There was no window into Streeting's office, but from what he remembered of the building's layout, there would be no other exit. To get out, Streeting would have to walk through this room.

And past Tom.

The picture on Mulligan's desk showed him standing with his arm around a smiling woman with blonde hair and freckles, a waterfall in the background that didn't look like it belonged in Britain. Was he married? Kids? Tom could have named half a dozen people Mulligan had put away, but he had no idea where the man lived.

Mulligan was back five minutes later, pushing a chair, and behind him another man with a box of wires, who introduced himself as Phil and said he could help Tom get set up here if he had his laptop with him.

Tom produced his laptop, and Phil slid under the empty desk and got to work.

"So," said Tom. "This is your team room, then."

Mulligan looked around the room. "I suppose it is a team room. Never been anyone except me in it, till now." He glanced at the corner. "And the boss keeps himself to himself."

Half an hour later, the man himself finally emerged,

spotted Tom sitting at the desk, pretending to focus on his laptop, and sighed. He marched straight through the room and out again.

Tom was up and on Streeting's tail before he'd made it to the end of the corridor. He followed him up a flight of stairs and along another corridor to a white door, more scuffed than the rest of the station. The DI stopped and turned to face him.

"What the hell do you want?"

"Just checking if there's anything you need doing."

Streeting pushed open the door to reveal a tiny kitchen.

"Yeah. Coffee. Black. No sugar." He turned, pushed past Tom, and walked away.

Damn. He'd lost him. He'd just have to be quick and find him again.

Tom made one for Mulligan too, guessing on milk and one sugar, which turned out to be close enough. When he got back to the team room, Streeting was standing at the desk Tom had claimed. He reached out and took the coffee without a word.

"Nothing back from forensics," Mulligan said.

"Why not?" Streeting asked.

"They said there's been a holdup. Bit vague, to be honest. Something about authorisations and backlogs."

Tom forced back a grin. That would be Stella, making things as difficult as she could. He didn't envy Streeting.

There was a short silence, and Tom examined the DI's face. He wasn't sure he'd seen a man look that tense before.

Good.

"Boss," said Mulligan, seemingly unaware of the stress the DI was fighting. "What's next?"

Streeting said nothing.

"Have we taken statements from the victim's other associates yet?" Tom asked, knowing the answer.

Streeting turned to him. The man's face was slowly turning red.

Excellent.

"I understand there's a couple of friends she worked with at the port." Tom pretended to check his phone. "Miles and Stacey. Probably worth speaking to them, isn't it?"

"You bloody do it," said Streeting, and disappeared into his office.

Mulligan stood and shook his head. "He doesn't like you, mate. What's that all about?"

Tom shrugged.

"Well, whatever it is, it's not my problem. I'm off. See you tomorrow."

Mulligan walked away, and Tom went back to staring at the door to Streeting's office.

Streeting was tense and angry, and, as Mulligan had just pointed out, he really didn't like Tom.

Which meant he was doing the job just fine.

CHAPTER FORTY-SEVEN

"An unfortunate accident."

Lynn had read the report four times now, and every time she returned to those same three words. Gabriel Morales had been crushed to death by a digger at the site he was protesting. In any normal situation, it would've been looked into thoroughly. Would've been the subject of multi-agency investigations.

But no. One quick report, based on two witness statements, and that was enough to write the whole thing off as "an unfortunate accident." Reading the whole thing four times had taken her less than ten minutes. Another five to hunt down the police officer who'd written it. DS Charlie Mickleborough, who'd since moved abroad. To Australia.

Convenient.

Then there was the Jan Calloway incident.

Again, a cursory report from a detective sergeant who didn't seem to have put more than the bare minimum into her investigation. Lynn read the report again and was noting down a reference to follow up when the door opened and DS Keyes walked in, holding his phone.

"Sarge," she said. DS Keyes nodded, but she noticed another movement to her side, turned, and saw DS Bateman watching her. "Sorry. I mean DS Keyes. Something I'd like to show you."

Keyes wheeled his chair over and peered at her screen while she took him through her findings.

"Australia?" he said.

She nodded.

"I don't know Charlie Mickleborough, but the name rings a bell. Might be worth seeing if anyone locally has contact details for her."

"Him," Lynn corrected. "And then there's this other one. Jan Calloway. Went missing in Maryport, while protesting a Conway Homes project."

She sensed him leaning further in and shifted slightly to allow him to move closer, resisting the urge to make some quip about aging eyes.

"This one got followed up, too?" he asked.

"Yes. Another cookie-cutter report."

"Cookie-cutter?"

"Mass-produced. She could have been writing about anything. You could put these words down in roughly the same order, and it would cover half the unsolved crimes in Cumbria."

"She?"

"Yeah. You might know this one, actually. Maryport. Would have come through the Hub."

"Hub didn't exist then. But..."

He leaned in further, his eyes flicking right across the screen, then back and down again, like an old-fashioned typewriter. He reached the end, and his eyes opened wide, his mouth set hard.

"Jesus," he breathed.

She frowned. "What is it?"

"Her." He pointed at the name at the bottom of the report.

Detective Sergeant Tracy Giller-Jones.

"You know her?" Lynn asked.

"Yes. I know her. And if I'd gone missing, she's the last person I'd want trying to find me."

Given DS Bateman was sitting not six feet away, that was quite the condemnation.

CHAPTER FORTY-EIGHT

"Bring. It. On."

Nina repeated the words as she drove.

For once, there was no Elvis. Elvis made her relax. Made her feel good. Elvis was what she listened to when she had no problems. Or wanted to convince herself she had no problems.

But tonight, there was a problem. The problem sat on the passenger seat beside her, the spine uncracked, the cover staring accusingly at her.

Blackstone's Police Sergeants' Manual, it said.

Nina had come up against murderers, rapists, pushers, and thieves. She'd dealt with the scum of the earth, on the street and in the interview room. She'd faced her own demons, out on the ice, days earlier.

She'd never had an enemy like this one. But she would beat it. She would read it, and read it again, and learn that bastard like it had never been learned before.

Just as soon as she got home.

She could smell it as she parked. Like one of her neighbours had thrown some plastic on the fire. She locked the car and approached the house and sniffed. It was stronger.

She slowed as she approached her own front door.

The smell was even stronger.

She stopped.

Was that smoke?

She froze, then broke into a run. The door was...

She pushed, and the door opened. She tried not to notice the marks on it. Scorch marks. There was no heat, but she couldn't ignore the sting that forced her eyes closed.

Not before she'd seen it. On the floor. Black and curling at the edges, like it was still thinking about bursting into flame. Like...

"Elena!" she shouted.

Silence.

Where the hell was Elena?

"Where are you?" she shouted. She moved further into the house. The smoke was thicker, but not so thick she couldn't see.

Elena could be anywhere. On the ground. Unconscious, suffering from the smoke. Choking to death.

"Elena!"

"I am here," she heard ahead of her, and saw a figure standing by the open back door. "It is OK. I am here."

"What happened?" Nina walked purposefully towards Elena. "Are you hurt?"

"I was upstairs," Elena explained. "No."

"No?"

Nina had stopped in the kitchen, her back to the fridge, looking around as if the answers to all her questions might be written on the toaster or the kettle.

"No. Not here. Smoke. Come in garden."

"But the fire..."

"I put fire out. Call 999. They will be here soon."

Nina followed her out into the rain, and sure enough, there it was. Sirens, getting louder.

"What happened?"

"I was upstairs. I smell smoke. I come downstairs. There is a rag on floor, by front door. Fire. All very fast. I run to kitchen, get pan, fill with water, throw on floor. It is OK."

"It is OK," Nina repeated. The sirens drew closer.

"But you must listen, Nina. There is something else—"

"You're not hurt?" Nina asked again.

"No. But you must—"

"Arse. Fuck. Shit." Nina muttered. "I was going to... No. It doesn't matter. The books are safe."

Elena watched her, eyes narrowed. The sirens were close now.

"Are *you* OK, Nina?"

"I thought... No. It doesn't matter. No one's hurt. I just—"

The sirens drowned everything out, then went dead.

"Nina," said Elena. "There is—"

She stopped. She looked up, past Nina, into the house. Nina turned. There were men there.

"Everybody OK?" one of them shouted.

Yes, thought Nina. Everybody would be OK. Everything would be OK. She turned to Elena and followed her gaze to her own hand. To the *Police Sergeants' Manual*.

Everything would be OK. But she wasn't going to get much studying done tonight.

CHAPTER FORTY-NINE

"THERE YOU GO."

Lynn set two pints on the table and sat opposite Aaron. He raised his lager in a toast and took a slug.

Wainwrights' Inn was busy for a weekday in January. It had been a while since Aaron drank here. The bar was as smooth and shiny as ever, the guest beers as tempting as they always had been. The lighting was gentler, and the slate and wood had been cleaned up. The food smelled better, but you could say the same about most pubs. There were maybe twenty drinkers in, mostly men. No protestors and hardly a tourist in sight. Just locals.

Aaron had exchanged nods with half a dozen of them. All OK so far. There would be no trouble here.

"So you think this is where Kevin was heading?" he asked.

Lynn nodded. "They show the women's matches. Quite popular. If he was going to watch the England-Germany game, it would have been here. And I've checked. They were showing it."

"Good work." She was a decent DC. Wasted in Langdale.

No. Langdale needed good police as much as anywhere. Wasted under Bateman and Jasmine Woolley, that was it. Wasted at that station.

"And Isaac didn't trace his movements?"

Lynn shook her head. Kevin Downes had been reported missing, and Bateman and Woolley had done nothing. Hadn't even tried to find out where he was going. This morning, it had taken Lynn half an hour to piece his movements together.

"Come on." Aaron stood, picked up his drink, and made his way to the bar. He'd taken three steps when he heard his name being called. He turned and headed back, past the table, Lynn two paces behind him.

Marc Langham was sitting with two men Aaron didn't recognise. His bushy black hair was as wild as ever, but now there was something almost stylish about it. Maybe it was the glasses. Narrow lenses, a hint of a pattern across the arms. Some designer brand or other.

"Aaron Keyes, as I live and breathe." Marc stood and offered his hand. "Idris," he said, pointing to the tall Asian man to his left. "Bill." The shorter white man on his right. "You remember these two?"

Aaron pulled a face, pretended to think back.

"No, sorry," he said. "I don't think—"

"After your time," Marc said. "Sit down, the pair of you. Lynn, isn't it?" He moved to the nearest table, exchanged a couple of words, and came back with two more stools. "Tell me what's been going on in your life, Aaron. It's been too long."

Aaron didn't need more than thirty seconds to set it out.

"Moved to Whitehaven, Marc. Married, lovely bloke called Serge. We've got a daughter. Not a lot to add."

Marc nodded.

"Tell me about life here."

Aaron and Lynn sat with Marc and his friends for half an hour, bar the two-minute break Aaron took to get another round. Three more locals joined them, including Trish Marston, who he'd known since she was a tiny blonde toddler named Trish Newman. He repeated his own brief life story three times, and no one pressed for more. They were more interested in their own lives.

"Thing is," Idris was saying, "a place like this needs a bit of life. Something new."

"And don't forget the jobs," Trish added.

"Bollocks to the jobs," Marc said. "It's a crime against the environment."

Aaron hadn't been paying attention, but this was interesting. Everybody seemed to be in favour of Sinead Conway's development, which was what he'd expected.

Everybody except Marc Langham.

"What's the problem?" he asked.

Idris gave a long, loud groan. "Don't ask him that, Aaron. He'll still be talking about it at closing time."

"Shut up, Idris," Marc asked. "Look, it's simple. The land can't support—"

"Give it a rest," shouted someone from another table. Aaron hadn't realised so many people were listening. There was a burst of laughter, and Marc shook his head, grinned, and shrugged.

"The ignorant masses will always attempt to silence the true prophet," he said, then lifted the glass in front of him and knocked back nearly half a pint in seconds.

There was, Aaron admitted to himself as he made his way back to the bar, something likeable about Marc Langham. But Aaron had seen the state of Sara. He wasn't ready to forgive the man.

Eliot at the bar had been knocking around the village since before Aaron could remember. Ten years older than Aaron, and friendly enough without being friends. He was more than happy to talk about Kevin Downes.

"Yeah, I knew the bloke. Came here time to time."

"Don't suppose you'd know if he was here on the twenty-seventh of November? Night of the England-Germany game?"

"No," said Eliot.

Aaron thanked him and turned to walk away.

"I mean, yeah, I remember, and no, he wasn't here," Eliot added.

"Really?"

"Yeah. I remember the night, coz of the match. Trish drinks too much and passes out in the bogs. Bill nearly gets in a fight with some tourist about how big Scafell bloody Pike is. Marc misses the first half, buys everyone two rounds to make up for it. Sally nicks Frank's keys and takes off on his bike for an hour, and he doesn't even notice till she's back. Not a night you'd forget."

"And with all that going on, you're sure Kevin Downes wasn't in?"

"I'd have noticed. I were keeping an eye out for him."

Eliot had lowered his voice. Aaron leaned in.

"Last time I seen him were a week earlier. Told him he'd better keep his nose clean, or he wouldn't be coming back in."

"Why?"

Eliot looked from one side to the other, but apart from Lynn, there was no one close enough to hear.

"Drugs. And before you ask, I know it were, coz my lass were back from uni, and even though she swears blind he didn't, I'm sure he sold her something."

Dealing to the villagers. A man could make enemies that way, on top of all the other enemies already made.

CHAPTER FIFTY

NINA WATCHED ENOUGH TV. Real life was always a disappointment.

It wasn't that there was anything wrong with the fire-fighters. They were young, fit, pleasant, and competent. But there was a stereotype. And these guys – they were all guys – weren't it. They were just...

Normal.

"This your house?" asked the one in charge. She thought she'd seen him before, at one of the many suspected arson attacks that turned out to be someone falling asleep with a lit cigarette.

She nodded.

"Looks like your friend put it out before there was any real damage." He pointed towards Elena, who was talking to one of his colleagues.

Elena had been trying to tell her something before the fire crew had turned up.

"You recognise this?" asked the man. He held a mass of blackened... Blackened nothing.

"I don't know. What is it?"

"It's the rag that caused all this trouble. Looks like it's been doused with petrol and shoved through the door."

"Christ," Nina said.

Elena had been in here, alone. She'd smelled it, put it out. But if she hadn't...

She could have died.

"I wouldn't worry too much," he continued. She hadn't caught his name, but the others called him Skip.

Skip. It wasn't really a name, was it? Just meant he was in charge.

"No?" she said.

"Nah. Very amateurish, this. Your friend put it out without much trouble, didn't she?"

"I... I don't know." She turned back to Elena, who met her eye and mouthed something. Nina couldn't figure out the words. "You'll have to ask her."

"My colleague's been doing just that. Don't you worry. Chances are, it's just teenagers."

She turned back to him. "Teenagers?"

"You know. Yobs. Hoodlums."

She grinned at that. "Hoodlums? Where are we, 1950s New York?"

He grinned back. "Yeah. Not sure why I said that. But you know what I mean."

And she did. Yobs, hoodlums, hooligans, louts.

It was just that she didn't believe him.

Nina's mum had let it slip. Posted it on Facebook. If anyone was looking out for someone called Elena in Whitehaven, they'd found her.

And twenty-four hours later, someone had tried to burn her house down.

Not hoodlums.

"Come with me."

Nina turned to see Elena standing next to her. The man – Skip – had moved away, talking with the rest of the crew, pointing up the stairs. Nina realised she didn't know whether she'd put her underwear away, or if it was still piled all over her bed.

Sod it. She had more important things to worry about.

"Come on," Elena said, taking her by the shoulders and turning her around, so the two women were facing each other.

"What?" Nina said.

"Come with me," Elena said again.

"Where?"

Elena was already at the front door, turning around and rolling her eyes.

"To Kay's house. Come. Now."

CHAPTER FIFTY-ONE

THE HANDOVER HAD BEEN SMOOTH, but DC Willis – Tom – had been nervous.

"What's wrong?" Denise asked. They stood under a small shelter outside Carlisle HQ, watching Streeting climb into his car.

"Don't want him knowing we're watching him, do we?"

Maybe Tom didn't. He had to work alongside the guy, or pretend to, at least. And Tom seemed like the kind of person who couldn't handle awkward situations and didn't like confrontation.

That always amused Denise. *If you don't like confrontation, don't become a copper.* Confrontation was one of the better parts of the job.

She shrugged.

"Be careful," he said, and walked away.

She shrugged again. *Be careful.* What was Streeting going to do, exactly?

She climbed onto her bike and made sure it wasn't too

loud when she started up, but even so, there was no way
Streeting wouldn't notice it.

She followed his shiny BMW all the way to an estate on
the edge of Cockermouth, overlooking Fitz Park. He parked
in the driveway of a large detached house that had Denise
wondering how much money he'd taken from Carter over the
years.

One man, living alone in a place like that. Like Bobby
Silver. But worse.

Because Streeting was a copper.

He looked up as she drove past. He frowned, then
walked to the front door and let himself in. The lights in the
front room came on a moment later. She drove to the end of
the road – The Parklands, it was called, like it was in a theme
park or something – and turned around.

She parked across the road from Streeting's house and
waited.

It was still raining, but Denise didn't care. Not in all the
gear she wore. The leathers, and the layers underneath, and
the helmet. He wouldn't know who she was, unless he ran
the plates, and then he'd realise who she was, and who she
worked for, and Tom Willis's worries about whether
Streeting knew he was being watched would be history.

After half an hour, she needed to stretch her legs. She
walked a little way down the road, and back up it again. A
man a few doors down from Streeting's house was staring at
her from a ground-floor window.

She gave him a wave and carried on walking, then saw
the look on his face.

He was terrified.

She walked back again, and even from the end of the
driveway, she could see his eyes widen. She glanced back.

No movement from Streeting's house.

She drew a little closer, flipped open her warrant card, and held it up. Streeting's frightened neighbour wouldn't be able to read it, not from this distance. But people watched TV. He'd know what it was.

Back she went. She stood outside, watching, beside her bike. After another half hour, she climbed back on the bike, revved a little, drove to the end of the road and back, and parked again.

The lights in the front room went off. A few seconds later, a light came on upstairs, and she counted down.

Ten.

Nine.

Eight.

The light went off.

She was hot now. Hot and itchy. And she had a long night ahead of her. Watching Streeting was important, but it was boring.

She needed something to distract her.

She reached into her bag, pulled out the first of the evening's sausage rolls, slid open her helmet, and tucked in.

CHAPTER FIFTY-TWO

"THIS HAD BETTER BE GOOD." Zoe glared at Nina.

"I don't know."

"You've dragged me out to the middle of nowhere in the middle of the night, and you don't know?"

They stood outside Kay Holinshed's house. It wasn't the middle of nowhere, and it wasn't the middle of the night, either. It wasn't long past ten.

But Zoe had been relaxing. She'd finished the chicken casserole Carl had made – heated, out of a packet, but still. She'd been looking forward to heading upstairs, not thinking about work for the first time in a long while, when the call had come.

"You need to get over here, boss."

And Nina didn't even know why?

The door was open. Nina turned to go in, and Zoe grabbed her shoulder.

"What's going on?"

"I really don't know, boss. Someone tried to burn my

house down, and then Elena said we had to come here. I had to call you and get you over, too. She wouldn't tell me any more."

"She wouldn't..." Zoe stopped, rewound what she'd just heard, and started again. "Someone tried to burn your house down?"

"Everything's OK, boss. No harm done. Shall we?"

Feeling more out of her depth with every passing moment, Zoe followed Nina into the house.

"No, thanks," Nina said when Kay appeared.

Kay stared at her.

"Sorry." Nina recovered. "I meant, thanks for having us over."

"Would you like a brew?" Kay asked.

"No, thanks."

Zoe fought back a smile. She'd sampled Kay's tea.

Elena was sitting in the kitchen with the two women from the warehouse. All three stood when Zoe entered.

"Sit down," Zoe said. "It's Maria, isn't it? And Alexandra?"

The women nodded.

"Thank you for coming," said Elena. "You will be pleased."

"Sit down," said Kay, who'd produced two more chairs. A moment later, five women sat around a kitchen table designed for no more than three, while Kay fussed around by the kettle.

"I will translate," said Elena.

"Translate what?" asked Zoe.

"You have the photographs? From the Port?" Elena asked.

Zoe felt her heart quicken.

It couldn't be.

Could it?

She pulled out her phone, scrolled to the right image, and passed it over to Elena, who leaned across the table, holding it up, first for Maria, then for Alexandra. She spoke quickly, barely a word comprehensible to Zoe, but the women nodded.

Then Maria spoke. Again, it made no sense to Zoe. There was the occasional burst of what sounded like English, but might not have been.

Elena turned to Alexandra, who nodded again and spoke.

There was a short silence. Zoe looked up and around the room. Kay was still fussing by the kettle. The three Romanian women were grave but resolute, as if something had been decided. Nina... Nina had never struck Zoe as the religious type, but she looked like a woman caught in the act of prayer.

"Yes," said Elena.

"Yes, what?"

"Yes, these women, Maria and Alexandra. They can identify themselves in these photographs."

For a moment, Zoe felt like praying herself. But Elena hadn't finished.

"And this man." She held the phone up to Zoe and tapped on the shape in the corner.

Ralph Streeting.

"They say yes, he was there. They remember him. He was in charge."

"They're sure?" Zoe asked.

"He gave orders. The other men obeyed. He said, 'bring them here.' He said, 'in the truck.'"

Bring them here. In the truck. Those were the words that had sounded like they might have been English.

Was it enough? Enough to bring Streeting in? Enough to keep him there?

Zoe could only pray.

CHAPTER FIFTY-THREE

"WHAT THE HELL did you just say?"

The shout came from inside Streeting's office. Tom looked around guiltily, though he hadn't spoken. At the other desk, Mulligan snorted and went back to his screen.

"I don't care about your bloody processes!" Streeting shouted. His door slammed open, and he appeared.

Tom had followed him into the building, meeting DS Gaskill in the car park and taking over. For someone who'd been standing outside all night in the middle of winter, the DS had looked fresh. Streeting, presumably, had slept, but the man's eyes were rimmed with red, and he'd missed a patch shaving.

"What is it?" Streeting barked.

Tom and Mulligan looked at him, then at each other. Neither of them had spoken.

"What are you working on?" Streeting stared straight at Tom.

"I... I'm looking into Bobby Silver's friends."

Streeting walked over and slammed a hand on Tom's desk. "Her friends? Her fucking friends? Why are you looking at them, you useless piece of shit? You think they killed her?"

Tom heard Mulligan take a sharp breath.

"Pull in the local dealers," Streeting said. "It was one of them."

"Which local dealers?" asked Tom.

"All of them!" Streeting shouted, and returned to his office.

Was this the way they did things here, just shouting out orders at random?

A moment later Tom's screen flashed with a notification: the task coming through. That was something, at least.

Mulligan broke the silence. "Sorry, mate."

"Is he always like this?"

Mulligan shook his head. "He can be difficult. But this is next-level stuff."

Tom turned back to his screen, to the job Streeting had just assigned him.

All of them.

It wasn't a real task. It was a distraction. Streeting's way of getting Tom off his back.

But there was more than one way to skin a cat.

"Mind giving me a hand?" he asked.

Mulligan looked over. "What you got in mind?"

"We could make a few calls, get them to come in themselves. Ones that don't show up, we'll hunt them down."

"Good idea," said Mulligan.

The next forty minutes passed quietly. Tom made calls. Mulligan made calls. Most people didn't answer. Most of those who did, having been woken up, took a few minutes to figure out who they were talking to, and when it sank in, didn't much fancy dragging themselves out to Carlisle in the rain.

Tom wasn't as firm as he might have been. It was a waste of time. A deliberate waste of time.

He was on his seventh call when things got heated. He could hear a raised voice from inside Streeting's room, which was something he was getting used to, and from beside him, which wasn't.

"You need to come in," Mulligan was saying.

A short pause.

"I'll fucking do it myself, then, will I?" shouted Streeting from his office.

"I don't care!" Mulligan said. He turned to Tom and shrugged apologetically.

"Who the hell is calling me at this time in the morning?" said someone else, and Tom realised the voice was coming from his phone.

"Karen Graves?" Tom said.

"You first," said the woman. "Oh. You sound like a cop. You a cop?"

"This isn't some shitty little drugs bust!" Mulligan said, his voice louder.

"Oi!" It sounded like the woman, Karen Graves, had put her hand over the phone, but he could still hear her calling out to someone. "There's some cop on the line. You expecting a call from a cop?"

"Karen Graves?" said Tom. His phone beeped, and he moved it away so he could read the message.

The boss.

Sit tight. Hopefully not much longer.

"Karen?" he said.

"Listen to me, you piece of shit," said Mulligan. "I want you over here, and I want you over here now."

"Bugger off, cop," said Karen Graves, and the phone went dead.

Tom looked up to see the door to Streeting's office was open.

"Where—" he began, but Mulligan was still talking to his dealer. Tom stood, walked to the office door, and peered inside.

No sign of Streeting.

Shit.

He was in the corridor a moment later, downstairs and at the exit within half a minute, just in time to see Streeting's BMW leaving the car park.

He was behind the wheel of his own car in fifteen seconds, silently thanking Mulligan for pointing out the space the previous day. Streeting had taken a right onto the Eastern Way. Tom followed a moment later and caught a glimpse of the BMW.

Right onto the A6. Fine. *Just keep him in your sights.* Traffic was building up, but Tom had done this before.

Not often. Not recently. But he knew the theory.

Keep them in your sights. Don't let them know you're following them. Close, but not too close.

He slid through a set of lights an instant before they turned red.

Left onto the A595, and Streeting could be heading anywhere. Bobby Silver's house. Cockermouth. Port of Workington, even.

The road opened up. Less traffic. And that BMW could shift.

Close, but not too close. Only...

Tom thought it through.

Streeting knew why Tom was at Durranhill. He knew he'd been watched last night. There was no real secret here.

Sod it.

He hit the gas on an open stretch and was pleased to see a handful of slow-moving vehicles ahead. Streeting wasn't getting away anytime soon.

They'd been driving for twenty minutes or more, and he'd closed to within a few car lengths, when Streeting took a sharp left, at the last second, without indicating, heading away from Wigton, down a road Tom wasn't familiar with that was signposted to Caldbeck and Ireby.

Tom slammed the brakes and made the turn. There was nobody ahead. Streeting opened up, putting some distance between them.

Shit.

Tom floored the gas, but it didn't make much difference. Not another car on the road. And Streeting disappeared.

Around a corner.

Gone.

Tom turned the corner and saw two things.

A long, straight road.

And a tractor pulling out of a farm entrance past the BMW. Behind the tractor was a trailer loaded with hay.

Streeting had slowed. Tom could almost feel the waves of anger radiating off the BMW.

There was a turning before the tractor. A holiday park, according to the sign. The BMW made a left, then reversed back onto the road, facing back the way he'd come.

Tom made his own quick turn, on the main road, empty of traffic apart from the tractor lumbering towards them. As Streeting passed Tom, their eyes met.

Streeting's face was expressionless.

Tom followed him back to Carlisle.

CHAPTER FIFTY-FOUR

"Sarge," Lynn said, then added, "DS Keyes." Aaron wheeled his chair over.

"What have you got?"

"The Gabriel Morales incident. I've tracked down one of the witnesses."

Aaron leaned in and rubbed his eyes. "One?"

"The other one's dead. Another protestor. She died late last year, it was in the local paper. Heart attack. Much missed."

Aaron raised his eyebrows. "But..."

"But Amos Briggs is alive and living in Clappersgate."

"That's not—"

"No, not the actual development Morales was protesting against. Not far from it, though."

Aaron knew Clappersgate. Anyone hiking, or camping, or messing around on the north end of Windermere, would pass through Clappersgate.

"What do we know about this Amos Briggs, then? Another protestor?"

"The report's a bit vague, to be honest. He saw it all. Was certain it was just an accident. I've got a phone number, Sarge."

Aaron noted down the number.

"Oh," he added. "Any luck on Charlie Mickleborough?"

"He's dead, Sarge," Lynn replied.

"What?"

"Yup. Retired to Australia, dropped dead two months later."

"Bloody hell. What was it?"

"Heart attack."

Another heart attack. *Coincidence?*

It had to be.

Amos Briggs had no voicemail and didn't answer the phone the first two times Aaron tried. In between, Bateman turned up, hovered, did nothing useful, and stomped through to DI Woolley's office before returning two minutes later and sitting down at his desk to carry on doing nothing useful.

No answer on the third go, but Aaron's phone rang as he put it down.

Chris Robertson.

"Aaron," said the pathologist. "Got some news for you."

"Yes?" Aaron prayed it wasn't going to involve yet another heart attack.

"The strap your colleague found. The one Keisha gave me. It's a match."

"What do you mean?"

"I mean... Hang on. I'll send you the images." Aaron heard his phone ping as Dr Robertson continued. "Long story short, the width, the material, the texture and strength, even the creases on your strap are a perfect match for the murder weapon."

"You're sure?"

"You could give me a thousand leather straps and this is the one I'd pick out, Aaron."

"Have you—"

"I've handed it back to Keisha."

Progress, finally. A murder weapon.

Amos Briggs answered the phone on Aaron's fourth attempt, sounding half-asleep.

"Yeah," he said. "It were me. I'm the one in the witness statement."

"Can I ask you—"

"Can it wait, fella? I'm not really awake, you know."

"You work nights, Mr Briggs?"

There was a short, bitter laugh.

"After what I saw? Lucky I can get out of bed at all. Nah, I'm still at home. Psychological trauma, they called it."

"What?"

"Post-something. Not sure what."

"Post-traumatic stress disorder?" Aaron said.

"That's the one. Full pay, mind."

A year later, and the man was still on full pay.

"May I ask who your employer is, Mr Briggs?"

"Conway Homes, of course."

Of course.

Aaron arranged to meet the man a little later. When he was up and about. A man on full pay, a year after witnessing the death of a protestor at a Conway Homes development.

Maybe he was suffering from PTSD. Maybe he needed the time off.

Or maybe he was being paid to keep his mouth shut about what he'd really seen.

CHAPTER FIFTY-FIVE

THE MEETING COULD HAVE BEEN HELD ANYWHERE. Harriett reckoned DI Whaley would have preferred the sixth floor.

But DI Finch had called it. Harriett had seen arguments between the two of them before, and this wasn't worth fighting over.

So there they sat in DI Finch's team room. DS Keyes was over in Elterwater, and Tom, who'd just called her from his car, breathing hard, telling her he'd almost lost the man he was watching, was up in Carlisle.

The man Tom was watching was Ralph Streeting. He was the subject of the meeting.

"Will they talk to us?" DS Gaskill asked. She leaned against the glass wall like she was about to fall through it. DS Gaskill had been up all night and had the look of someone held upright through caffeine alone.

"They say they will," DI Finch replied. "Or at least, Elena says they say they will."

Harriett frowned. "I don't want to imply anything, but can we trust Elena?"

Four pairs of eyes turned to look at her. She held up her hand.

"I don't mean she's lying. But she's the only person who's spoken to these women. Are we sure she's translating accurately?"

"She's been living at my place for long enough." Nina stopped pacing and stared at Harriett. "Her English is good enough. So with all respect to your little disclaimer, I think you do mean she's lying."

DI Finch shot a glare at Nina that would have had most people needing to take a seat. Nina remained standing. Harriett decided it was best not to say any more.

"Is it enough, though?" asked DS Gaskill.

"They're willing to state in interview that they were trafficked," DI Finch said. "They can identify themselves in the photos, and if you look closely, there's no doubt it's them. They're willing to confirm Streeting was there, and they remember exactly what he said."

"Isn't that a bit suspicious?" asked DI Whaley. "All this time later, and they don't speak a word of English, but they remember a man saying... What was it?"

"'Bring them here,'" said Nina. "And 'In the truck.'"

"Right. Isn't that a bit..."

He looked around, realising there were four women looking at him and trying not to shake their heads.

DI Finch cocked her head. "It's the situation, Carl. Sort of memorable, don't you think? And the man who's running the show, he'd stick in your mind. And as you say, they don't speak a word of English. I've met these women. If they understood what we were saying, I'd have clocked it. They don't. This is all they've got. It's real."

"But is it enough to bring Streeting in?" asked DS Gaskill.

All eyes turned back to DI Whaley. There was silence. One beat.

Two.

Three.

"Yes," he said.

CHAPTER FIFTY-SIX

AARON WALKED into the Lakehead Inn to find one customer. When he'd suggested meeting up, Amos Briggs hadn't been keen. When Aaron had explained that he was investigating a murder, and it wouldn't look great if Briggs failed to cooperate, the man had suggested the Lakehead Inn. It was a smaller, dirtier cousin to the smart Ambleside inns overlooking Windermere.

It was half past ten, and the pub had been open for thirty minutes. Aaron saw a bearded, overweight fifty-something slouched over a table in the corner, nursing a half-empty pint glass. And an empty one beside it.

Aaron went straight for the table. He'd buy Briggs a drink if he had to, but it was best to get some sense out of the man while he could.

"Mr Briggs? Aaron Keyes."

Briggs grunted a greeting, took a swig from his beer, and looked up. Aaron had been expecting something obvious in that look. Scared, maybe. Or just shifty. But all he could see was tired.

"Get me a drink, will you?"

There was a glass of clear liquid beside the second, now empty, pint glass. It might have been water. But it probably wasn't.

"Can we chat first?"

Briggs shrugged. "Go on, then. Let's chat."

"Tell me about Gabriel Morales. What did you see?"

Briggs laughed. "See? If it were just seeing, I wouldn't be sitting here doing this, would I?" He gestured at the empty glasses.

"So tell me," Aaron said.

Briggs explained. He hadn't been there protesting. He hadn't been a bystander, either.

Amos Briggs was the driver of the digger Morales had slipped and fallen under.

"I couldn't have seen him. He came from the side, see." Briggs held out his right fist and slipped his left finger underneath it. "No visibility there. Think they've changed that now. But there was no way I'd have seen him, poor bastard."

Amos Briggs was still on full pay, a year later. He'd already pointed this out on the phone and was at pains to repeat it.

"Company pays for the lot, too. Counselling. Don't reckon much of that, just talking, really."

"I'm not so sure, Mr Briggs. I've..."

Aaron hesitated. Could he trust this man?

"I've been through something difficult myself. I found counselling invaluable. If you give it a chance, you might—"

"Yeah, maybe. But company also pays for these."

He slipped a hand in his pocket, pulled out a blister pack, removed a pill, and swallowed it, chasing it down with the clear liquid.

Vodka. It smelled like vodka.

You could talk to people like Amos Briggs. You could try to convince them to talk to someone else. But until they decided to care about tomorrow, you wouldn't get anywhere.

"When do you get back to work, then?"

Briggs shrugged and looked over at the bar.

He seemed lucid enough. Aaron pointed to the empty glasses, and Briggs named a local ale.

Fortified by the sight of a fresh pint, Briggs was happy to talk again.

"Whenever I want. She says I can come back when I'm ready. No rush. She'll pay me till then."

"She?"

"The boss. Ms Conway."

Aaron nodded.

"And what about Gabriel Morales?"

Briggs looked confused. "Well, he's not working, is he? He's dead."

"I mean, had you come across him before?"

Briggs took a large swig from his glass and set it back on the table. "Nope. He'd just come up that day. That's what his parents said."

"You met them?"

Briggs nodded. Somehow, the pint was almost finished. The man had a talent. Just not a very valuable one.

"There was a memorial thing. It was all very..." – he finished the drink and signalled to the barman – "civilised."

"They weren't angry?"

"Yeah. But not with me. Or Ms Conway. They were angry with the company that made the bloody digger, and can't say I blame 'em."

"They're really not angry with Sinead Conway?" Aaron asked.

Briggs eyed him with suspicion. "What's your game, then? You trying to pin something on Ms Conway?"

Am I?

Aaron shook his head. "I'm just trying to get to the bottom of an unexplained death, Mr Briggs, and the more you can tell me, the easier it'll make my job."

"Go and get that, will you?"

Briggs was pointing at the bar, where another pint had just been poured for him. Aaron made his way over, where he found, unsurprisingly, that he was expected to pay for this pint, too, and made his way back.

"I'll tell you this," said Briggs after the obligatory mouthful of beer. "Ms Conway's a very generous woman. She's still paying me. And I don't know what she paid the Morales family, but they weren't angry with her. Grateful, more like."

Grateful? Their son had died.

Just how much was Sinead Conway prepared to pay to keep people quiet?

CHAPTER FIFTY-SEVEN

"WHAT HAPPENED?" Mulligan asked as Tom ran into the team room.

"Is he in there?"

When Tom had driven back into the car park, fifteen seconds behind Streeting, there'd been another car in the space he'd used before. One of those stylish little Fiats for people with more money than sense. He'd driven past, cursing, and noticed the woman standing next to it. Small, with oriental features, staring at him like she'd heard every word he'd said.

That was the least of his problems. Finding a space had meant another minute getting into the building, by which time Streeting could have been anywhere.

Mulligan nodded, just as a shout from the inner office confirmed it.

"You spoken to those dealers yet?" Streeting bellowed.

"Erm, some of them," Tom replied through the wall.

The door opened, and Streeting emerged, blinking as if

blinded by the light. Which was hard, in the murk of the team room.

"What d'you mean, some of them?"

He wasn't blinking. It was a tic. A spasm. That was new. And in response, Tom realised his own mouth was moving, but there didn't seem to be any words coming out.

"Get those arseholes in here and get them questioned. Neither of you goes home until you've interviewed every bloody dealer from Bowness to goddamn Barrow. You got that?"

Tom said nothing.

"Yes, boss," Mulligan muttered. "Oh, I heard from CSI. They've traced calls on one of the burners found in the victim's house."

"And?" Streeting shouted.

"Not much, I'm afraid. Calls to another burner that's been traced to Cummings. And calls to Josh McKenzie. Her own network."

Streeting frowned as he absorbed the information. Tom already knew it; he'd heard it yesterday from Caroline Deane, who'd been instructed to drip-feed information to Streeting's team, slowly and uselessly.

"McKenzie is dead," Streeting said, "and Cummings is locked up, so I don't think they did her in, did they?"

No one replied.

"Useless pricks," Streeting said, and retreated back into his office.

"Bloody hell," Mulligan said. "I've never seen him this bad. What happened?"

Tom was saved from making something up by voices coming from the corridor. He looked to the open door to see a man and a woman standing there, watching them both.

"Boss being a prick again?" the woman said, addressing Mulligan.

"Like you wouldn't believe. Oh, this is Tom."

Tom stood and shook hands as introductions were made. DS Sharon Virgil. DC Nigel Shaw.

"You like it here?" Sharon asked. "Working for that guy?"

She pulled a face as she pointed towards Streeting's office. Tom wasted a few seconds trying to think of a diplomatic way to answer before his phone rang.

"Sorry," he said. "Got to get this."

The conversation continued around him as he heard DI Finch's voice.

"Tom. Have you got eyes on Streeting?"

"Sort of."

"Do you know where he is?"

"Yes."

"Good," she said. There was a seriousness in her voice that he hadn't heard before. "Stay on him."

"Is there anything I need to know?" he asked.

"Nearly there, Tom. We're nearly there."

CHAPTER FIFTY-EIGHT

"WHY?"

Aaron should have known this was coming. He sighed. "I'm over in Elterwater. Murder investigation."

"I've heard," replied Tracy Giller-Jones.

Was that jealousy? If Markin had been halfway competent, this might have been her case.

"The victim was protesting against one of Sinead Conway's developments."

"Right."

"Your missing woman, Jan Calloway. She was also protesting against one of Sinead Conway's developments."

"Yeah," she said. "Rings a bell."

He tightened his grip on the phone. "You wrote a report. Doesn't seem like there was much of an effort to find her."

"If you're making an accusation, DS Keyes, you'll find I don't break easily."

Christ, she was hard work.

"I'm not making an accusation. I'm trying to find out what happened. If there's a link. Or a pattern."

"There's a pattern. We do our work, you get on our cases. If you want to hassle cops, join PSD, Aaron."

"Just..." He forced himself to breathe. "Just tell me what you know about Jan Calloway."

"It's all in the report. She went missing. Didn't show up to work, didn't answer the phone, didn't answer the door. Gone. She worked at a bar. I spoke to her employer. That was it. She wasn't a priority."

"Why not?"

"No reason to think she was vulnerable. Look, she's just skipped town. It's not exactly unknown."

"Fair," he conceded. He'd have looked harder than she had, but he wouldn't have kept pushing, not without cause. "Look, I'm not saying anyone did anything wrong. What you had back then, it looked like nothing. Now, with this new case, things might be different."

Would she soften?

"Whatever," she said. "Like I said, it's all in the report."

He sighed. The usual level of cooperation from DS Tracy Giller-Jones. Aaron glanced over at Bateman and wondered which of them was worse.

It was a close-run thing. But no one got under his skin like Giller-Jones did.

He turned to Lynn, who'd just ended a call of her own.

"Any luck?"

She shook her head. "Nope. No one I've spoken to remembers seeing Kevin that night. It's all too vague. Sounds like half the village was drunk, and as for the rest, well, it's a random day a couple of months ago, isn't it?"

Aaron nodded. People wouldn't remember. Not unless they had good reason to.

"No one remembers anyone talking about meeting him, though? Even if he didn't show up?"

"Sorry. I'm thinking maybe he wasn't going to the pub after all."

"You think the people at the camp are lying?"

She shook her head. "I didn't get that sense. But Kevin might have been."

"What, lying to them?"

"Yes. I just can't figure out why."

They fell silent, both of them thinking it through.

It couldn't be drugs. Everyone knew he was dealing. There was no need to keep that secret.

And whatever it was he'd been lying about – if he'd been lying – why had it taken him to Baysbrown Wood?

CHAPTER FIFTY-NINE

"HEADING OUT, BOSS." Tom stood and walked out of the team room, talking into his phone.

"What the hell's going on?" Mulligan asked.

No time to explain.

DI Finch had called again. This time, it wasn't *nearly there*. It was happening. And that meant Tom had to be on top of Streeting, so of course Streeting had picked that moment to stride through the office and away down the corridor.

Down the stairs. Tom couldn't see him, but he could hear his footsteps. He knew where he was parked.

"Nearly outside, boss," he muttered. "He'll be at his car any second."

"It's OK. They're on it."

Not just seriousness now. A breathless excitement. He could feel it himself.

He'd just made it outside and into the early afternoon rain when it hit him. Not a fist, but two hands on his shoulders, hard.

"Stop. Fucking. Following. Me."

Streeting didn't just look angry. He looked insane.

Tom said nothing. They stood there staring at each other for a moment, then the DI's voice punctured the silence.

"Tom?"

Both men looked down at Tom's phone.

"Get back in the building," Streeting said. "Get back and do your job."

Tom didn't move. He looked past Streeting, over his shoulder. Two figures were approaching.

"Are you ignoring me, DC Willis?"

Tom said nothing. The woman he'd seen earlier, the one with the Fiat who'd stolen his parking space, walked out of the building, staring at the two of them, then continued past them into the car park.

"If you're not back inside that building within thirty seconds, I'll be instituting disciplinary proceedings against you. And you can bet—"

"DI Streeting," said a voice.

Streeting whirled around, fists clenched.

"DI Whaley." There was an odd note in his voice.

"Yes. I'm DI Whaley, from Professional Standards."

"I know that, Carl. What's this—"

"This is my colleague, DS Gaskill."

"Right. Hello, DS Gaskill." There was a forced cheeriness in Streeting's voice. A few yards away, the woman with the Fiat had stopped, watching.

"DI Ralph Streeting," said DI Whaley, stepping closer. "I'm arresting you—"

"What? This is ridiculous."

The Fiat woman took a step towards them.

"I'm arresting you in connection with—"

"Come on, Carl," said Streeting. "You know me. I don't know who's put you up to this, but—"

"Ralph," said DI Whaley. "We're in no rush, but the sooner we get this done, the fewer people will see it happening."

To Tom's surprise, Streeting nodded.

"DI Ralph Streeting," said DI Whaley. "I'm arresting you in connection with offences under section two of the Modern Slavery Act."

Streeting nodded again. "This is ridiculous."

"Please come with me," said DI Whaley.

Streeting took a long look around. Then he followed DI Whaley across the car park, DS Gaskill close behind, to an unmarked vehicle parked by itself against a low wall.

"Bloody hell," said someone.

Tom looked up to see the woman with the Fiat. She was older than he'd expected. Not old. But older than Tom. Older than DS Keyes. Maybe closer to the DI's age.

"That was tense," she said. "Thought things might get a bit exciting there."

"Tom Willis." He stepped forward, hand outstretched. "DC Willis. Based in the Hub, usually. Here on special assignment."

"Special assignment? Get you." She shook his hand. Firm grip. "The Hub, is it? Bloody Southerners."

Tom looked up from his hand. She was smiling.

"DI Hae-Won. Song Hae-Won. Or just Song."

He nodded.

"I never liked Ralph Streeting," she said. "Can't say I expected to see him dragged away by PSD, mind. That your doing?"

"I can't really... I'm sure you'll understand, Ma'am."

She shrugged and took a step away from him, then stopped and walked back.

"I like young coppers with a bit of attitude, DC Willis. And I like a bit of creativity, too. But if I ever hear you swearing at a senior officer the way you swore at me earlier, I won't be quite so charming. Got it?"

"Got it," he said, as she turned and walked away.

CHAPTER SIXTY

JAN CALLOWAY's last known address had been on Moorside Drive, Maryport. The phone line for the house next door was registered to Sue Goodman, who picked up the phone on Aaron's first try.

"Yeah?"

"Sue Goodman?"

"Who's asking?"

"This is DS Aaron Keyes, from Cumbria Police."

"Right."

"I was wondering if I could talk to you about Jan Calloway."

He waited.

Nothing.

"You're aware of the person I'm talking about? Jan Calloway?"

"Course."

"And you're aware that she disappeared two years ago?"

Another silence, followed by a snort.

"Mrs Goodman?"

"'Disappeared,' you said?"

"That's right."

"More like 'left.'"

"Hang on."

"I'm not going anywhere."

"You're aware of the circumstances of her... Her leaving?"

"Yep."

"Did any of my colleagues interview you at the time?"

"Nope."

The neighbour. They hadn't even bothered speaking to the neighbour. Aaron cursed Tracy Giller-Jones.

"Do you mind if I head over for a chat?" he said.

"Depends on when."

He checked his watch. "Are you around later today?"

"I can be."

He waited, expecting a catch.

But not everybody was Amos Briggs.

"Good. How about I come over around four?"

"Fine." She hung up.

An odd woman, but if what she had to say helped find Jan Calloway, she could be as odd as she damn well pleased.

CHAPTER SIXTY-ONE

"I suppose I should congratulate you," said Fiona.

Zoe raised an eyebrow. "You're not going to, though."

"If what you've told me is true, and you can prove it, then yes, congratulations. But this is Ralph Streeting, Zoe."

"And?"

"He's not the sort of man to stay down. He'll come back fighting. You can be sure of it."

"We'll be ready." Zoe tried to sound confident. "In the meantime, I take it you're OK with my team picking up the Bobby Silver case again?"

Fiona frowned, then returned to her desk and sat. "Shouldn't I hand it to Alan?"

Zoe fought back a shudder. Alan Markin, on a case like this one? He'd arrest the parrot.

"You were fine with us handling it before Streeting took over."

Fiona shook her head. "No, Zoe. Not fine. I thought it was just about acceptable. And now I'm not so sure. You've got Elterwater, and yes, you had that before. But now you've got the people trafficking case."

"We had that before, too."

"You didn't have a suspect in custody for it. You just had a couple of witnesses and no way of knowing if they'd say anything useful. It was a slow burn. Now it's a live case."

"Yes," said Zoe. "Which means you can be sure we won't have it for long."

"Explain."

"People trafficking? Modern slavery? NCA's going to be all over it. Not to mention the fact that PSD made the arrest, not us. Yes, we've been involved. And we'll continue to assist as needed. But my guess is, this'll end up being run jointly by PSD and NCA. PSD will want to be involved in Bobby Silver, too. If my theories on that are correct."

"It's a murder case, Zoe. They won't take that off you."

"Oh, I know. But they'll want to be involved, and that'll mean they can help. So yes, it sounds like I'm asking if I can run three major investigations at the same time. But it won't be for long."

Another pause.

"Aaron's in Elterwater," Fiona said. "Can you manage everything else with what you've got here?"

"If you can dig out some extra resources, I'd be grateful. If this had been last year, I'd—"

"Please don't mention Kay Holinshed, Zoe. I don't care how good she was, I don't care how helpful she's being now, and I don't care that she was set up by Cummings. She broke the rules."

"Fair enough. But what about Harriett Barnes?"

"What about her? She's PSD, as far as I'm aware.

Although it seems she's been working under your authority lately."

There was something in Fiona's voice that Zoe didn't like.

"Hasn't she?" Fiona prompted.

Shit.

"I'm sorry, Fiona."

"Sorry for what, precisely?"

It was like being back at school.

"Sorry I didn't clear it with you first."

And she *was* sorry. It was a screw-up. The sort of thing that drove a senior officer mad, and with good reason. How could you run a team, or a department, or a station, if you weren't kept up to date with who was in it?

"I arranged it informally with Carl," Zoe explained. "It all seemed natural. And I messed up."

"Good."

She looked back at the super. "Good?"

"Good that you can see that, at least. There's hope for you yet, Zoe. Now, I assume you'd like me to have a little chat with our friend Douglas Branthwaite to formalise Harriett Barnes' temporary secondment to your team?"

"That would be extremely helpful," Zoe said. "She can act as a DC within my team, which is her actual rank, and she can act as liaison with PSD at the same time."

"Liaison with PSD? Good thinking. I have a feeling you're going to need it. Is that everything?"

"Yes. Thank you." Zoe stood up, but didn't move.

"What?" said Fiona.

"The IOPC investigation. How's it going?"

Fiona slumped forward, rested her forehead in one hand, and looked up at Zoe.

"You've spoken to them?"

Zoe nodded.

"How was that?"

"They seemed reasonable. Fair."

"That's good. It's... It's not easy, this. It doesn't reflect well on me, but that's not your problem. I'm more worried about morale here."

"In that case," Zoe said. "I'd recommend a more positive outlook."

Fiona stared at her. "I beg your pardon?"

"I'm sorry, Fiona, but if your main worry is morale, you sitting around acting like the world's coming to an end isn't likely to help."

"How... What... I really..."

Fiona was shooting for outraged, but it didn't suit her. After three attempts, she stopped and gave Zoe a grin.

"OK," she said. "I'll give it some thought. Now, off you go and crack your murders. That'll improve morale no end."

CHAPTER SIXTY-TWO

MOORSIDE DRIVE WAS a tree-lined street with terraced houses and a green space cut away to make room for cars. Aaron pulled into a space and was greeted by a bald man in his thirties or early forties, standing by the car, shaking his head.

"Can't park there, mate."

Aaron flipped open his warrant card. "Won't be long."

He walked past the man and up to Sue Goodman's front door. He waited, resisting the urge to check if the man was watching him. Eventually, the door opened, and Aaron found himself facing a hallway.

He looked down. Sue Goodman, he assumed. She looked up at him from a height of around four and a half feet.

"What you waiting for, then? Shoes off. In you come."

"Mrs Goodman?"

"Yes, Mrs Goodman, and you're the policeman I spoke to earlier. Shoes off. In you come."

Aaron looked back. The man was still watching him.

"Shoes off, I said. Come on."

Aaron removed his coat and shoes. His phone buzzed. He ignored it.

The next room was the living room. Aaron stopped on the threshold.

"Smile, Inspector," said Sue Goodman.

There was a flash. Then another, and another. Aaron smiled.

The walls and ceiling were lined with photographs, small prints of people, most of them apparently taken in this room. Many of the subjects were frozen in the same fearful confusion Aaron felt.

"My little hobby," she explained, setting her SLR camera down on a coffee table piled high with more portraits. "Everyone who enters this house gets snapped."

"Why?" Aaron asked.

"Most people don't ask that. Funnily enough, she did, too."

She lifted a black-and-white print from the top of the pile. It showed a woman in her late twenties. Thin face, long hair, serious eyes. Underneath it, the same print in colour. Now Aaron could see the green in the eyes and the auburn in the hair, and with the colour came a sort of mischief.

"Is that Jan Calloway?" he asked.

"Aye, that's her."

"And what did you tell her?"

"I told her she should mind her own business, like I'm telling you."

"Oh. Right."

"I'm joking. I told her it's so I can remember. Got this terrible fear of my memory going."

"Is it?" he asked.

"Is what?"

"Is your memory going?"

"No sign of it so far, DS Keyes."

"But—"

"But I called you 'Inspector'? Yes, I did. I did do that. Just wanted to see what you'd say."

"I didn't say anything."

"No, you didn't, did you? Was starting to worry about your memory, to be honest. Now then, what was it you wanted to know?"

Aaron looked around. "This is quite a collection."

"Yep. I remember her leaving. It was me that drove her, after all."

"You drove her?"

"Up to the ferry port at Cairnryan. You know it?"

Aaron nodded. "Why did you take her there?"

Sue Goodman stared at him. "She asked me to, of course."

"Of course." He forced a smile. "And do you know where she was heading?"

"Northern Ireland, she said. Didn't say any more than that, and I didn't ask."

"Any idea why?"

"Nope."

"And this wasn't... it wasn't just a holiday, then?"

"She said she were off and she weren't coming back. That sound like a holiday to you, DS Keyes?"

"No. No, it doesn't. Did she seem scared?"

"What do you reckon?" She held up the photographs Aaron had just been looking at.

"Were they taken that day?"

"Yep."

Aaron examined the photos again, the black-and-white shot and the one in colour. Was the woman in it scared?

He couldn't tell.

"What happened that day?"

"She just turned up, knocked on the door, asked if I could take her to the ferry port. It's a fair way, that. I didn't say nothing for a minute, then she said she'd pay my petrol plus two hundred quid."

"So you took her."

She nodded.

"Did she say anything? On the journey, maybe?"

"Not really, no."

"And did you have the impression she was trying to get away from anyone, or anything?"

"Well, she were leaving, so I'm guessing she were getting away from here, but that's all I can tell you."

Aaron looked around the room. Every photo had been taken here. Inside.

"I don't suppose you noticed anyone hanging around her house, next door, before she went? Or after? Anything unusual?"

"Nope," said Sue Goodman. "I tend to mind my own business."

Which was an admirable trait, Aaron thought, as he thanked her, put his shoes back on, and headed outside.

The man was still standing in the rain, arms folded, watching. Admirable, except when you actually wanted to know what had happened next door.

Maybe...

He approached the man, but it turned out he'd only lived there a year.

"I'd have noticed," he assured Aaron. "I keep an eye out. I'd have spotted any funny business."

And there had been some funny business. Aaron was sure of it. Jan Calloway had upped and left without warning, only telling her neighbour. She'd been running from something. Or someone.

And Aaron had a pretty good idea who that someone might be.

CHAPTER SIXTY-THREE

"INTERVIEW WITH DETECTIVE INSPECTOR RALPH STREETING," said Denise. "Conducted by Detective Inspector Carl Whaley and Detective Sergeant Denise Gaskill of the Professional Standards Division. DI Streeting is accompanied by his lawyer, Trevor Singleton."

She stared at Singleton for a moment before the interview began in earnest. She hadn't seen the lawyer for a while, and if there had been any doubt about who Streeting was working for, there wasn't now.

Singleton looked innocuous enough. His face unlined, his attitude calm, his voice low, his white hair lending a friendly, avuncular charm to a man who couldn't have been much past forty. And he knew his stuff, as Denise had found in the past.

The most interesting thing about Trevor Singleton was who his clients were. Exclusively friends, or colleagues, of Myron Carter.

DI Whaley kicked things off, and as they'd agreed, he went in hard.

"Who killed Bobby Silver?" he asked.

Streeting said nothing.

"Why did you do it, Ralph? Why did you have her killed?"

Again, nothing.

Denise took over.

"I can think of a reason. She'd stolen from Myron Carter, hadn't she? From his clients, really. But he was the one she'd betrayed. You had to send a message on Carter's behalf. If you cross Carter, you'll pay for it."

"Makes sense," DI Whaley added. "And of course, if she'd made an enemy of Carter, and there was any danger she was going to be picked up, there was a risk she'd talk. Tell the police what she knew about Carter's operation. That couldn't be allowed to happen, could it, DI Streeting?"

"Oh, good," said the lawyer. "A question. I thought for a moment the two of you were just having a little chat among yourselves."

Streeting said nothing.

"Who killed Bobby Silver?" asked DI Whaley again.

Streeting turned to Singleton and whispered something. Denise watched the lawyer's face change from inscrutable to mildly intrigued.

The lawyer nodded.

"Who killed her, Ralph?" said Denise.

Streeting finally spoke. "I don't recognise your authority in this investigation."

Denise looked to DI Whaley, who seemed as bemused as she was.

"We've arrested you, DI Streeting," she said. "Mr Singleton can check the arrest sheet. Everything is in order, as far as I'm aware. If you believe otherwise, by all means, do tell."

"I've been arrested under section two of the Modern Slavery Act. Trafficking. Right?"

"Right," said the lawyer, before either police officer could reply.

"If I'm in for trafficking, I expect to be dealt with by the National Crime Agency, not a pair of..." He waved dismissively. "I don't know what you are. Cops who prey on other cops. If I'm here about the murder of Bobby Silver, then by all means, ask me questions about it. But first, I'd suggest you actually arrest me for that offence, rather than some other one."

"We'll take a break," said DI Whaley, before Denise could formulate a reply.

Probably a good thing, she thought, as she followed him out of the room. *Streeting was right.*

They couldn't arrest him for Bobby Silver; plenty of grounds for suspicion, but no real evidence, and no sign of where to find any. Even the trafficking was on shaky ground. They'd decided, between themselves, that the statements from Maria and Alexandra were enough to bring him in. But were they enough to charge him?

She wasn't sure the CPS would think so. Same for the NCA, who'd be pushing to take the case off their hands, and would then probably forget about it, because they didn't have the resources to follow it up.

Politics. It always went the same way. Grab as much work as you can, more than you can handle, use it to plead for a bigger budget for the next year. And the work you've let slide? The cases you've dropped, as part of your campaign?

Just the collateral damage.

CHAPTER SIXTY-FOUR

THE CLOUDS PARTED as Aaron skirted Workington. He hadn't learned much from Sue Goodman, but he'd learned enough.

Sinead Conway wasn't in the clear. Not by a long shot.

But Sinead could wait. He'd got everything done that he needed to. Which meant he had time to pop home.

A surprise would be perfect. Serge would pretend he'd somehow known Aaron was coming. Annabel would either jump up and down like a lottery winner, or she'd act like he hadn't even been away.

He was looking forward to it. Smiling, even. Right up to the point where he glanced right, at the forbidding edifice of Moresby Hall, and his phone rang, and he made the mistake of answering.

"Sarge," he heard.

It took him a moment to place the voice. Not Nina. Definitely not Tom.

"Lynn. Everything OK?"

The pause before her reply was as good an answer as any.

"You nearby, Sarge?"

"Not exactly," he replied, with a sinking feeling. "Why?"

"There's been an incident."

He swallowed. "What kind of incident?" he asked, indicating right into Parton.

"A fight, Sarge. Bunch of locals, bunch of protestors."

He exhaled. "Anyone hurt?"

"Some bruises," she said. "Some pride. It's broken up now, but there's a lot of ill feeling."

"Right. And that's..." Aaron tried to work out a way of putting it politely. "Is that something you need me for? If it's broken up? Can't DS Bateman handle it?"

The sound from the phone grew muffled. Aaron heard footsteps, then the patter of rain.

"Sarge, it's DS Bateman that's messed everything up. Could have just given them a talking-to, but he pulled out Uniform and dragged everyone back to the station."

Aaron pulled out into the slow-moving traffic heading north, earning a hoot from a frustrated driver behind.

"Not your station?" he said.

"Langdale nick."

"Christ." The place was barely big enough for the police who worked in it. "How many are we talking about?"

"Thirteen of them. Nine locals, four from the camp. We're doing our best to keep them apart, but it's in danger of getting out of hand."

"Christ," Aaron said. "What's DS Bateman holding them for? Breach of the peace?"

"That's the thing, Sarge. He hasn't arrested them at all.

Not formally, anyway. He just said they had to come, and Henniker and Fraser turned up, so they did."

"Christ." Aaron took a deep breath. "Fine. Let's see if we can make the best of this, shall we? I'm heading back. Shouldn't be much more than an hour. If you can, keep them all there. But if they want to go, you can't stop them."

"Got it, Sarge." Lynn sounded relieved.

What it must be like to be stuck there working with Bateman and Jasmine Woolley, every day. Not for the first time, Aaron thanked his lucky stars he'd ended up where he had.

CHAPTER SIXTY-FIVE

"You must have known this would happen, Zoe," said Fiona.

Zoe wasn't sure how to respond. Not because she didn't know what to say. But because of the other person in Fiona's office.

He crouched in the corner, inserting wires into ports, sucking his teeth every few seconds.

"Is this…" Zoe gestured towards the man. "I'm not sure…"

"Jeff," said Fiona. "You mind leaving us for a moment?"

Jeff stood, slowly uncurling himself. He was tall, thin, wearing a dirty cardigan and jeans.

"Won't take long," he said, pointing back at the wires he'd been working with. "We can get you linked back up."

"I know." Fiona smiled sweetly at the man. "And I really appreciate it. But I just need a few minutes' privacy with DI Finch, and you can get back to it. Is that OK?"

Jeff nodded and walked out, still clutching his wires.

"He's a sensitive sort, is Jefferson," Fiona said. "You have to keep his spirits up, or he just moans all day. And I get enough of that with Alan Markin. Now, as I was saying. You can't be surprised."

Zoe wasn't the slightest bit surprised. Streeting had ways of getting in touch with the right people, even when he was locked up. No doubt Trevor Singleton had passed on some messages.

"Becca Grey called me earlier," Fiona told her. "The usual outrage and nonsense."

Zoe had looked up Becca Grey, Joe Carghillie's policy advisor. The woman was younger than she'd expected, barely out of her thirties. Cambridge, followed by a brief but successful stint as a lawyer, then as a local councillor, and finally as a civilian worker with the police, where she'd risen swiftly to her current lofty height. People only had good things to say about Becca Grey, and that alone was enough to set Zoe's antennae twitching.

"Well, she can't give the Bobby Silver case back to Streeting. Not while he's locked up."

"True," Fiona acknowledged. "But it's Streeting being locked up that she's taking issue with now. Or, as she puts it, that Little Joe himself is taking issue with."

"You believe her?"

"Who knows? Joe Carghillie and Streeting know each other. I have no idea how friendly they are. Could be golf buddies for all I know."

That would be like Streeting. Just like him.

"Anyway, the way Becca Grey tells it, we're wasting resources and pressing unfounded accusations on an important member of the constabulary."

Zoe's jaw dropped. "She used those words?"

"She likes her words, does Becca Grey," Fiona replied with a sigh.

"She can't really do anything about it, though, can she?"

"She tells me she understands proper procedures haven't been followed. The NCA should be involved, but they're not. She reminded me I've got the IOPC breathing down my neck and this isn't the time to be making mistakes."

"There are no mistakes," Zoe said.

The super was always giving Zoe warnings, telling her to tread carefully, not to antagonise the powerful, but she'd backed her up every time she'd needed backing up.

She wouldn't cave. Not now.

"No. I believe you're right. But Becca's right about the IOPC. Branthwaite can get away with whatever he wants; no one can touch PSD. But if anything goes wrong, it's my neck on the line, Zoe."

"Understood."

"Good. Remember that. The pressure's on."

CHAPTER SIXTY-SIX

"Sit down and do some bloody work," said DS Bateman.

Lynn stared at him. *The nerve of the man.*

"Sarge, we've got them all here. It's worth asking them, isn't it?"

No need to mention why they were there, who'd brought them, and the fact that he shouldn't have. Talk about exceeding your authority.

"Oh, so it's me that gets called 'Sarge' now, is it? All very easy when it suits you."

Her jaw dropped.

Every time she thought Bateman couldn't get worse, he proved her wrong. He'd brought half the village in for no reason. But there was still a chance to ask them what they knew about Kevin Downes. All of them, in one place, watching their friends getting led off to be questioned. Wondering who was saying what.

It was the sort of situation that made people talk. The sort of situation you couldn't engineer.

And Bateman was wasting it.

"Fine," she muttered, and sat down.

She'd had another call with DS Keyes as he drove back east, and she'd taken note of everything he'd said about his interview with Sue Goodman. Like DS Keyes, she found it difficult to escape the conclusion that Jan Calloway had been running from someone. And the likeliest candidate was Sinead Conway.

But if Jan Calloway had run, unlike Gabriel Morales and Kevin Downes, chances were she was still alive. And if she was still alive, Lynn could find her.

It took less than three minutes to find Jan's Facebook profile and the linked Instagram account, but she'd gone silent as soon as she'd disappeared.

So whatever Jan Calloway was, she wasn't stupid.

Lynn spent another ten minutes trawling through the accounts Jan had engaged with most frequently before she found what she was looking for.

Not completely stupid, but no genius, either. If you wanted to disappear, you didn't pop up again less than a week later with a new Facebook profile under a different name – and a handful of the same friends.

Hello, 'Jan Smith.'

Jan Smith had come into existence six days after Jan Calloway had left for Northern Ireland – if that was really where she'd gone. Lynn had checked the ferry destinations, the obvious road and other routes. Northern Ireland was still the likely candidate, but if you were trying to put someone off the scent, Cairnryan would be a handy place to do it.

But only if you were smart. If you were the sort of person who wouldn't set up a new Facebook account in the name of Jan Smith.

Jan Smith claimed to be based in London, but there were

no personal photos. Just images grabbed from the web: favourite bands, favourite films and TV programs. Her conversations ran along the same lines, although from time to time she'd ask how her friends were getting on, and either congratulate or commiserate, as appropriate.

Nothing about herself. Nothing at all. Jan Smith could be anyone.

The cursor hovered above the blue box. Lynn looked up and caught DS Bateman staring at her. He looked guiltily away.

She tapped the mouse.

Friend request sent.

CHAPTER SIXTY-SEVEN

AARON SHOULDN'T HAVE EXPECTED any better, but it came as a shock to walk into the police station and find half a dozen men standing around, leaning against the walls, chatting and sipping drinks from mugs. Actual mugs, not plastic cups.

He hadn't realised there were mugs in the building.

"Hello," he said. He was mostly ignored, but two of the men looked up and gave him a friendly greeting as he walked past. Marc Langham. And his friend, Idris. Aaron nodded back and made his way to the team room.

No sign of Isaac Bateman, but Lynn Hedley was at her desk, frowning at the screen. She turned as he walked in, her entire body tense, and visibly relaxed when she saw who it was.

"Sarge." She nodded. "You've seen our guests?"

"I thought you said there were thirteen of them."

"The four from the camp are still downstairs. We've got a little cell under the station. DS Bateman's put them in there."

"Is it safe?"

"Depends how long they're in there for."

"Right." Aaron turned, then stopped. "And the others? I counted six. Didn't you say there were nine?"

"DS Bateman told them they could go home."

"Right." He paused. "And we've still got six of them here because..."

"Because he's been bringing them tea and biscuits, and it's warm and dry, and they're having a nice chat."

Things were going from bad to worse. Aaron stood for a moment, torn between the entrance lobby and the cell, before he made up his mind.

Welfare had to come first.

The room Lynn led him to was even smaller than he'd expected. The smell of damp hung over everything like a thick layer of paint. He couldn't see the water dripping from the walls, but the light was so poor he could barely see the men in the cell. It wasn't just about welfare. Keeping people here wasn't even legal.

"Why didn't Bateman say this lot can go home?" he'd asked as they made their way down.

"Said they were too drunk," Lynn had replied. "Said it was for their own good."

He recognised Paddy, and the man who Lynn had spoken to, who called himself Pete, which apparently stood for something much less normal than simply Peter. The two others he hadn't met. Sly and Wolfgang, apparently.

None of them were drunk.

Outside the cell, he turned to Lynn. "We've got their prints? DNA?"

She nodded. He turned back and opened the door.

"Go on," he said. "You can head back to the camp."

Off they went, quietly, apart from Pete, who paused to give Aaron something that was either a blessing or a curse. No way of knowing which.

By the time they made it back to the team room, Bateman was waiting for them, hands on hips, wearing a glare that looked like he'd been practising it.

"What d'ya let them go for?"

"You hadn't arrested them," Aaron replied. "There were no grounds to keep them here. What about the others? Have you at least got prints and DNA for them?"

Bateman grinned, showing his teeth. "Nope."

"Is this normal?" Aaron asked.

"Listen, Keyesie," Bateman said, and Aaron felt his skin tighten. "You might be a big-city cop these days, but some of us still live here, and we actually know everyone. Don't need DNA. Don't need prints."

There were things Aaron might have said to that, but what was the use?

He stood in the corridor, watching the men in the entrance lobby. They looked relaxed enough. Tea and biscuits.

If there was a right mood to be in, they were in it. Worth a chance.

He stepped out into the lobby and cleared his throat.

"Evening," he said. The hum of conversation ceased, and all six turned to look at him. "All OK?"

There were a couple of nods. The rest just watched him, curious.

"I'm sorry about all this." He gestured vaguely. "But since you're here anyway, I was wondering if you might be willing to help us clear up some other matters."

"What other matters?" Idris asked, suspicious.

Aaron pressed on. "If you wouldn't mind us taking your fingerprints and DNA, it would be very—"

"Whoa," said Marc. "We haven't been arrested, have we?"

"No, you haven't, but—"

"So we don't have to do this, right?"

"No, not at all. It's entirely voluntary."

"Sod that, then," said Marc. Around him, there were quiet noises of agreement.

"Look," said Aaron. "I appreciate you're not exactly thrilled about being dragged out here. And I imagine you're not in the mood to help us when you don't need to. All I can do is apologise. I don't know—"

"Don't know?" Marc stepped towards him, his voice louder. "You don't know what happened at all, do you? I'll tell you what happened. There was a little disagreement. Nothing much. None of us needed to be dragged to the bloody police station. I wasn't even involved, and if I had been, I'm not sure I can tell you which side I'd have been on, 'cause this lot" – he pointed at the others in the room – "they might be my friends, but they're all wrong about the quarry development. And the others might be assholes, but they're actually right."

There were grumbles, but good-natured. "A little disagreement" sounded about right.

"So no, you shouldn't have dragged us here, and there will be complaints because this isn't a police state. You can't just do what you want and expect to get away with it."

The grumbles turned back into murmurs of agreement. Aaron's phone buzzed, and he ignored it.

"We have rights," said one of the others.

"Exactly," said Marc. "And you lot" – he jabbed a finger in Aaron's direction – "have a vastly inflated sense of your own importance."

Worth a chance, Aaron had thought. But now things were getting away from him so fast he could hardly keep up.

CHAPTER SIXTY-EIGHT

"Zoe?"

Zoe had picked up the phone, expecting a routine update, but there was a note in Stella's voice she hadn't heard before.

"Yes, what's up?"

"It's... Shit... It's not good. This shouldn't be happening. Not after..."

Now she had it. *Panic.*

"What's happened? Are you OK?"

There was a short silence, a silence Zoe filled with the worst possibilities. Had someone else died?

"Stella, you've got to tell me what's going on."

"There's been an attack." Stella's voice trembled.

Stay calm.

"An attack on who?"

"Caroline. She was moving the evidence." Stella's words were uneven and staccato, like they were being fired from a damaged gun. "The stuff from Bobby Silver's place. It was in... Well, you don't need to know where it was. No one knew. Just me and Caroline. I don't know how they..."

"Calm down, Stella. First, is Caroline OK?"

"She's fine."

There was another silence, less fraught than the previous one. But only slightly.

"Good. Talk me through it, Stella."

The crime scene manager took a long breath. Her voice lost its tremble.

"We moved everything. When Streeting took over. You asked us to make sure he couldn't get hold of the evidence, so we put it somewhere he'd never find. And it worked, right? He lost the case, you've got it back, so I sent Caroline with a truck to bring everything back here."

"Here?" Zoe interrupted.

"The lab. Thought it would be fine. Anyway, she picked it all up. Load of furniture. The sofa from the living room. The bed from the room Bobby Silver died in. The bookshelf from the hall. Bunch of smaller things like door handles. Window fittings. TV remote—"

"Stella, focus. What happened?"

"Right. Sorry. She got rammed. How the hell they found her, I don't know. But—"

"Where did she pick up the truck?"

"Oh," said Stella. "Of course. She drove it from here. All they had to do was follow her. Wait till she picked everything up."

"OK. So that answers that question. And you're saying Caroline's OK? She's not hurt?"

"She's fine. A bit shaken, but she's tougher than you'd expect. She's been through a lot lately."

Zoe was well aware of that. Caroline Deane had been

the one to examine the crime scene at Huz's house. Her friend lying dead in the middle of it.

"And the evidence?"

"All fine. The truck took a bit of a bashing, but she's a good driver. She got hit from the side. Lost control for a moment, she says, then steered back and forced them off the road."

"Them?"

"Land Rover, she thinks. It wasn't clear. No lights until they were on her, then full beam. Right in the middle of nowhere, too. She just kept going until she was back here. Shit, Zoe. I was on the phone with her when it happened. I thought..."

She didn't need to complete the sentence. Not after Huz.

"Right. We need to focus. We'll find the Land Rover, but if they couldn't move it, odds are they'll have burned it. But that's secondary. Whatever they wanted, they didn't get it. You have it. You need to get everything you can. Prints. Fibres. DNA. Anything on the furniture and fittings and all the stuff you've got. You need to move fast."

"What's the hurry?"

"I don't know how long we can hold Streeting. If he gets out, he'll be doing everything he can to get the case back. And then—"

"Leave it with me," Stella told her. "If there's anything there, we'll find it."

CHAPTER SIXTY-NINE

AARON HADN'T REALISED DI Woolley was in the building. The men around him fell silent, looking over his shoulder.

He turned. There she was.

There was something different about her.

Her face. She'd always been pale, but now she was ash-white.

"What the hell is going on here?" she said.

No one answered.

"I asked a question. What are these people doing in my police station?"

"I believe they were brought in by DS Bateman, Ma'am," Aaron said.

She turned her glare on him. "You believe, do you? And where have you been, DS Keyes? Solved your murder yet?"

"No, I—"

"Well, get cracking, then. Sooner you do that, sooner you can bugger off back to Whitehaven. You lot," she added, turning back to the men. "Out."

"DI Streeting's a friend of the boss," Lynn told him, as Marc and his friends sloped quietly away.

Aaron frowned, confused. She passed him her phone, an arrest sheet open on it.

Ralph Streeting had finally been pulled in.

Aaron pulled out his own phone, annoyed to have been out of the loop, to see three missed calls from Nina.

It might say PSD on the arrest sheet, but it wouldn't have taken much for DI Woolley to figure out that DI Finch's team – Aaron's team – had been involved in the arrest of her friend.

No wonder she'd been angry.

"Do me a favour," he said. "Look up the bunch who've just been in. See if we've got them on file for anything."

Two minutes later, Lynn had what he wanted.

For Frank, there was a list of driving offenses so long and varied it was a wonder the man was still alive. For the other five, nothing. No run-ins, no arrests, nothing.

There wasn't anything surprising or suspicious about that. The lack of prints or DNA on file was just an inconvenience.

And inconvenience was something Aaron was used to.

CHAPTER SEVENTY

IT WAS SUPPOSED to be miserable, coming home to an empty house in the depths of winter. Lynn was supposed to miss Gerry while he was away – one week gone, another to go – travelling around Europe with the telecoms business he'd worked at for six years.

And she did miss him. But she liked the space. Liked a bit of time to herself. When you spent most of your working day with Isaac Bateman, an hour or two of quiet reading or watching TV was a joy.

Gerry had called earlier, and she called him back now, catching him asleep in his Frankfurt hotel room. Confused at first, then pleased to see her on the screen. She *did* miss him. She couldn't wait to have him back.

But she liked the space.

Lynn ended the call when Gerry's yawning became too much to ignore and sat down with the novel she'd been enjoying. Historical fiction, technically, set in the sixteenth century, but really just another fast-paced, well-written drama. Racier than she'd expected, and absorbing. An hour had gone by when she looked up and realised how late it was.

She checked her messages and got ready for bed. Then she remembered the friend request she'd sent to Jan Smith. She reached for her phone.

The request hadn't been accepted. It hadn't been rejected, either. But "Jan Smith" had seen it. She'd changed the privacy settings on her account, and from being able to see everything, Lynn could see nothing.

She put her phone down, switched off the light, and lay down with her eyes closed, waiting for sleep to come.

Half an hour later she sat up again, wide awake. She picked up her phone, scrolled to "Jan Smith," saw nothing had changed, looked for the old Jan Calloway account, and found it had been deleted.

Good thing she'd taken screenshots.

There were three of them. Isla, Emily, Francesca. The three names Jan Calloway had shared with "Jan Smith," the ones she'd interacted with.

All of them local. All of them in West Cumbria.

She checked their feeds, saw nothing that rang any alarm bells, closed her eyes, and tried to sleep again.

This time, the attempt lasted no more than ten minutes.

She picked up her phone and began to type. The longer she took, the more chance she'd change her mind.

She didn't want to change her mind.

My name, she wrote, *is Lynn Hedley. I am a Detective Constable with Cumbria CID, stationed at Langdale Police Station. Please feel free to check my profile and the public information the police have about me.*

That was OK, wasn't it? She wasn't lying. Not yet, anyway. And she was taking a risk, certainly, but not with her privacy. Anyone who wanted to track down Lynn Hedley wouldn't exactly struggle.

She continued to type.

I am trying to contact your friend Jan Smith, and would appreciate it if you would forward this message on to her.

This was the tricky bit. Jan had disappeared, and she might not have done it as effectively as she'd hoped, but she'd done it deliberately. She wouldn't want anyone coming after her. Including the police. If Lynn was going to get anything out of this, she'd have to blur the line between truth and fiction.

She'd have to lie.

Jan, she wrote. *We know who you really are.*

That was good. That was fine. Short, punchy, accurate.

We're investigating a murder, and while we know you weren't involved in it, we believe you might be able to assist us as you may have had your own difficulties with one of the suspects. We appreciate your need for secrecy, but if we found you this easily, the people you're hiding from will be able to find you too.

Still good. Still true. It was a wonder Sinead Conway hadn't already found the woman. She might be sending people over to Northern Ireland even now. Or – Lynn shivered as she sat up in bed – she might have sent someone over months ago. Someone who'd finished Jan Calloway off, taken her phone, and continued to update her Facebook feed so as not to alert the few people Jan had stayed in touch with.

Lynn held out her phone, looked at it for a moment, and pulled a face.

She might be sending a message to Jan Calloway. She might be sending a message to Jan Calloway's killer. Using her real name. Her real identity.

All the more reason to add the last bit. The blurry bit. The lie.

Given the importance of the matter, she wrote, *you should be aware that we will be alerting our counterparts in Northern Ireland should you not respond.*

If someone had killed Jan Calloway and taken her phone, it was unlikely they were still in Northern Ireland. But it wouldn't do any harm.

And if the real Jan Calloway got the message, then it would be harder for her to ignore it.

She pulled up tabs for Isla, Emily, and Francesca. She copied the message, and pasted it into a window, a second window, a third. She paused.

Talk about exceeding your authority.

Sod it, she thought, and pressed send.

And send again.

And, for a third time, send.

CHAPTER SEVENTY-ONE

Aaron smiled as he got in his car the next morning and headed out towards Elterwater, imagining the DI arresting Streeting. He might not have been there when it happened. But he could still enjoy it.

He reached Elterwater. He drove up to the station.

And he kept going.

Marc Langham lived in an enormous farmhouse near Loughrigg Tarn, on the road to Ambleside. Marc wasn't expecting him, and it was early, but when Aaron buzzed at the set of wooden gates set into an imposing red brick wall he couldn't see past, he was answered within seconds.

"Aaron? Come on in. See you in a minute."

The house was one of those places Aaron had driven past a thousand times but never noticed. It was set behind those gigantic walls that the Lake District was full of.

Marc stood at a tall glass door, gesturing for Aaron to come in. Stepping inside was like stepping into a different world. The moment his boots came off, the underfloor heating made itself known.

"Come on through," Marc said. Aaron followed him into a wide kitchen filled with more appliances than he'd seen in professional kitchens.

"You like to cook?" he asked.

"You guessed?" Marc smiled.

Marc had been friendly each time Aaron had seen him, even last night at the station. It would have been helpful if Aaron could have picked out a false note in all that friendliness, but there was none.

The man was rich, successful, and, it seemed, perfectly pleasant. Difficult to dislike, in some ways. But very easy to hate in others.

Over coffee so good even Aaron could taste the quality, Marc directed his attention outside, where half a dozen acres stood wild and rolling, buildings dotted here and there.

"There's even a stable block," he added, pointing to a long, low building not far from the house. "Woman who sold me the place used to keep horses, apparently."

"Not you?"

"I don't ride. Maybe one day."

"Why did you buy a place with stables, then?"

"Did I not just show you the half a dozen acres of wild Lake District countryside?"

Aaron grinned.

"Look, mate," said Marc, his voice lowering. "I don't blame you."

"Blame me?"

"Last night. All that stuff about prints and DNA. I understand."

Aaron frowned. "You do?"

"You were just doing your job, right?"

"Right."

"Even if your job is being a bit of a fascist," Marc added. Aaron looked up in time to catch the wink.

Although he wasn't sure it was a joke.

"But listen, I'm sorry I couldn't help you. It's just, I'm not keen on the state possessing information about me that it has no need to hold or right to hold."

"The state?" prompted Aaron. "You mean me, though. Me and my colleagues."

Marc shrugged. "Look, I made my money coming up with ways of using the blockchain, so centralised information is always going to be something that winds me up."

Aaron didn't understand any of that, but he nodded. Serge had worked in tech. If he needed to know, he'd ask his husband to explain.

"But that's the thing about a database you can't control. If someone said to me, 'Can Aaron Keyes have your prints, just Aaron Keyes, maybe that pretty DC who's following him round, but no one else, and definitely not Isaac bloody Bateman?' I'd say, 'Yeah, go for it.' But it's not that, is it? It's Bateman. It's that mad woman who runs the shop up there." He pointed west, Aaron assumed, towards Elterwater. "It's not that I don't trust you. But I've got no idea who's going to be around after you've buggered off back to Whitehaven."

Aaron had heard worse. And it wasn't unreasonable.

After that, the conversation spread out. Old friends, mutual friends, successes and failures. Marc didn't mention Sara, the woman he'd been engaged to, the woman who'd been Aaron's closest friend for so many years, and Aaron didn't think it was his place to, so there was a hole at the centre of the discussion, but it didn't feel like something they had to skirt around.

It just didn't come up.

Aaron was interested in what Marc had achieved, and how he'd achieved it, and Marc was happy to tell him.

"My business," he said, "is more than just a way of making money for me."

Aaron looked up from his coffee, expecting another wink, but Marc was deadly serious.

"It's my entire way of life, Aaron. I only create things I think will help people, you understand?"

Marc had lost him a couple of minutes earlier, during his in-depth analysis of the impact of AI on how algorithms were used, or of algorithms on how AI was used, Aaron wasn't sure which.

"Yep," Aaron lied.

"All of it has to be part of something bigger. My business. My house. My contributions to the community."

Aaron had heard all about those contributions from Lynn the previous evening. Marc gave generously. To everyone and everything, it seemed. He'd made himself a popular man.

"And then there's my work in London. I don't mean the business, Aaron. I mean my initiatives."

"Initiatives?" asked Aaron, even though he was growing bored with the conversation.

"I've got a couple of groups. One in Camden. One in Morden, you know?"

Aaron nodded. He'd never heard of Morden. Somewhere in London, presumably.

"They participate in community actions. They're activists, demonstrators, instigators, innovators. They are whatever the community needs them to be. And my funding allows them to continue."

On the one hand, it sounded impressive. On the other, it sounded like a load of nonsense.

"I'll tell you what, at one point I was even contemplating putting some money into the cemetery idiots."

"The cemetery idiots?" Aaron asked.

"The protestors. The ones up here. Their camp's right by the cemetery. I thought they were on to something. Still do, as it happens. But they're unreliable. And after the trouble last night, I'm glad I didn't. My people need to have more focus. I'm not sure this lot are capable."

Which brought Aaron back to the reason he'd come here in the first place.

"Did you know him? Kevin Downes?"

Marc took a sip from his coffee cup, and shrugged. "Yes. I mean, not well. But I'd chatted to him. About the protest. Tried to size him up."

"And did you?"

"Size him up? Yes, I think so. One of those who thinks he's better than everyone else – and I can see that look, Aaron Keyes, I know people say much the same about me, but they're wrong. Besides, he'd done nothing to justify it. I can't say I was fond of Kevin Downes. But still." He shuddered. "To die, out there, like that. No one deserves that."

Aaron thanked him and left. During the short drive back to Elterwater, he mused on the little he'd learned, and concluded that Marc was fixated on what people deserved. Even more so on what *he* deserved.

And on what he owned. On *his* business, *his* house, *his* initiatives, *his* people. More than anything.

CHAPTER SEVENTY-TWO

LYNN WOKE with a headache and a sense of something foreign in her throat. Her mouth was dry, and where the sheet touched her elbow, there was heat and pain.

Every winter, without fail. She'd made it as far as the new year and dared to hope it wouldn't come back, but it had. The same fever, cold, flu, not-Covid-but-something-like-Covid.

It would floor her. No one else would catch it, or if they did, it would be a sore throat that lasted twenty-four hours. It would send her spiralling so far down she'd feel like she was never coming back up again. It would last a week, eight days tops. And then it would leave her as suddenly as it had come.

She had twenty-four hours before it hit her with its full force. Thirty-six if she was lucky. She'd gone downstairs and swallowed four paracetamol with a glass of water before she remembered the messages she'd sent. Only the frailty of her legs stopped her from running back upstairs to her phone.

There was a message from Jan Smith.

I hear you're trying to reach me.

What do you want?

How do I know you are who you say you are?

Lynn had an answer for the first question, but wasn't about to blurt it out. The second one was easier. Lynn spent a minute tapping out the reply and editing it before it went. She suggested a video call. *That way we can both see who we're talking to. And if you're worried about who I am, my photo's right there on the Cumbria Police website.*

Lynn wasn't expecting a reply anytime soon, but the three dots appeared before she'd put her phone down. The reply came a minute later.

Fine. But not now. I'm on my way to work. Later this afternoon.

Fine, agreed Lynn. She considered throwing in a smiley face, but decided against it. *Where's work?*

Just a bar.

Of course. Just like back in Maryport.

It took longer than usual to get showered and dressed, but that was OK. She'd already made progress. Lynn was reaching for her coat when her phone rang, and she recognised the main number from the station.

"DC Hedley," she said.

"It's PC Henniker, Lynn," said a hesitant voice.

"Everything OK, Chaz?"

"Fine. But someone just dropped in a phone. Some tourist. Found it in the mud when they were walking."

"Right." She nodded. "That's great, Chaz. Do you really think that's a matter for CID, though?"

He laughed. "Not normally, no. But it was found in Baysbrown Wood. Not far from the body. I thought... I wanted to let you know straight away."

"That's great," she said again, meaning it this time.

"It's probably nothing," he added. "I mean, not sure it'll even work."

"Why not?"

"It's like an antique. One of those Nokias from the old days."

Lynn tried not to laugh. *The old days*. He was only a few years younger than she was.

"Right. Doesn't matter how old it is. We need to treat this as potential evidence in a murder investigation. Can you bag it and make sure it's not touched by anyone who hasn't already touched it?"

"Already done," he told her.

"Brilliant. You've done well, Chaz. I'll arrange for someone to pick it up."

Keisha. She'd said something about tech. Phones. This would be right up her street.

CHAPTER SEVENTY-THREE

THE FIRST THING Tom noticed when he walked into the team room was the antimacassar hanging on the back of Nina's chair.

Last time he'd seen that antimacassar, it had been on his.

"I see victory is mine," he said.

Nina turned to him. Anger? Sadness? A little of both.

"I didn't get to study the other night," she told him.

"Hence my victory."

"I haven't finished," she said, just as Harriett walked in. They'd agreed it would be diplomatic to walk into the team room separately, even if they arrived at the Hub together.

"Haven't finished what?" asked Harriett.

Nina continued, "I wasn't able to study the other night, because some bastard thought it would be a nice idea to try to burn my house down."

"Shit," said Tom.

Harriett took three strides to Nina's desk and wrapped her arms around her shoulders.

"Are you OK?"

"Yes." Nina extracted herself from Harriett's embrace. "I'm fine, Elena's fine, the house will be fine. The fire brigade thinks it was just local yobs, but I'm not so sure."

"Carter?" said Tom.

Nina nodded. "That stupid bloody post my mum put up on Facebook. They know Elena's staying with me. Carter and Streeting. And the way the boss tells it, the bastards tried to take out the evidence from Bobby Silver's house last night, too. And we've got a matter of hours till Streeting's out, so I don't want to think about anything except how we can stop that happening."

"What can we do?" Harriett asked.

Nina shrugged. "Hope for a miracle?"

Nina's phone rang. All three of them stared at it for a moment before she picked it up.

"Yes?" she said, then listened for a minute. Her eyes widened. "The handle?" she asked. "They're definitely his? Thanks, Caroline. You're a legend."

She put down her phone, turned to the others, and said, "You're not going to believe this."

Caroline had been analysing the evidence all night. She'd found fibres on the furniture and feathers and dog hair on everything, even the window frames. She'd found all the things you'd expect in the places you'd expect them.

And then she'd picked up a door handle – the handle from Bobby Silver's bedroom door – and found that it was smeared in petroleum jelly.

"Vaseline," Nina said.

"Oh," said Harriett. "I remember that."

"You do?" Tom asked.

"I remember seeing it on the handle when we went upstairs at the house. When we found her. I didn't know it was Vaseline. Thought it was just an unusual pattern. But..." She turned to Nina. "Vaseline. Makes it slippery. Makes it harder to turn the handle."

"If you were wearing gloves," Nina said, "you'd probably have to remove them."

Harriett picked up the thread. "And if you did that, if you took off your gloves and turned the handle, the Vaseline would hold your fingerprints nicely."

"And," added Tom, "if you had to run downstairs and jump into your Jeep because the police were coming, you might not have time to wipe that handle clean."

"Feels like Bobby Silver did it on purpose," Harriett said. "Maybe she knew. Maybe she was sending us a message."

Tom looked at Nina. "And did we get that message?"

"Yes." Nina's face broke into a smile. "There's a print on the handle. A clear print, with a match. For a certain Ralph Streeting."

CHAPTER SEVENTY-FOUR

"JUST LIKE OLD TIMES," said Zoe. She turned and remembered there was no one next to her.

She'd been here before. The tiny viewing room where, if you were privileged enough, you could watch people being interviewed in the sixth-floor custody suite.

Since the sixth floor was reserved for PSD, the people being interviewed were either police officers or civilians who worked for the police. In the past, when Zoe had sat here, or in the interview room itself, she'd faced people she knew. People she'd worked with. On one occasion, someone she'd liked.

And she'd generally had someone sitting next to her. Someone to bounce ideas off. Someone to share the shock, or disappointment, or disgust.

It was just her today. And on the screen, Ralph Streeting. Next to him was his lawyer, Trevor Singleton, who Zoe hadn't seen since her first case. Mick Halfpenny's lawyer.

Another friend of Carter's.

Opposite them were Carl and Denise Gaskill. Carl was

poker-faced. If she hadn't known what he had up his sleeve, she'd have assumed there was nothing.

Denise was struggling to hold it in. She kept opening her mouth, shutting it, waiting for the right moment, changing her mind. Every now and then, a smirk crossed her face.

Streeting didn't know her. But he'd be suspecting something.

After a few minutes of formalities and a recap of the previous day's interviews, Carl broke it. He produced four sheets of paper and placed them on the table, face down, but didn't slide them across to Streeting and the lawyer.

Not yet.

"I'm sure you won't be aware of this," he said, the sarcasm so sharp it almost hurt, "but there was an attack on a vehicle last night."

"There are attacks on vehicles every night, DI Whaley," replied Streeting.

"This particular vehicle was carrying evidence from Bobby Silver's house."

"That's a shame," Streeting said. "Wouldn't have happened on my watch."

"I'm sure it wouldn't. Thankfully, the attack failed, and the evidence made it to its destination, where it was thoroughly examined overnight."

Streeting's smile dropped.

"I'm now producing a list of these items," said Carl, "as well as images marked X, Y, and Z, representing photographs of the item referred to as Handle 4 in the list, and a printout from IDENT 1, the national fingerprint database."

It was glorious. The moment. The expression on Streeting's face. If time had frozen and Zoe had been forced to live in that instant for eternity, looking at that expression, the dawning realisation, the horror, she wouldn't have got bored for centuries.

She didn't even mind that she wasn't in there. It felt more than ever like they were one team, acting in concert, with a common purpose.

They were so close.

Zoe listened as Carl and Denise outlined the evidence. The fingerprint. The match. She smiled as Streeting sat back, frowning, then leaned across to whisper to his lawyer, who asked for ten minutes alone with his client.

They had to give him the ten minutes. They could watch. They couldn't listen.

She left the side room and found Carl and Denise waiting for her at the round table in the entrance area.

"Going well," she told them.

Carl's frown suggested he didn't agree.

"He'll come back hard," he replied. "He'll go political."

"We've got evidence now, Carl. He can't make that disappear using his contacts."

"You watch."

She watched. Back in the side room, on the screen, ten minutes later, she watched as Streeting did exactly what Carl had predicted.

"Yes, I was there," he said.

"Did you murder her?" asked Denise.

"No. I was there the day before she was killed."

"Why? And why haven't you said anything?"

"I don't want to say anything now," Streeting replied. "I just don't have a lot of choice, under the circumstances."

Zoe noticed with growing alarm the way his expression had turned. He was relaxed.

The bastard was enjoying himself.

"What were you doing at Bobby Silver's house, then, if you weren't murdering her?" asked Carl.

"I was there as part of my own investigation into activities at the Port of Workington. You'll be aware that area is within my purview. My activities at Bobby Silver's house were part of an important ongoing investigation into organised crime."

"Go on," said Carl.

Streeting smiled and shook his head. "I don't think so."

"Why not? With the evidence we have, we could rearrest you for murder, DI Streeting. It's in your interest to be as open with us as possible."

"No, it isn't. Because with the exception of my lawyer, I don't trust anyone either in this room or watching this interview remotely. I don't trust you not to leak."

"You..."

"You think *we're* going to leak details of your investigation to the people you're investigating?" Denise said. "*You* think *we're* going to do that?"

Streeting eyed her. "Precisely. I understand there's already an IOPC investigation going on into incidents at this station. I understand it involves DI Finch's team and PSD, as well as at least two corrupt officers, one corrupt crime scene investigator, and a corrupt civilian police employee. In the circumstances, I'd be foolish to trust you."

Carl sat back. Zoe was impressed with his calm.

She couldn't have managed it. Couldn't have coped.

"What do you propose, then, if you're not willing to talk to us?"

"I'll talk to the Assistant Chief Constable's team. And no one else. If you can arrange for me to speak securely and privately with Becca Grey, the ACC's policy advisor, then we can put an end to all this nonsense, and I'll be out there finding the person who *actually* killed Bobby Silver."

Zoe cast her mind back. Fifteen minutes. Just fifteen minutes ago, she'd been watching this same man as his world collapsed around him.

Now, the boot was on the other foot.

CHAPTER SEVENTY-FIVE

"Come on, love," said Val.

Sara eyed her mother.

"Go on. It'll do you good," added Joe.

Aaron stood behind them, silent. He'd spent ten minutes persuading Sara to come out of her bedroom, but at least she was dressed.

She looked past her parents and met his eye. A tiny movement. Not a roll. Just a flicker upward, then back down, followed by a nod. He couldn't help but smile.

His old friend was still in there somewhere. And she was coming out for lunch with him.

Twenty minutes later, she sat opposite him at the Eltermere Inn, studying a menu she probably knew by heart. They'd been twenty mostly silent minutes, and she was studying the menu to avoid eye contact. But still. She was out. In public. It was, according to Joe, a big improvement.

"What do you fancy?" he asked.

She shrugged.

"Come on, Sara. Pick something, or I'll order you a scotch egg."

She hated scotch eggs.

She looked up. "I'll have a pie."

"And a pint." He went to the bar and ordered for them both.

The pint loosened Sara's tongue enough to answer his questions, but the pie did it. After two mouthfuls, she was laughing about the colony of peahens that had surrounded them on their way in. After three, she asked Aaron how he was. After four, she remembered he had a husband and a daughter and asked about them.

After five, she looked around the room, made sure no one could see or hear her, and burst into tears.

"I think... You know, Aaron, I think I actually loved him. I think I was in love with him."

Aaron reached across the table and took her hand. "I'm so sorry. It must be terrible." He paused, wondering if this was the right time. "Why did he break it off?"

Sara stared at him, a frown spreading across her face. There was a smear of brown on her left cheek, gravy from the pie. He resisted the urge to reach forward again and wipe it off.

"Not Marc," she said. "I mean Kevin. Kevin Downes."

He sat back so fast his knee hit the table, and the half pint he'd been nursing tumbled onto the floor.

"Shit!" he said. At least the beer hadn't hit the food. The muscle-bound Australian who'd served him emerged from behind the bar, armed with cloth and mop, winked, and silently cleared the mess away.

Two minutes later, they were alone again.

"Sorry," he said. "I just..."

"I know." She gave a small, sad smile. "No one knew. No one knows."

"You were..."

She nodded. "I don't feel good about it. It was an affair. I was engaged. It wasn't the right thing to do. And Marc is... He was always kind to me. Until the end, anyway. But with Kevin, there was something different."

Over the next fifteen minutes, Sara went from a silent ghost to a woman who wouldn't stop talking, and everything came out.

She'd been sleeping with Kevin Downes. He'd tried it on a few times, and she'd found him funny and clever and fun to be with, but that had been the sum of it. Nothing physical. Until there *was* something physical.

"He just got me. Got people. Could see through their falseness and pretensions to what they really were, underneath."

Aaron was getting an idea of the sort of man Kevin Downes was. The sort of person who set himself apart from everyone else and took advantage of those unlucky enough to fall for it.

In short, an arsehole.

But Sara had loved him. That was the theme she returned to, time after time. She'd loved Kevin Downes.

This was why she was so sad. Why she'd retreated to her room. Why she hadn't spoken to anyone. Not because Marc Langham had broken off their engagement. But because Kevin had left her, which was what she'd assumed at first. He'd disappeared, without a trace. And then, finally, because Kevin had died.

"Is this why Marc broke it off?" he asked. "Did he find out?"

Sara nodded.

"He found my messages. On my phone. I couldn't hide it then." She looked up from the remains of her pie and must have seen something on Aaron's face, because she shook her head so vehemently it was almost violent.

"No, Aaron. Marc wouldn't hurt anyone. He's not like that."

More nods. More sad smiles.

"I'll have to take your word for that," he said.

It was a throwaway comment, cast out with an easy smile, but it was a lie. When it came to murder, Aaron wouldn't be taking anyone's word. For anything.

CHAPTER SEVENTY-SIX

THERE WAS a look on Luke's face that Zoe hadn't seen before.

He looked concerned. Genuinely worried. Not just pale, but somehow even whiter than usual. Almost gaunt, like he'd been stretched.

Maybe that was what working for Fiona Kendrick did to people.

Zoe approached him, smiling, expecting the usual shake of the head, but something in his eyes made her stop.

"It's bad."

"It can't be that bad." She kept her smile fixed in place.

"It is. But she's expecting you. You'd better go in."

Inside her office, Fiona was standing, facing away from the door. She pointed to the chair without turning. "Sit."

When she finally turned around, Zoe was shocked. Luke had just been the taster. Fiona looked like she hadn't slept in a week.

"Are you OK?" asked Zoe.

"Remember when I told you it was my neck on the line, Zoe?"

"Yes."

"I've had the ACC on the phone. Not one of his minions. Not Becca Grey or Mickey White or Nicky Pink. The ACC himself."

She fixed Zoe with a glare. Becca Grey was real. The other names weren't.

"Somehow, Ralph Streeting managed to get to him. No, I don't care how," she added, seeing Zoe open her mouth to comment. "I don't care if it's the lawyer, or a leak, or anything else. The point is, Joseph Carghillie knows all about our little IOPC investigation. He knows all about Tel Cummings and Carrie Wright, Hussein Mahmoud and your precious Kay Holinshed. And thanks to Ralph Streeting, he's decided to draw lines that don't exist between all these things."

Some of those lines did exist. Some of those lines were the reason they were here, the reason Streeting was in custody, the reason Bobby Silver was dead.

"Joseph Carghillie has informed me that both PSD and the Hub are riddled with officers who've got into the habit of doing whatever they want whenever they want to."

"That's ridiculous," Zoe said.

"I know it's ridiculous. So does Ralph Streeting. But thanks to the timing of this IOPC investigation, it's not so ridiculous that a serving Assistant Chief Constable can't be convinced it's true. He's concerned there are, what he calls, 'problem officers' here."

"What does that mean?"

"Search me. But it gets worse. Or better, if you're looking at this whole thing as a bad black comedy where you don't really care what happens. Because Streeting's convinced the

ACC that he, Ralph Streeting, has identified these so-called 'problem officers,' and that's why he's been arrested."

Zoe stared back at the super.

"Joseph Carghillie is furious. He doesn't know if it's true, but he does know something's badly wrong here. He wants Streeting released."

"Shit," said Zoe. She wasn't sure she'd ever sworn in front of the super, but Fiona didn't bat an eyelash.

"Twenty-four hours are nearly up, Zoe," Fiona continued. "It's charge or release time."

"But—"

"But you want me to authorise an extension?" Fiona asked. "Another twelve hours?"

Zoe said nothing.

"My neck is on the line, Zoe."

"I know."

"How sure are you?"

"That Streeting's guilty? One hundred percent."

"You know that's not what I mean."

Zoe swallowed. "That we'll get enough to take it to trial? Fifty. Maybe sixty."

"What are we looking for?"

"Truthfully? I don't know. Something else in the forensics, I'd imagine. That, or cameras, or a mistake from one of his associates. Something that can put him not just in Bobby Silver's house, but in her house when she was killed. Ideally something that puts him in the Jeep or holding the gun."

Fiona nodded, glanced at her watch, then back to Zoe.

"Twelve hours," she said. "That's a bit after two a.m. And Zoe?"

"Yes?"

"My neck on the line."

There was an expression very much like relief on Luke's face when Zoe emerged. Maybe he'd thought she wouldn't make it out of there alive. She thanked him, noticed a missed call on her phone, and answered it on the stairs when it rang a moment later.

"You've got to get him," said Olivia Bagsby, breathless, panicky.

"What?"

"Carter. His people are close. I think..."

There was a pause. The sound of passing vehicles. The hoot of a train, suddenly muffled by a window being closed. Birdsong. A seagull, Zoe thought. She'd heard enough of them over the last year or so.

"What is it?" Zoe asked.

"You've got to put him away, Zoe. I think they know where I am."

The line went dead.

Zoe looked back down at her phone, to a second missed call.

Both of them from David Randle.

CHAPTER SEVENTY-SEVEN

AARON CALLED Lynn the moment he'd dropped Sara back at her parents' house. He asked her to find out everything she could about Marc Langham. She reminded him that there wasn't anything on Langham. The man had never been arrested, never charged, never even brought in for questioning. No prints, no DNA, not so much as an interview.

"See if there's anything else," he said. "You OK?" Her voice sounded off.

"Yeah. Just didn't sleep well."

"It's going around."

He took a detour to the quarry site on the way back, hoping for another glimpse of Sinead Conway. There was no sign of her, or of anyone else. A quiet day.

At the station, it was obvious Lynn had been lying. Her eyes were bloodshot, and she was fighting back a sneeze every time she opened her mouth.

"Go home," he said.

"Not yet." She popped a handful of pills into her mouth and chased them with water. "These'll keep me going a while longer. Look at this, though." She stood and moved away from her screen.

There had been a complaint made against Marc Langham.

Last summer. August, to be precise. An allegation from a pair of ramblers that he had assaulted them when he caught them walking across his land. That he had driven his Land Rover at them.

"Bloody hell," Aaron said. He turned to Lynn, but she was squeezing her eyes shut.

Why hadn't Langham been arrested?

Aaron turned back to the screen and found the answer. The allegation had been dropped before anything could be done about it.

"Seen this?" Lynn was holding up her phone. "Email."

He returned to his desk and pulled up the message she was referring to.

The subject was *Fucker's alive.*

The sender was Keisha Middleton.

Aaron opened the email. Just a photo of a phone, an old Nokia 3310, battered and muddy but intact.

The message underneath was clear.

Got the thing charged. It's not dead. Doesn't mean I can actually open it, though. On to the next challenge. Will let you know if I recover any data.

No "kind regards." No sign-off at all. Just the photo and the facts.

Still. It was progress.

CHAPTER SEVENTY-EIGHT

Nina didn't mind it up here, in the side room, watching the interview.

It would have been nicer if there'd been someone else with her. But there was something about watching Streeting getting grilled by a couple of no-nonsense interview experts that sent a pleasant tingle down her spine.

At least, that was the way it started.

Once the formalities were out of the way, DI Whaley reminded Streeting of what he was facing. Not just the fact he'd been identified by Maria and Alexandra – their names had been kept out of it. Not just the photos. Not the host of circumstantial evidence that, by itself didn't mean a lot, but with everything else, might tip the scales.

The kicker was the fingerprint. And yes, Streeting could talk all he wanted about how he'd been in the house earlier, how he'd had nothing to do with the murder, but he hadn't mentioned that at the time, had he? Footage was being pulled from all the cameras on surrounding routes that covered the day in question. So far, there was no sign of Streeting's car.

DI Whaley had all the facts. DI Whaley had the evidence.

But Streeting simply shrugged.

"I've told you what I'm going to tell you," he said. "I don't recognise your authority in this case and I expect to be released shortly, following which I'll be back on the case and tracking down the perpetrators."

DS Gaskill sat forward, ready to say something, but Streeting held up a finger.

"That being the case, DS Gaskill, DI Whaley, is there anything *you* might want to tell *me* about your involvement in all this?"

And like that, the tingle was gone.

It was his confidence that did it. Anyone could say the words, could act the part, but Streeting was really living it.

He thought he'd be fine. He truly believed it. Which meant he was probably right.

Nina turned her attention to Denise Gaskill. This was why she'd jumped at the chance to watch the second part of the interview when the boss had asked her to. The boss had calls to make, things to follow up, stuff that couldn't wait.

And Nina could watch how a great DS interviewed a suspect.

It wasn't that she *liked* DS Gaskill. But Nina couldn't help admiring her. She went in hard. Aggressive.

So far, she hadn't said a thing. But now she sat forward again and spoke, and if anything, Nina's admiration grew.

"Are you familiar with this man?" the DS asked, sliding a photograph across the table. "His name's Victor Parlick. *Was* Victor Parlick, but I'm sure you know all about that. Now, you don't have to answer this, and I'm quite sure you'll deny everything, but we know he was killed on your orders, following instructions from Myron Carter."

Streeting opened his mouth to speak, but now it was DS Gaskill's turn to hold up a finger and silence him.

"It's OK. We're not questioning you over Mr Parlick's death," she said. "Yet. I just wanted to remind you of what happens to Myron Carter's employees when he decides they've become a liability. Look, here's someone else."

She slid another photograph over.

"This is Dean Somerville. Remember Dean? He was one of Mr Carter's customers. Or is it 'clients'? 'Purchasers'? I'm not sure how you refer to people who buy women. Anyway, that's not the point. The point is, Mr Somerville is currently enjoying the hospitality of the infirmary at Wakefield Prison. He's not dead, not quite, but it was a near thing. Again, someone who'd been a close associate of Myron Carter. Someone who ended up in a position where Carter thought he might talk. Someone who paid the price."

"Are you threatening my client?" asked the lawyer. Nina didn't recognise him, but she knew exactly who he was. When he'd been in the Hub, a year or so ago, acting for Mick Halfpenny, she'd been out cold in the basement Halfpenny had locked her in.

Halfpenny was serving life for the murder of Daria Petrescu. Hopefully, Trevor Singleton's current client would have the same sort of luck.

"Far from it," DS Gaskill replied with a smile. "I'm trying to show him that he's already under threat. And that it makes sense to get ahead of the threat. Come clean. Help us get Carter locked up, and it'll be harder for him to get to you, DI Streeting."

Streeting just smiled back at her.

The bastard really thought he was untouchable, didn't he?

Nina was worried. Worried that he wouldn't talk. Worried at his confidence, at his apparent certainty that he'd be out soon, and fitting someone up for a murder he'd orchestrated.

Most of all, worried that he might actually be right.

CHAPTER SEVENTY-NINE

THE WELCOME this time was less warm.

The gates buzzed open again, but Marc stood at the front door, arms folded.

"Mind if I come in?" Aaron asked.

Marc shrugged and stepped aside. Aaron walked through to the kitchen.

"What are you actually doing here, Aaron?" Marc asked.

Aaron sat. "I was hoping to ask you a few questions. I'll be honest with you, Marc, I'm a little disappointed."

The look of surprise on Marc's face came a second too late to be spontaneous.

"How so?" Marc asked. He leaned against a stark white cupboard door. He was trying to look casual, and at first glance, it was working. But that pause, the way he was standing...

The man was nervous.

"I don't think you've been completely open with me. You didn't lie," Aaron added, spotting the objection forming on Marc's lips. "But you weren't forthcoming, were you?"

"I don't know what you mean."

"Would you like me to read from my notes of our conversation this morning?" Aaron pulled out his phone and scrolled to the record. "We were talking about Kevin Downes. I asked if you knew him. You said you'd tried to 'size him up.' Said you weren't 'fond of him,' that he thought he was 'better than everyone else.'"

"That's all true."

"And yet, despite the fact that you know I'm investigating a murder, you didn't think it was worth mentioning that your fiancée – sorry, your former fiancée – was having an affair with Kevin Downes? That you found out about this affair and broke off the engagement?"

"Now, look here, Aaron," Marc began. "This isn't any of your business. It's my private life, and I'll thank you to—"

"Enough!"

Aaron stood. Marc went to take a step back, realised he couldn't, and almost fell.

"Enough, Marc. Don't bullshit me. What's going on? Why didn't you tell me?"

Marc held up one hand. "Fine." He walked over, and both men sat down. "I didn't tell anyone about Kevin Downes, because I was embarrassed."

"Embarrassed?"

Marc nodded. "Imagine losing a woman to *that*!"

Aaron kept his expression neutral.

"It wouldn't have looked good, would it? I knew you'd jump to conclusions. No, I didn't think much of Kevin Downes, and after I found out he'd been screwing my fiancée, I thought even less of him. But I didn't kill him, Aaron. I wouldn't do that."

Aaron nodded. As far as he could judge, the man was telling the truth. But he could be a good liar.

"Fine," he said. "Let's move on."

"Thank you," Marc replied and went to stand.

Aaron held up a hand. "Let's move on to Guy and Ava Townsend."

Marc's smile froze. "That incident was resolved. Nothing happened. The complaint was withdrawn."

"So you didn't drive your Land Rover at them when you spotted them on your land?"

"I've just told you. Nothing happened. It was withdrawn. And frankly, if you're over here investigating a murder, I'm not sure why you'd be looking into that sort of petty nonsense."

"You weren't even asked about it at the time. There's no record of anyone interviewing you, taking a statement, any of that. The complaint was withdrawn so fast, there wasn't time."

Marc shrugged. "I suppose they saw the error of their ways. Now listen." His face hardened. "I've had enough of this."

"I don't suppose you'd reconsider your decision not to provide fingerprints and DNA, Marc?"

"No, I wouldn't. And if you want to speak to me again, you can call my lawyers first."

"You have lawyers? I mean, on some sort of retainer? Why would you need that?"

"For the protests. My people, sometimes they fall foul of the authorities. I employ lawyers in London to ensure their rights aren't infringed."

"Human rights lawyers?"

"Yes, that's right. Do you have a problem with that, Aaron?"

"Not at all."

"I know what the police can be like, *DS Keyes*," Marc continued, making the title sound like an insult. "If you continue to harass me, you can be sure I won't take it lying down."

"That's fine. That's your right."

"I'm glad you see that. Then you won't be surprised to find yourself the subject of an official complaint."

"You do what you have to do, Marc. Oh, and while you're dropping in your complaint, do remember to hand over the contact details for your human rights lawyers." Aaron stood. "Because I intend to speak to you again, one way or another."

CHAPTER EIGHTY

THREE TIMES, Zoe had checked the corridor. Three times she'd shut the door. Twice she'd gone back to make sure.

It was fine. No one was hovering. She wouldn't be disturbed.

It was time to speak to David Randle.

He picked up immediately. "What's happened?"

This wasn't like Randle. He'd usually spend a few minutes easing his way in, engaging in small talk he must have known she loathed, relishing her discomfort.

What did he know?

"What do you mean?" she asked.

He sighed. "Last time we spoke, you were in something of a quandary. Olivia Bagsby wouldn't come in, but she wouldn't leave you alone, either. And your friendly Detective Inspector Streeting was trying to take over a murder investigation that would almost certainly have implicated his friends. I called for the latest news. And to offer you some advice on how to move forward."

There were plenty of things Zoe might have said to that,

mostly about just how welcome David Randle's advice would be. But she held back. Because, under the circumstances, he'd have a better idea what to do than she would.

"Brace yourself," she told him. "There have been some developments."

She started with Olivia Bagsby. That was easy. Maybe Carter had caught up with her, and if he had, there wasn't a lot Zoe could do if Olivia wouldn't tell her where she was. On balance, Zoe suspected Olivia was jumping at shadows, but that was hardly surprising. What was it they said? *It's not paranoia if they're really out to get you.*

Streeting took longer. Losing the case, arresting him, the ramming attempt, the print, the intervention of the ACC, the impact of the IOPC investigation.

There was a lot.

"Well, you have been a busy girl, haven't you?" Randle said when she'd finished. "And it must be hard."

"It's always hard."

"No, I mean for you, Zoe. You never were very good at all the politics, were you?"

"I'm sorry?"

"I'd advise you to leave it to the big boys, but it's the big boys you're up against, so that won't work."

She wondered for the hundredth time how she'd got here, taking advice from a man she hated, hiding it from her partner, aware that even if she wasn't actually breaking the law by speaking to him, Randle certainly was by contacting her.

"The best you can do is find something you can charge Streeting with," he said, "and that's the sort of solid, old-fashioned policing you can handle without me looking over your shoulder. I'm more interested in your Olivia Bagsby. Run through it all again, will you?"

Zoe took a breath and went through it all. Right up to the most recent call. Everything she'd said. Everything she'd heard.

"Those words, please," Randle said. "Exactly."

"She said, 'I think they know where I am.'"

"And she didn't say why?"

"No, David. And no, I don't know where she is, and I've told you everything we've got and everything we've done, and we can't find her."

"That's because you're not trying hard enough," he said, his tone so matter-of-fact he might have been talking about the weather.

"I beg your pardon?"

"Don't get offended, Zoe. But if Olivia Bagsby was a murder suspect, you'd have found her by now."

"We almost did. In Glasgow, we were so close, we—"

"Spare me the almost-had-her, Zoe. Almost is nothing. Now, I'll have a think and get back to you if I come up with anything. In the meantime, don't leave it so long before updating me."

He ended the call.

It was astonishing, really. In a twisted, psychologically damaged sort of way, it was extraordinary. After all they'd been through, David Randle still seemed to think he was her boss.

CHAPTER EIGHTY-ONE

"Lo," said Lynn into her phone.

"What the fuck's wrong with you?" said the woman on the other end. Lynn hadn't recognised the number, but it was obviously Keisha.

"A cold."

"Sounds like someone's ripped out your throat and replaced it with Bob Dylan's. If that's your idea of a cold, you're in trouble, girl."

"Any luck with the phone?" The words didn't come out quite right, but it was close enough.

"Der phobe? Yeah, got the bastard open. Next step's recovering the messages. I'll let you know. But that's not what I was calling about. I've heard back about your strap. The thing you found at the scene."

Lynn had been leaning back, one hand across her forehead, but now she sat forward.

"Yes?"

"Two things. At least two sets of DNA on it, and one of them we can't match, but the other one matches the victim's, so, well, you add that to what Doctor Death said about the shape of the thing, and it looks like you're talking murder weapon, right?"

"Right." Lynn didn't have to ask about Doctor Death. Had to be the pathologist.

"And the animal hair I found on it? Horse. My guess is it's part of a saddle strap. So either you're looking for a killer horse, or you're looking for a killer jockey."

"Right."

"Jockeys are small. Hide easily. Let's hope it's a horse. Though that fucker Shergar's been in hiding for decades, hasn't he? Clever bastards, horses. Oh, and we did manage to pull some prints, too. No match on them, either, in case you were wondering."

"No, you'd have led with that if there were. Thanks, Keisha." Lynn ended the call, wondering how Keisha managed it, all day, all the time, just *being* like that. And even more, how the people who worked with her every day could stand it.

"Shit," she added to dead air. She'd just noticed the time.

She'd have to do it here in the team room. DS Bateman wasn't around, thankfully. DS Keyes was, but he wouldn't make any difficulty. She explained what was about to happen, then set her phone on the desk, leaning against a book. She spent a minute adjusting the angle so her nose didn't look too red or too prominent, then a frantic thirty seconds unscrewing and shifting the screen DS Keyes had set up, detailing all the evidence in the murder investigation.

Probably best a random member of the public didn't see that.

Jan Calloway answered the call quickly enough. She was sitting in a dark room, but as Lynn's eyes adjusted, she made out the woman's face, the hints of auburn in her hair, and the surroundings she'd expected.

A bar. Not even the back room. Jan Calloway was standing at the bar, bottles lined up behind her, the gentle hum of conversation in the background.

"Are you OK to talk?" Lynn asked.

"Yeah, fine." Jan peered at the screen, then down again. "You not well?"

"Just a cold."

"If that's just a cold, remind me never to come back to England. OK, I reckon you're legit. What do you want?"

"You sure you're OK to talk?"

"No one can hear me. Anyone comes close enough, I'll tell 'em to bugger off."

"Won't you get in trouble for that?"

"It's my bar." Jan laughed. "I can say what I like."

"Fair enough." Lynn stopped.

Had she heard that right?

"Your bar?"

Jan looked at her. For a moment, Lynn thought the call had crashed. But then Jan started talking.

"Look, I don't like talking about this," she said. "But it's not what you think."

Lynn waited.

Jan sighed. She scratched her arm, glanced to one side, and continued talking.

"Sinead Conway... I was a thorn in her side, see? She didn't like me." Another scratch. "She didn't threaten me, or 'disappear' me, or whatever you want to call it. She paid me off. Gave me money to leave the area."

Lynn frowned. That made sense. But...

"Why go to all that trouble to disappear?" she asked. "As

far as I can see, there's only a handful of people who know you're alive, and I'm not sure even they know where you are."

"You come across protestors before?"

"A little. Why?"

"How do you think they'd feel about someone who'd been one of them, taking a fat payoff to throw the whole thing over and buy her own bar?"

"Ah. OK. But why Belfast?"

"Sinead had contacts over here. Told me they'd help set me up. Find a place to stay, help me scout out a decent bar without getting ripped off. You need something like that when you're setting up in a new place."

"Right." Lynn considered. "So clearly you don't have any issues with Sinead Conway."

"No."

"But what do you reckon would have happened if you hadn't accepted the payoff?"

"What d'you mean?"

"Did you ever get a sense that you might have been in any danger? Were there any threats?"

A shrug. "It never got that far. She offered the money, it was a good deal, I took it."

Lynn thanked her and ended the call. It hadn't given her what she'd hoped. But it hadn't ruled anything out either.

When she turned to DS Keyes, who'd watched the whole thing, he seemed inclined to agree, but more worried about her health than anything else.

"I'm fine," she told him. *I'b fibe.*

"Sure you are."

She ignored the jibe and told him what she'd heard from Keisha Middleton. He seemed unmoved by the news on the phone, but when she mentioned the matching DNA on the strap, the horsehair, and Keisha's theory that it had been part of a saddle strap, his face came to life.

"That's good," he said. "That's very interesting indeed."

"Why?"

"Because Sinead Conway rides."

Lynn nodded. Sinead Conway was just the sort of person who'd ride.

"She has a horse called Jenkins," he continued, lost in thought. "A thoroughbred. They're sensitive creatures, apparently."

"DS Keyes!" shouted a voice from behind them. They both turned.

DI Woolley was standing at the entrance to the team room, arms crossed, murder in her eyes.

"Yes, Ma'am?" DS Keyes replied.

"I gather your friends over in Whitehaven still haven't released Ralph Streeting."

Lynn turned to DS Keyes and watched, open-mouthed, as he shrugged.

"I don't know what you want me to say, Ma'am. It's got nothing to do with me."

"I beg your—"

"Now, if you'll excuse me," he went on, "I've got a murder to solve."

He smiled at her.

He turned back to Lynn, and she remembered what she'd heard about him offering himself as a hostage, stripped and cuffed, to a crazed killer with a knife.

She'd known he was brave. What he'd done last year, only a brave man would do that.

But she hadn't known he was *this* brave.

CHAPTER EIGHTY-TWO

"You lot do like to stir things up, don't you?"

Zoe frowned. She was used to this sort of comment from the super. It was the "you lot" that threw her.

Tall women? Redheads? Brummies? What did she mean?

Fiona must have read the expression on her face. She slid a sheet of paper across the desk, and things became clearer.

Not tall women. Not redheads, or Brummies. Just the team.

It was a letter, addressed to a number of senior officers, lodging a complaint against Aaron.

"You know this lot?" Fiona ran her finger across the four names, half of them double-barrelled, on the letterhead.

Zoe shook her head.

"Fancy London lawyers. Human rights, that sort of thing. They claim Aaron's been harassing their client. A Marc Langham. You heard anything about this?"

"No. But if there was a problem, Aaron would have let me know. I trust him. If he's stirring things up, they need stirring up."

Fiona nodded. "Good. In that case, I'll report back to the chief constable that you have my complete confidence."

Zoe widened her eyes. "You told Big Jo?"

"I'd had enough of the ACC meddling. I managed to get a message to her."

"Thank you."

Fiona nodded. "She said she'd back us up. But she made it clear that we need to move quickly. She said she can't risk the political exposure."

"What does that mean?"

"It means that if it gets out that we've arrested a senior officer, held him for a couple of days, then released him without charge, it'll look very bad for us. And the chief constable won't want to be associated with it. So the longer we hold him without charge, the less solid her support. She said she wishes she could be more helpful, but that's the way things are. And this didn't help." She pointed at the complaint.

"Politics." Zoe had been expecting this. Not the complaint. Not even the support. But the fact that any support would be weak, liable to be withdrawn the moment it became politically inconvenient.

"It's a fucking disgrace," Fiona replied, earning a look of shock from Zoe. "I'm sorry, Zoe, but it makes me sick. All of it. Enough to throw the whole thing in. Not that I have any intention of doing that. It would give them all too much satisfaction."

Zoe had always thought of Fiona as being a million miles from her old boss, Lesley. But in some ways, they were more alike than she'd realised. Impatience with the political manoeuvrings of the higher echelons was clearly something they had in common.

"Well, the bad news is we haven't made any progress since I last saw you," Zoe admitted. "I'm not confident we'll find anything we can use to charge him by tonight's deadline."

Fiona pursed her lips. "And if you had another twenty-four hours?"

"I couldn't promise anything. But I'd be more hopeful."

"Put a number on it, Zoe."

Zoe closed her eyes. It wasn't like there was any one thing they were looking for, a specific witness or piece of evidence they might find.

She couldn't lie.

"Thirty percent. Maybe forty," she said. It had been fifty or sixty just a few hours earlier.

"Fine. That's good enough for me."

"It is?"

A nod. "We'll apply to the magistrate later tonight to keep him in custody. It'll be strongly opposed, but I'll support the application. All we can do is try."

"You heard what I said, Fiona? Thirty percent?"

The super nodded again. "Thirty, maybe forty. But if you think he's guilty, then I think he's guilty, and we've got to give it a go."

"Thanks." Zoe found herself remembering another thing Fiona had in common with Lesley.

Both women always had her back.

CHAPTER EIGHTY-THREE

GUY AND AVA TOWNSEND might have withdrawn their allegation, but the initial report was still on file. *Yet another reason for Marc Langham to dislike databases*, Aaron thought as he pulled up their contact details.

A home number. Not local. Manchester. The phone rang half a dozen times. Aaron was about to give up when it was answered.

"Hello?" said a male voice.

"Mr Townsend?"

"Yes, who's speaking?"

"This is Detective Sergeant Aaron Keyes, Cumbria Police."

A pause.

"How can I help you, DS Keyes?" Guy Townsend didn't sound nervous.

"I was hoping I could talk to you about an incident that took place in Cumbria last August."

No response. Guy Townsend seemed polite, but he wasn't making things easy.

"There was a report at the time that while you and your wife were walking in the area, you were assaulted. Someone drove a vehicle at you."

"We made a complaint, yes. But we withdrew it."

Still polite. Still nothing Aaron didn't know.

"I understand that, and I'm not trying to make things difficult. I was hoping to discuss the incident in more detail. I'm not trying to get you to change your mind."

"Well," began Guy Townsend. A series of noises came down the phone. There was a muffled quality, like a hand had been placed across it. Then footsteps, and clicks, and a series of urgent whispers.

"No," said a female voice.

"I'm sorry?"

"I don't think so, no." Guy Townsend's accent had been barely detectable. His wife, if this was her, was pure Manchester.

"I just wanted to ask about—"

"Look, I'd appreciate it if you'd leave us alone. This was all resolved months ago, and we've got no interest in dredging it all up again."

"Mrs Townsend—"

"So if you don't mind, I'll not be expecting to hear from you again."

The line went dead.

CHAPTER EIGHTY-FOUR

ALL THE EXCITEMENT over the fingerprint on the door handle had faded.

Somehow, Streeting wasn't even bothered.

Tom could hardly believe it when Nina came back downstairs looking glum. She'd gone up there with fire in her eyes, excited to watch the bastard finally brought to book. Half an hour later, she dragged herself back into the team room and told Tom and Harriett that Streeting wasn't bothered by the evidence, which was what the DI had already told them.

"But this was different," Nina said. "Bastard was actually enjoying himself. Even asked DI Whaley what *his* involvement was in the case, like there was something PSD were hiding."

Tom waited for the kicker. No way Nina would pass up the opportunity to put the boot in on PSD, on how secretive they were, how lying was in their DNA. Especially with Harriett there to take the hit.

But she didn't.

"And then DS Gaskill reminded him how Carter treats people who might be a threat. Parlick. Somerville. He just shrugged. I—"

She stopped, looking over Tom's shoulder. He turned to see two people, a man and a woman, smartly dressed and smiling neutrally at them all.

There was something menacing about the pair. A cold professionalism that reminded him of TV versions of FBI agents.

"DC Willis?" said the woman.

Tom nodded.

"I'm Catherine Silverman. Senior Investigator, IOPC North West. This is my colleague, Ravi Sharma. Ravi's an investigator on my team. I was hoping we could have a little chat with you."

Tom cast a helpless glance back at Harriett and Nina, and followed the pair into the corridor.

The interview took place upstairs, in a meeting room with a small round table. He stood frozen when they invited him to choose a seat. Was it a test? Eventually, the two investigators took pity on him and sat down themselves, leaving him only one option. The woman pulled some papers out of a briefcase and started recording. Tom felt something solid in his throat and swallowed.

The man turned to him, a look of concern on his face.

"Are you quite well, DC Willis?"

Tom nodded.

"You have nothing to worry about," the man continued. "We're just here to get to the bottom of things. All we're asking for is your help, and your candour. Is that OK?"

"Ye-es," Tom stammered.

He'd heard that sort of thing before. Hell, he'd even *said* that sort of thing before.

To people he suspected of being criminals.

It wasn't so bad, in the end. He waived his right to a lawyer or a Police Federation representative. Catherine Silverman asked him about Huz, and he answered, all of it, his relationship with the man, how he'd felt about him, both before and after they'd learned of his extracurricular activities.

"I understand you were present when your colleague DC Kapoor telephoned DCI Branthwaite to question Mr Mahmoud's release. Is that right?"

"Yes," Tom admitted. "But Branthwaite held his hand up. He apologised. And it wasn't like Nina thought Huz was in danger. It was just a judgment call."

"Very good," said the man, Ravi Sharma. He did a lot of smiling, but Tom wasn't green enough to be fooled by a smile. "And you were the one who found the photograph of PC Cummings with the late Josh McKenzie, is that right?"

"Yes," he agreed. *There couldn't be anything wrong with that, could there?*

"What were your general impressions of PC Cummings?" asked Catherine Silverman, and Tom felt himself on safe ground.

"Tel Cummings was a bully," he said. "No one liked him. I didn't think he was bent, but when I saw the photo, it all sort of made sense."

"Why? Because you assume it's natural that a police officer you don't get on with would be corrupt?" asked Ravi Sharma, still smiling.

Tom smiled back. He'd been wrong about that *safe ground*.

"No. Because we were actively looking for a corrupt police officer, and Tel Cummings was an unpleasant man who had a reputation for stretching the rules."

"Stretching the rules?"

Tom shrugged. "He used to boast about what he did to suspects. Nothing you could really point at and discipline him for, probably, but always on the line between acceptable force and unacceptable violence."

Both investigators nodded.

"Do you believe it's possible that more than one person was involved in Vicky Speares' death?" Catherine Silverman said.

Tom just stared at her.

"DC Willis?"

"Sorry," he replied. "I hadn't... It hadn't even occurred to me. No. No, I don't."

"Excellent. And finally, what are your general impressions of the culture of this station?"

Tom stared again.

"It's the only station I really know," he said.

"And?"

He shrugged.

"I don't know." His eyes roamed around the room, hoping to find an answer. "I suppose... I suppose it's a good culture?"

The investigators looked at each other, thanked him, and told him he could go. He took his time, walking slowly back downstairs, wondering if that line, if that last thing he'd said, was going to make it into the IOPC Hall of Fame for the most stupid thing any police officer had ever said under interview.

Still. Could have been worse. If they thought he was stupid, they wouldn't think he was bent.

CHAPTER EIGHTY-FIVE

IT WAS NEARLY nine when Aaron reached his destination, a wide side street in an affluent suburb north of Manchester. The light snowfall had become heavy rain by the time he parked.

He checked his messages, then his watch. It would take nearly two hours to get back, and he didn't want to wake his parents.

He smiled. Here he was, a grown man with a husband and a child, worrying about getting in trouble if he was back too late from a night out.

The quality of the nights out had changed.

He dashed for the house, a large detached one with a Victorian frontage and a short driveway. He huddled under the porch while he waited for the door to be answered.

If it got answered at all.

It wasn't as if he'd called to say he was coming. It wasn't as if he knew there was anyone in.

The Townsends were in, thankfully. In, and in the shape

of Mrs Townsend, as polite and welcoming as they could be without actually throwing him out.

"I did tell you we've got nothing to add," she said. "I did say, didn't I?"

"You did, Mrs Townsend."

"You can call me Ava. And you might as well at least have a cup of tea now you've driven all this way on a godforsaken night like this."

He followed her into a spacious living room where Guy Townsend sat in an armchair, the *Times* crossword open on his lap. Aaron explained again who he was, and why he'd come.

Guy looked past him for his wife, who'd disappeared into the kitchen. He shook his head and returned to his crossword.

"Here." She returned with a tray laden with teapot, cups, and accoutrements. They were an odd pair. They spoke and acted like people in their sixties, or older, and the house was decorated in a style Aaron associated with people of that generation. But neither of the Townsends looked much older than forty. They ran a design and website-building business from home, and if the home was anything to go by, they did it well.

"Thanks for the tea."

"You're welcome. I'm just sorry you've wasted your evening."

"Are you sure you have nothing to add?" Aaron looked at Guy, who seemed to be avoiding eye contact.

"Nothing, I'm afraid," replied Ava. "It was all just a misunderstanding. Nothing more."

"You alleged that a car was driven at you."

She shook her head. "He wasn't driving *at* us. He just didn't see us."

And still, Guy remained silent.

"That isn't what you told my colleagues at the time."

Ava took a sip from her tea and set it down on a saucer on an antique table beside her wing-backed chair. "Everything was a bit fraught at the time. We were angry. We were probably irrational. We made something out of nothing."

Aaron turned to Guy, who had put his newspaper down but now seemed to be finding the curtains fascinating.

"Thank you," Aaron said. "You've been very helpful."

Ava gave a small smile.

"But in case it helps," Aaron said, "this is a murder investigation. If there's anything else you remember, it could be invaluable. Even things you think might not be relevant could turn out to be crucial."

The colour drained from Ava's face. Her husband gripped his teacup, his knuckles white.

Damn.

Aaron hadn't mentioned the murder. Hadn't even said there was another case involved.

"Murder investigation?" Ava said.

"I'm sorry. I should have said earlier. There's been... A young man's body was found, near the area you were in back in August."

"He's been dead that long?" asked Guy, finally breaking his silence.

"No, no. A matter of weeks. We're just trying to build a complete picture of—"

"And the man, the one with the Land Rover. He's a suspect, is he?" asked Ava.

"I can't really go into that. As I say, we're just building a picture of the area, the people, that sort of thing."

Even as he said it, Aaron knew it sounded weak.

But it changed nothing. He finished his tea, and Ava was still insisting it had all been a misunderstanding, while Guy had lapsed back to silence.

He thanked them and began the long drive back. He called Serge en route, and had a fun, flirty conversation which might have improved his mood if he'd been able to stop thinking about the case.

He tried Keisha when he'd said goodbye to Serge, in the hope that she might have cracked Kevin's phone, but when she answered he knew he'd made a mistake.

"Right?" she said. "Aaron? How's it going?"

He could hear music. People talking. People shouting. People singing, badly.

"Are you—"

"In the pub, mate. You coming? Oh, shit. You're in Elterwater, right? Can't come here, then."

"I was just—"

"See you, mate." She ended the call.

CHAPTER EIGHTY-SIX

It was seven-thirty in the morning, and Luke wasn't in yet, so there'd been no one to offer the usual warnings or encouragements. All Zoe knew was what she'd heard five hours earlier, on a conference call with the super, one magistrate, and what sounded like half a dozen lawyers. Someone else muttered in the background, sounding pissed off to be woken. As if everyone else there was overjoyed to be on the phone at that time of night. A senior officer, Zoe reckoned. Someone from the ACC's office, or even the Chief's.

Either way, they'd got what they wanted. Twenty-four more hours. That was the good news. The bad news was that meant the pressure was on.

"Bad news," said Fiona.

Not just the pressure, then. Something else.

"Yes?"

"The complaint about Aaron. Somehow the IOPC have got hold of it. I was woken at six by the ACC's office telling me I was clearly struggling to keep control of my people."

"Shit. I'm so sorry, Fiona. You know it'll just be a malicious complaint, don't you? No truth in it."

"I know that. I expect the IOPC and the ACC know that too. Doesn't mean they'll act like it. I tell you, if we don't win this one, Zoe, I'll be tempted to throw it all in."

Zoe blinked at her. "What do you mean?"

"I mean quit. I mean move to another force."

Just sixteen hours earlier the super had insisted she'd never give up. Things moved fast. Even faster, with no sleep.

"Stick with it," Zoe told her. "We've got them on the ropes."

"You really think so?"

There was a vulnerability about Fiona that Zoe hadn't seen before. A need to be reassured.

"They don't throw everything they have at you until they're desperate. That's why you're getting all this shit."

Fiona opened her mouth for a sigh, which turned into a yawn. She tried to cover it before giving up. She looked beaten.

She needed coffee, and when Luke finally turned up, no doubt he'd provide it. But before that, she needed something else.

"Fiona, can I tell you something?"

"Yeah," said the super, clearly not expecting much.

"I've only been with two forces, but I've worked for a lot of people. A lot of senior officers. DCIs, DSups, ACCs. Some of them have been incompetent, some of them have been corrupt, some of them have been half decent, and a tiny minority have been the sort of people who reminded me why I've stuck with being a detective so long. I can count those people on half the fingers of one hand, Fiona."

"Get to the point, Zoe."

"You're one of them." Zoe stood up and walked out.

CHAPTER EIGHTY-SEVEN

AARON LOOKED across the room at Lynn and shook his head. In his right hand was his phone, pressed to one ear. In his left was his third coffee of the day.

It had only just gone eight.

"I'm sorry," the man said. "Ms Conway's offsite."

"Yes," he said, trying to remain patient. "I appreciate that. But as I've been trying to explain, I'd very much like to meet with her to discuss an extremely important matter."

"Do you have an appointment?"

Aaron had already answered this question twice.

"No. I do not have an appointment. I am, however, investigating a murder, so I'd hope Ms Conway could spare a few minutes of her time to see me."

"Well," said the man, "let me see." There was a short pause, broken by the sound of fingers on a keyboard. "I'm sorry, Mr... What did you say your name was again?"

"Detective Sergeant Aaron Keyes," Aaron said, for the fourth time.

"I really am terribly sorry, but as I say, Ms Conway's not

here at the moment, and she'll be tied up for the foreseeable future. I'll be sure to pass on—"

"Sod it," said Aaron, and ended the call.

His plan had been to show her a photo of the saddle strap. Just to see how she would react. Maybe doorstep her if she refused to see him. But if she wasn't there, he'd just be wasting his time.

Two feet away, it sounded like Lynn was having similar luck, compounded by what looked like the worst cold he'd ever seen.

"Fibe," said Lynn, and ended her call.

"Are you sure you're OK?" Aaron asked. He tapped his nose, in case his meaning wasn't clear, but you'd have to be blind or an idiot to miss it.

Lynn's nose wasn't just red. It was guide-your-sleigh red. It positively glowed.

And not in a good way.

"Fibe," she said again. She didn't sound it, but she'd insisted she didn't want to go home. "Keisha said chill out, she's god a hangover, she'll ged to the phobe later."

The day didn't continue well.

Jasmine Woolley walked in, scowled at him, then walked out again, and he'd just decided that was actually a positive thing when Isaac Bateman lumbered in and sat down at his desk, sighing and stinking of last night's beer.

Definitely *not* a positive thing.

It was in this frame of mind, with no one apart from a single sickly DC being helpful, and surrounded by a fug of alcohol, that Aaron reached for his ringing phone and answered it with an irritable, "Yes?"

"DS Keyes?" said a voice he recognised. He stood up.

"Yes," he replied. "Mrs Townsend."

"Ava," she corrected. "Hello. I'm here with my husband. We have you on speaker."

"Hello," said Guy Townsend.

"Hello," replied Aaron, wondering whether the Townsends were in the habit of phoning people at eight in the morning just to exchange greetings.

"We've changed our minds," said Ava.

Aaron felt his chest constrict. "Go on."

"It's true. What we said at first."

"One moment," he told them. "Do you mind if I put you on the speaker here? I'd like my colleagues to hear this."

Colleague, really, but this wasn't the time to go into Bateman's shortcomings.

"That's fine."

He moved to Lynn's desk and stood over it, holding his phone.

"Please go on," he said.

"As I say, it was all true," repeated Ava. "The man was a maniac."

"You mean Marc Langham?"

"Yes. He simply drove his car at us."

"I had to throw myself into a bush," said Guy.

"He was badly scratched," added Ava. "And yes, we might have been on private land, but the path was marked as a public right of way on our old Ordnance Survey maps, and we've checked since, and it still is."

"Did he speak to you first, or anything?"

"No," said Guy.

"We'd have left if we'd been asked to," said Ava. "But he went straight to driving at us."

"Right," said Aaron, his mind racing. It wasn't just the

attack. It was what had happened afterward. "Why did you drop your complaint, then?"

There was a short silence.

"We did agree to tell them everything," said Guy.

"I know," said Ava, irritably. "Fine. Well, I just hope this doesn't come back to bite us."

"I'll do what I can to protect you, Ava," Aaron said. "But I really do need to know what happened."

"What happened was we got a letter from Marc Langham's lawyers. Poncy London outfit."

Aaron moved back to his desk, picked up his own letter, and read the name on the top.

"Harris-Caney, Levens, Brake-McMaster and Lupton?" he asked.

"That's the one. They... Well, they're lawyers, aren't they? So they know how to make a threat sound perfectly reasonable and legal, but leave you in no doubt that you've been threatened."

"What do you mean?"

"He's big in tech, is Marc Langham," said Guy. "And we have a little web business. Sort of thing he'd never even notice, in the normal course of events. But this wasn't the normal course of events. It was..."

The rustle of paper was followed by Ava's voice.

"'It would be a great shame,'" she read aloud, "'if Townsend Web Design were to find itself the victim of this unfortunate misunderstanding, and we are confident that any decision on your part to drop proceedings would serve to prevent such a situation arising. In contrast, continuing this action might well have unforeseen adverse consequences.' You see what I mean?"

"So you dropped it. I can see why."

"Yes," said Guy. "But you said someone had died. And...
Well, it was fine when it was just us. We had nothing to gain
and a lot to lose. But I don't want that on my conscience.
That I didn't help when things got serious. Neither of us do.
We're willing to revise our statement. Put the allegation
again. Whatever is appropriate."

Aaron thanked them, promising he'd be in touch soon,
and ended the call.

"Enough to bring Langham in?" he asked.

"Ebough," agreed Lynn, and sneezed.

CHAPTER EIGHTY-EIGHT

"THERE HAS TO BE SOMETHING," said Tom.

The other three stared at him. Fair enough. He'd said the same thing three times in the last ten minutes.

But there did have to be something, didn't there?

They'd all got the same message from the boss, shortly after three in the morning: *Extension approved. 24 hrs.* He'd been awake, waiting for the news. Harriett had been pacing the floor. She'd wanted to head into the Hub immediately and get working, but he'd persuaded her to try to sleep for an hour first.

He'd managed it. He wasn't sure she had.

They'd been in by half-five. DS Gaskill had been waiting for them. She hadn't slept at all, she said, but she looked pretty much the same as usual. Nina had turned up ten minutes later, which was something of a record. They'd spent the last few hours sitting in the team room, walking around the team room, running through forensic reports, pulling up maps and photos on the big screen, and poring over data from cell towers and ANPR cameras.

"Go through it again," said Nina.

"Christ," said DS Gaskill. "OK. I was watching the house all night. He didn't leave."

"What about on the way in, or the way out? Any unusual route, any notable stops?"

"Nothing. And we've got his phone data, and there's no sign of a burner in his house or his office or his car."

"OK," said Nina. "That was the easy one. Your turn, Tom."

"I had eyes on him the whole time. I mean, not when he was in his office. But you can hear everything in there. And like you say, no burners. We went to the shop near Bobby Silver's house."

"Mrs Gillespie's," said Harriett, with a shiver.

"I followed him there, followed him back again. Mulligan thought I didn't know the way. There was just that one trip... Oh." He stopped.

Three faces turned towards him.

He closed his eyes.

Too tired. Too tired for this, now.

But now was when it had to be.

"He tried to lose me. Did a runner from the building. I caught up with him and followed him. Thought he was heading to Bobby's house, but he turned off."

"Where?"

"Here." He pulled up the map on the big screen, scrolled, and pointed. "He spotted me. Figured out I was tailing him. Turned around and came back. But I assumed he was going to Bobby Silver's house again."

"And?" said Nina.

"If he was going to the house, why go that way?"

The four of them stared at the map in silence.

Harriett stood and traced a route with her index finger.

"You could get there that way," she said.

"Yeah, but why would you? Adds fifteen minutes to a half-hour journey. And it's not like he had all the time in the world. *And* he ended up going down a long straight road, which is how I was able to find him again."

"*Again?*" said DS Gaskill.

Tom pulled a face. "I may have lost him for a moment. His car's faster than mine."

"Fair enough." She turned back to the map.

"Clea Hall Holiday Park," Tom said. "That's where he turned. Which suggests he was heading somewhere after that. But there isn't anything after that."

"Hang on," said Harriett. She tapped a few keys, and the map changed to a satellite view.

Nothing. Farms. Farmhouses. A set of holiday cottages.

"He might have been meeting someone," Nina pointed out. "Any of these places."

"True," agreed Tom. "But why there? Why not somewhere more convenient?"

More silence.

Harriett pointed. "What's this?"

She'd found a line so thin it was barely there at all. A footpath, Tom assumed. Until he saw what lay at the end of it.

Buildings. Well, one building, and what might have been a handful of huts.

And vehicles.

Even from however many miles up the satellite was, you could see the vehicles. Cars, vans, tractors, trucks. What looked like a bus. Parked haphazardly, like the drivers hadn't really thought about how they were going to get them out again.

Some of them weren't really vehicles. Just half vehicles. Like someone had sheared off a chunk, or it had been in an accident so bad there was no longer any hope for it.

A place where vehicles went to die.

Harriett tapped the screen, the vehicles, the huts, circled the whole area.

"That's a breaker's yard," she said. "That's where Streeting was going."

CHAPTER EIGHTY-NINE

AARON STEELED himself before he went in.

He'd had less-than-positive relationships with colleagues before. He'd worked with homophobes, bullies, and racists. He'd worked with idiots, cowards, and moral relativists. But he'd never had to deal with someone who so clearly hated him.

He knocked on DI Woolley's door, waited for her to invite him in, and entered. Inside the office, he didn't sit, just launched straight into it. The Townsends. The Land Rover. The threat.

"I'd like to bring him in," he concluded.

"No." She bent back down to her desk, an effect ruined only by the fact that it was empty apart from a blank sheet of paper.

He waited for her to expand, but she said nothing.

"I believe we have enough here to arrest him," he said.

"I don't care what you believe. *I* believe that arresting Marc Langham wouldn't serve the interests of justice, and last time I checked, *I'm* the real DI here."

"But—"

"But nothing. Unlike you, Marc Langham is an important member of this community, and unless I'm mistaken, you weren't tossed in here to investigate arguments between landowners and irritating trespassers."

"With respect, I—"

"I said no. Even if I thought arresting him was the right thing to do, I wouldn't trust you to get it right."

Aaron walked away without another word, back to the team room.

He opened his mouth to unleash all the anger he hadn't let out on Jasmine Woolley, then noticed Lynn was on the phone. A moment later, she put it down, frowning.

"Dat was Keisha," she said.

"Any news?"

"She got the phobe open. Looks like it was his. Kevin's."

Some good news, at least.

"Thing is, on that last afternoon, he got a text message. Someone asking to meet him in the wood."

"The wood?"

"Baysbrown. Named a spot not far from where his body was found."

"So he wasn't going to the pub after all."

"No. But that was the cover. The person who texted suggested he tell anyone who saw him he was heading out to watch the match."

"It was deliberate, then." Aaron scratched his chin. "Can we trace the number?"

There was a look on Lynn's face that he couldn't follow. A sort of awkwardness. Pain.

"We don't need to. It was stored under the sender's name. And I've checked. It's right."

"Who was it, then?" he asked, and the look seemed to deepen.

"It was from your friend," she replied. "It was from Sara Miller."

CHAPTER NINETY

"Found it," said Nina.

The others turned from the screen to face her.

"Found what?" asked DS Gaskill.

"A number. Not well advertised, but I tracked it down."

She winked at Tom. The breaker's yard didn't have a name, didn't advertise or appear in any directories, but Tom had shown her ways of tracking down phone numbers.

"No public presence," she said. "If you know, you know. If you don't, the place might as well not exist."

"Interesting," Harriett said. Nina picked up her phone, put it on speaker, and tapped the number in as the others gathered around.

It rang a dozen times before a man answered.

"Yo," he said.

"Is that the breaker's yard down from Clea Hall?" Nina asked.

"Might be. Who's asking?"

She looked to the others. Harriett shrugged. Tom did nothing. DS Gaskill nodded.

"This is Detective Constable Nina Kapoor. Cumbria Police. I've got a few questions for you."

She'd not wanted to play her hand that early, but there hadn't been much choice. Now the man would turn hostile, or evasive, or hang up.

"Oh. Right. God. Is everything OK?"

"I was hoping you could tell me that, Mr..."

"Carmichael. Saul Carmichael. What d'you mean?"

"Well, has anything unusual happened on your site lately?"

There was a short pause.

"Dunno if it counts as unusual, but yeah, sort of."

"Go on. Anything you've noticed might be helpful."

"Right. Well, we usually get the shit here. I mean, it's smashing up cars, right? They're either old or knackered or both. Bit like me, right?"

Another pause. Nina forced out a chuckle.

"Thing is, other day, right, I turn up, and someone's dumped a lovely motor, decent condition, bit scratched and that, but nothing you couldn't sort out in half a day. And it's been sitting there ever since."

"What sort of car?" asked Nina.

"Jeep. Wrangler. Green one. Like I say, it's a decent motor."

Nina looked up from her phone and around the room. Six eyes stared back at her. Three open mouths.

"And no one's come to claim it?" she asked.

"Nah. That's the thing. I thought maybe it had been dumped by mistake, and someone would turn up, but it's still here. I called the boss and he said I should leave it alone and he'd send someone to deal with it personally."

"Is that normal?"

"No. It's smashing up cars. Even I can do that. Doesn't take a specialist."

"And did someone come?"

"No. I was told to expect them on— Hang on, what day is it?"

"It's Friday," Nina told him.

"Right. So I was told to expect this guy two days ago, but he never showed up."

Tom was mouthing something, but Nina didn't need to see it. *Two days ago.* When Streeting had tried to lose him.

"What did you do, then?"

"Well, I didn't know what to do, did I? I called the boss, and he said he didn't know, and he'd call *his* boss, and in the end, I just sat there waiting. And eventually, the big guy calls. Says not to touch a thing. So it's still sitting here, been nearly a week now, and I haven't even popped the boot." He laughed. "Think there's a body in there or something?"

"Not a body, no. But this is all very..."

Harriett was trying to get her attention. Whispering something. Nina moved towards her.

"Big guy," Harriett was saying.

"Who's the big guy?" Nina asked. "The one who called you?"

"Oh, him? He's, like, the ultimate boss. The boss's boss's boss. End of level boss, right?"

Another laugh.

"What's his name, though?"

"Well, it's Mr Carter, of course."

CHAPTER NINETY-ONE

"I'M FINE," Lynn insisted.

DS Keyes didn't look convinced, but he didn't object when she climbed in beside him.

It was just a cold.

In better weather, they might have walked to the Miller cottage, but it didn't look good to turn up at someone's house looking like you'd just swum there. And Lynn felt terrible. Even a ten-minute walk in the freezing drizzle sounded like hell.

DS Keyes parked up outside the cottage, and she eyed it nervously before following him to the front door. She'd seen this cottage a thousand times. Walked past it, driven past it. Never been inside.

Sara Miller hadn't just been one of the older kids. She'd been one of the cool older kids. A group that Lynn Hedley was always outside.

Sara's dad opened the door, spoke quietly with the sarge, and pointed them upstairs. Lynn followed DS Keyes up there, but the bedroom door was open, the room was empty, and there were animal-like noises coming from the bathroom.

"Sara?" DS Keyes tapped on the door, and the noises stopped.

"Sara!" he shouted.

There was a muffled sob.

"Sara. You've got to come out."

There was a short silence, then a voice.

"I'm sorry," said Sara Miller. It was Sara Miller, it couldn't be anyone else, but it didn't sound like her. It sounded like an old woman. A dying woman.

"You've got nothing to apologise for. Just come out and talk to me." The sarge turned to Lynn and gave an apologetic shrug.

Talk to me.

They'd come here as police officers, to interview a woman about the messages they'd found on her lover's phone. But now he was here as a friend, talking Sara out of whatever state she was in.

And Lynn? She wasn't sure why she was there at all. Suddenly, his earlier suggestion that she either stick around at the station or go home and get some sleep sounded remarkably attractive.

"I tried," Sara said. "I really tried."

"Tried what? Just come out."

"It's all my fault."

There were footsteps on the stairs. Mr and Mrs Miller. Joe and Val. Lynn turned.

"Do you know what she means?"

"Not a clue," said Joe.

"No," agreed Val, looking close to tears. "We've tried

everything. For weeks now. But this? It's not been this bad. I just don't understand."

"Sara." The sarge's tone was firmer. "You have to come out. Please."

Nothing. Not even a sob. Lynn held her breath, straining to listen.

Nothing.

"Sara!" shouted the sarge.

Nothing.

He looked past Lynn to Sara's parents. "I'm sorry. I'm going to have to break it down."

Lynn turned to see Val nodding, tears in her eyes. Joe muttered something about a screwdriver, but Val patted him.

"There isn't time for that, Joe."

He nodded too.

It only took one kick, just by the lock, and the door was open.

Lynn stayed where she was, acting as a barrier. Whatever was in there, it was best Sara's parents didn't see it. Not yet.

But she could see it. She could see Sara Miller, cool, beautiful Sara Miller, wrapped in a dingy grey dressing gown, lying on the floor, her eyes flickering, her face a blotchy mess of red and white.

And beside her, an open medicine bottle, lying on its side.

Empty.

CHAPTER NINETY-TWO

"Can you hear me?"

"Yes," Carl said. "I'm in..."

A pause.

"Fifteen minutes."

"We didn't get that," Zoe replied. "But can you hear us?"

"Yes. I won't be..."

She turned to the others. Tom and Nina. Denise and Harriett. Half of them were hers and half of them were Carl's, but Carl wasn't here, and she could hardly hear a word he said.

"Run through it again," she said. "And be quick."

Denise Gaskill spoke.

"We think we've found the Jeep that Harriett and Tom followed. The one used by whoever killed Bobby Silver."

"Where?" said Carl. *Good.* At least he'd heard that.

Denise pointed at Tom.

"Not far from Bobby Silver's house," Tom said. "The day you arrested DI Streeting, that morning, I followed him out into the sticks. He saw me and turned around. But there's a breaker's yard there—"

"Owned by Myron Carter," said Nina.

"Owned by Myron Carter," Tom agreed. "A green Jeep Wrangler was dumped there on the day of the murder. Someone was supposed to deal with it the day you picked up Streeting. No one's touched it. It's still there."

"So we... Was... Rid of it?"

Zoe could interpret this one herself.

"We think Streeting was heading out to get rid of it, get rid of the evidence, but never got round to it thanks to Tom and Denise watching him. Yes. Exactly."

"So we need... it up."

"We need to pick it up, yes."

There was a squeak, then static, then a moment's silence, followed by Carl again. "... who to trust."

"Look, Carl, we can only hear half of your sentences, but I think what you're trying to say is we don't know who to trust."

"... actly."

"I don't want this getting past the people in this room, and Stella."

"Stella?"

"Whatever's in this Jeep, she'll need to look at it. I want her to recover it. But I want someone with her. After what happened to Caroline, with the ramming."

Silence. Zoe took that as agreement.

"I'll go," said Denise.

"... think... right..." said Carl.

Zoe looked around the room. No one was objecting.

"We'll call you in a bit," Zoe said, and ended the call.

The call to Stella was easier, if only because they could

actually hear each other. It was agreed in the space of two minutes.

Stella would take a low loader and meet Denise at the breaker's yard. She'd conduct a brief check of the Jeep in situ, before the two of them got the car onto the trailer.

And then Stella would drive it back. Denise would act as an escort. They'd get it to the lab, analyse it, find something.

And find it fast. Zoe glanced at her watch.

They had until half past two in the morning. Less than fifteen hours.

CHAPTER NINETY-THREE

It had all been so fast. Aaron was still standing there, staring at Sara in horror, when Lynn rushed past him, dragged her to her feet, over to the toilet, and stuck her fingers down his friend's throat.

Whatever she'd taken, it wasn't inside her anymore. Most of it was in the toilet. A fair chunk was on the bathroom walls. They wiped Sara down and wrapped her in a blanket, and now she was sitting on the armchair that had been reserved for Joe for as long as Aaron could remember. Sitting there, sipping from a glass of water, looking nearly as bad as she'd looked lying on the bathroom floor.

Nearly as bad, but not quite.

She was breathing more easily, the sobs still coming and catching in her throat, but less often.

Aaron didn't want to think about the germs. Lynn's cold. Lynn's fingers in Sara's throat. No time to put on gloves.

But at least she was alive.

Alive, and talking.

"It's all my fault," she said. She'd been saying it

constantly since they'd brought her downstairs and forced a little water down her throat.

Aaron was starting to make sense of it. "You mean Kevin's death?"

Sara nodded. He could see the sadness in her eyes, but relief, too. That someone had finally understood.

"We should go," said Lynn. "She needs some space."

Lynn had been calm and efficient in a crisis, and when all this was over, she'd receive the credit she deserved. But now the cold had taken hold of her again, and she was wrong.

"It's OK," Aaron said. "I've got this."

He'd been there himself, so recently he remembered every moment of it. Every moment of the hell, the pain, the guilt.

And every step he'd taken back up again.

"Why?" he said.

"What?" asked Sara.

Lynn shook her head. She didn't understand. If she stuck around, she would.

"Why do you feel that way?" he asked.

"Because... Well, it's obvious, isn't it?" said Sara, and he tried not to smile.

She couldn't answer. She could see it all, so clear, so obvious, but she couldn't explain it, because it wasn't real. It was twisted. It was wrong.

"No. Did you kill Kevin?"

She shook her head.

"Do you know who killed Kevin?"

Another shake.

"Do you know why he was killed?"

"No, but if I hadn't been... If we hadn't..."

"If you hadn't been seeing each other, then what? He

might have died a fortnight earlier. He might still be here, waiting to die next week."

It sounded cold, but it had to be said. Dr Filey had done it for him, and now he could do it for Sara.

Simple questions. Simple answers.

It's not your fault.

It hadn't been Aaron's fault. It wasn't Sara's fault.

Fifteen minutes later, she was nodding. She didn't agree with him, not yet, even though she was pretending she did. But the seed was there.

It would come. It would take some work, but it would come.

"We need your help, Sara," he said. Beside him, Lynn looked up from her steadily growing pile of tissues.

"What?" Sara said.

"We need to find whoever did this to Kevin. You want to help us, don't you?"

Sara nodded. He opened the photos app on his phone and scrolled to the image Keisha had sent.

A photo of Kevin's phone. The screen. The message from Sara.

The message that had lured him to his death.

"Did you send this?" he asked.

Sara stared at it, bewildered. "No."

"You're sure?"

"I'm sure. I don't... That's not the way I talk. And I don't... Why would I tell him to go there?"

"Right."

"And I don't... I wouldn't have known about the football."

Sara had never been a big football fan. Another rare trait they'd bonded over, back in the day.

"The only reason I remember it at all is that's the day Marc found out about me and Kevin," she added.

Aaron caught Lynn's eye and dipped his head slightly. *Gently does it.*

Lynn nodded back at him. *Understood.*

"What happened, Sara?" he asked.

"Marc. He... I was in the kitchen. I came back into the living room and he was looking at my phone. At my texts." She shuddered. "He had... He read them to me. Out loud. Made me listen. He made it sound horrible. Nasty. But it wasn't."

The sobs were back. Fine. That was fine. Take it slow.

"Then he... He just grabbed his coat and stormed out of the house. Said he was going to watch the match. Said I shouldn't be there when he got back."

"What did you do?"

"I didn't know what to do. I didn't know what I *wanted* to do. I stayed here that night. I thought it would all blow over. Either that, or it would all come out, and I'd be with Kevin. But..."

More sobbing. Another glass of water.

"It's OK, Sara. Take your time."

"Here," she said, reaching behind her for her phone. He hadn't even realised she had it with her. She held it out, then pulled it back, unlocked it, and passed it to him.

She hadn't exactly been subtle.

Kevin's number was saved under his first name, followed by three heart emojis. And the messages...

She was right. They were fine. Loving, almost. Fun, crude, from time to time, but not nasty. Unless you wanted to make it sound nasty.

Messages going back months. Starting casual. Ending anything but.

A dozen messages in the days after he disappeared, asking where he was, begging him to reply, to say something, anything.

Desperate.

But between the casual messages and the loving messages and the desperate messages, the one message Aaron was looking for was missing. Deleted, if it had ever existed, and it had. Keisha had checked. It hadn't been spoofed. It had come from this phone, but it wasn't there anymore.

The message inviting Kevin to meet in the woods had been deleted.

CHAPTER NINETY-FOUR

BIKE OR CAR?

Denise had spent too long deciding. She looked between the four-wheel-drive Audi she'd been offered and her own Yamaha. A former police bike, it had been powerful enough even before she'd spent time, money, and love converting it into something most bikers could only dream of.

Bike, then. Faster, more manoeuvrable, better visibility. She was more at home on the bike anyway.

She went for the straight road, wanting to be there before Stella Berry. Scope the place out. Make sure no one touched anything.

The guy they'd spoken to had seemed decent enough. Willing to talk to the police. Clearly ignorant of the sort of business his boss's boss's boss had him mixed up in. They'd wasted two minutes, debating whether to call him back and make sure nothing happened to the car, or to just head straight over there, and risk Carter's people happening to show up in the meantime.

In the end, they hadn't called. If Carter's people showed

up, the poor guy at the end of the phone wasn't going to stop them from doing whatever the hell they wanted to do.

She took the main road, cutting through traffic whenever it appeared, skirting around Cockermouth as she headed towards Carlisle.

She'd driven this route so many times she could have done it blindfolded, but now she found herself slowing at every junction, alert for something bigger than her, pulling out and ending her journey prematurely.

It wasn't an accident she was worried about. Accidents she could navigate around. That was the whole point of taking the bike.

Faster, more manoeuvrable, better visibility.

But if someone actually *wanted* to stop her from getting to her destination, things might get trickier.

Although this was the easy part. No one would know anything yet. There couldn't have been a leak, not with the few people who knew about this, and if the guy on the phone had blabbed, no one would have been able to get anything in place this soon.

The return journey, though, *that* would be different. Carter's people had time to make plans for that. So she wasn't just slowing to spot threats.

She was slowing to spot where the threats might be when they came back the same way.

And they would come back the same way. Main roads. Busy roads. Harder to block, and if someone did block one, you'd know about it before you hit it.

Piece of piss, this. Denise hadn't done anything that involved serious driving for a while, and she'd been jealous of Harriett Barnes, getting to chase down that Jeep, even if it had got away. She'd stuck her hand up for this job because she knew she was the best person for it, but it wouldn't be hard.

Secure the vehicle. Mount it on the trailer. Get it back to Whitehaven.

Piece of piss.

CHAPTER NINETY-FIVE

SARA HAD REFUSED to go to hospital. She didn't look so bad, physically, so Aaron had made her promise she'd talk to him later. And arrange to talk to a professional.

He'd said goodbye to Joe and Val, and walked to the car, Lynn following behind, no doubt wondering where they were going.

DI Woolley would lose her mind. She'd been angry before. Now, with Streeting still locked up on top of what Aaron was about to do, she'd be so far beyond anger that part of him was curious as to how it would come out.

A larger part was worried. But he wouldn't let that stop him.

Don't lose your nerve.

"Where are we... Ah." Lynn's voice was flat as they pulled up outside the gates and Aaron hit the buzzer. "Are you really going to..."

"Yes."

The gates buzzed open without a word.

At the front door, they had to wait in the rain for Marc to

appear, then while he stared at them through the glass, walked away, and returned with a key.

So it was power games, then.

Fine. This particular power game would be over quickly enough.

"You sure about this?" Lynn whispered as she followed him inside. Marc still hadn't spoken.

"Yes."

"What was that?" asked Marc, walking ahead of them. "And take your shoes off."

"I was just talking to my colleague here, Mr Langham."

Marc might have suspected before, but that was the moment he knew. There was a fraction of a second in which he froze, and his shoulders went down. He knew what was coming.

Might as well get to it, then.

"Marc Langham," Aaron said.

"I asked you to take your shoes off," said Marc, still without turning around.

"Marc Langham," Aaron repeated.

"Do I have to ask a third time?" said Marc.

Aaron bent down and began to unlace his shoes. Marc began to walk away.

Aaron straightened up. Power games were for idiots.

"Marc Langham."

Marc finally turned and opened his mouth to object, but he must have seen something in Aaron's expression that shut him up.

About time.

"Marc Langham," said Aaron. "I am arresting you in connection with the murder of Kevin Downes."

CHAPTER NINETY-SIX

"WHAT'S THE SITUATION?" Zoe asked.

"I'm here." Stella's voice came through with a high-pitched buzz. Too much interference to bother with the live feed from the bodycams. At least she wasn't cutting out. It was clearer than it had been for Carl. He was listening in on a conference line, muted.

"Is DS Gaskill with you?"

"Yeah, she's just arrived."

"Shut up," said another voice. Denise. "I've been here fifteen minutes waiting for you."

Zoe looked around the room. Nina. Tom. Harriett. Fists clenched. Faces set. It was good that Denise and Stella could banter like this. No one else could.

"Do you see the vehicle?" she asked.

"Yeah," said Stella. "Helpful bloke's just pointed it out to us. Even apologised for not having the keys. I'm approaching it now. Hang on."

A familiar rustling noise. Transferring to headphones and getting her gloves on.

And that buzz.

"OK. I'm at the vehicle. I'm trying the handle. It's unlocked."

"That makes life easier," Zoe observed.

"Unless it means someone's got here before us," Stella said. "Right. I'm opening the driver's side door. It's open. Looking inside. Looks relatively clean. Nothing major here. I'm coming out and approaching the boot."

Zoe looked up from the phone. The other three were still staring at it, as if they expected to see the actions Stella was describing.

"The boot's unlocked, too. I'm opening it. There's a box. It's open. There's... Bloody hell."

"What?" Harriett asked.

"The gun. Well, *a* gun. It's here. It's actually here. Bloody hell."

Bloody hell indeed.

"This could be what we're looking for," said Denise. "Could have DNA or prints. I'll take it."

"No you bloody won't," said Stella. "What's the point? You'd only be driving it to my lab and giving it to me."

"Are you an expert driver?" Denise retorted. "What will you do if there's trouble on the way?"

For Christ's sake.

"Stop it," said Zoe. "The pair of you. First you need to make it safe."

There was a brief silence. They'd have to call an AFO, wait, bring more people they couldn't necessarily trust into the operation. But there was no alternative.

"Done," said Stella.

"What?" asked Zoe. There wasn't already an AFO on the scene, was there?

"I've seen this done enough times, Zoe. I know how to make a gun safe."

Another brief silence. *Not ideal.*

But it was done now.

"Fine," said Zoe. "Stella's perfectly qualified to drive back to her own lab with an evidence bag containing a gun. I assume you have sterile compartments in the cab for that purpose, Stella?"

"Yes," Stella replied.

"Good. You need to preserve the chain of evidence. Denise, you can watch Stella load it up, capture it on your bodycam."

"No problem," said Denise.

It took two minutes to transfer the gun to the cab. Three minutes to move the low loader into position and prepare the trailer.

"Right," said Stella. "I've lowered the trailer. You really want me to talk you through this? It's putting a car on a trailer. It's not *Star Wars*."

"Just stay on the line, Stella," Zoe replied. "I'm not relaxing until you've got the car and the gun back at the lab."

"Fine. Right. DS Gaskill has her forensic suit on. Took her long enough. You can tell she's PSD."

"Bugger off," said Denise.

Beside Zoe, Tom laughed nervously.

"She's leaning into the car," continued Stella. "She's just taking off the handbrake."

The buzzing noise cut out.

"The Jeep's rolling forward," said Stella. "I—"

And then there was a noise like the end of the world.

CHAPTER NINETY-SEVEN

THE PAIN PASSED through Denise like a train, then it was gone. All she could feel was vibration, a humming, loud, then quiet, then loud again.

Why couldn't she see?

She forced her eyes open, but nothing made sense. The world was on its side. Bits of it were upside down, others the right way around.

She looked down to see the handle of a car door sticking out of her chest.

That couldn't be right. She had to be imagining it. Or dreaming. Where was she? Half of her was freezing cold, the other half so hot she wanted to take her jacket off and jump in the snow.

She reached for her jacket but felt nothing. She looked down at her arm, which hadn't moved.

Why hadn't her arm moved?

There was a voice. A woman, talking. Denise tried to turn in the direction of the voice, but nothing moved.

She was lying down. *When did that happen?*

"It's blown up," the woman was saying.

What had blown up? Was it a bomb? That would explain the door handle sticking out of her chest.

She looked down again, and yes, there it was.

"The Jeep," said the woman.

The Jeep had blown up.

The woman was still talking.

"I need an ambulance," she said. "The Jeep's blown up. It's on fire."

Denise forced her gaze back up and to the side, where she felt hot, and yes, there it was.

A fire.

"I need to pull her away from it," said the other woman.

Yes. Pull her away from it. Up into the sky and floating off like a balloon.

"No, I don't care, I can't leave her there. She'll burn to death."

Something touched Denise, like metal claws shredding her skin. She tried to scream and felt herself moving, not up into the sky and floating off like a balloon, but sideways or down or along the sharp edge of a cheese grater, and it all came together, the noise, and the heat, and the cold, and the pain.

And then, everything stopped.

CHAPTER NINETY-EIGHT

HARRIS-CANEY, Levens, Brake-McMaster, and Lupton weren't solely confined to London. They had an office in Liverpool. Just the one office outside the capital, compared to four inside it.

Tristram Bothwell-Jones didn't have his name on the firm's letterhead yet, but he had the right sense of self-importance. He'd made them wait three hours. Three hours Marc had spent in the cell, complaining incessantly about the conditions. Then Bothwell-Jones demanded another half hour to "freshen up." He seemed personally offended by the quality of the bathroom facilities.

Then it was another half hour in private consultation with his client.

It was nearly seven when they finally got started. Aaron and Lynn on one side of the table, Marc Langham and his solicitor on the other. The recording commenced, and the formalities were covered.

"Mr Langham," Aaron began. "Can you tell me where you were on the night of Kevin Downes's presumed murder?

The night we're talking about is the twenty-seventh of November last."

Marc frowned and reached for his phone, only to remember he didn't have it. It had been checked in with a set of car keys and a thin wallet.

"I don't know," he said. "Probably London. I spent a lot of time there, tail end of last year."

"London?" Aaron couldn't keep the incredulity from his voice.

"I'm not sure how my client can be expected to remember a random night, Officers," said Bothwell-Jones.

"Perhaps it might help," Lynn said, "if I remind your client that this was the night of the England women's football match. Against Germany. The night you ended your engagement with Sara Miller."

She'd downed a load more pills, with tea and hot water, and her voice was closer to normal than it had been all day.

"Oh," said Marc.

"Would you like to reconsider your answer?" Aaron asked.

Marc nodded. "Yes. Of course. If it was that night, then yes, it's true, I was at home with Sara, and then I went to the Wainwrights' to watch the match."

"And you were there for the whole match?"

"I think so," Marc said.

"Are you sure about that?" asked Lynn. "We've spoken to a number of people there."

Aaron glanced at her, then away again before the lawyer noticed.

That was clever. They *had* spoken to a number of people at the pub. The fact that only one of them, Eliot from behind the bar, had said anything about Marc's presence or otherwise was irrelevant. Good memory, too. Aaron had only mentioned the conversation to her in passing.

"Would you like to reconsider your answer?" Aaron asked.

"I don't know," said Marc, his voice quieter. "It was a while ago."

"Right," said Aaron.

There was a knock on the door. Without being invited to, DI Woolley pushed it open, marched in, and stared around the room in horror.

"DI Woolley has entered the room, interview paused," said Lynn, and stopped the recording just in time.

"What in God's name is going on?" asked Woolley.

"I beg your pardon?" said Aaron.

The lawyer frowned in confusion. Marc sat back, looking smug.

"I believe I told you not to arrest this man," said the DI.

"New evidence has come to—"

"With me," she said, turned, and walked out of the room.

CHAPTER NINETY-NINE

CARL MUST HAVE BROKEN every speed limit in Cumbria. He'd beaten Zoe to the West Cumberland Hospital.

She turned the final corner into the final corridor on the final floor. There he was, leaning against a wall, his head in his hands.

It was a hospital. You weren't supposed to run. You were supposed to stay calm and in control.

She ran to his side and put her arms around him. She tried to look into his face. When he moved his hands away, she saw horror there.

She'd come for news on Denise's condition. It looked like she had it.

"Oh God." Zoe breathed.

Carl shook his head.

"She's not..." he began, then stopped.

"She's not dead." The lump of solid matter that had taken up residence in Zoe's stomach felt a tiny bit lighter. "Yet."

A doctor strode past, ignoring them.

Zoe had still been on the line when the paramedics arrived. She'd heard the shock, the swearing, the unreality of it all. And these were people who dealt with this kind of thing every day.

Touch and go, she'd heard. *Anything could happen.*

"What's... How is she?" she asked.

Carl's face was blank.

"How is she?" Zoe asked again.

"Induced coma."

Two nurses walked by, one of them laughing, the other trying not to.

"What's the—"

"Major injuries to major organs. Significant blood loss. They don't know..."

Zoe took him in her arms and held him as he shook. They stayed like that for five minutes, maybe ten. She closed her eyes and tried to figure out if they could have done things differently. If they should have done things differently.

She couldn't see it.

And where was everybody, anyway? Where was Denise's family?

Zoe opened her eyes. She knew nothing about Denise Gaskill beyond her name. Her temperament, the way she pushed you away, all spiky, then relented and let you in once you'd proved yourself. Her competence in the interview room, in a debrief, in finding the angle no one else had thought of. Her bravery in everything she did.

Did she have any family? A partner? Children?

Please God, don't let her die.

"Carl." He'd stopped shaking a minute or two ago, but he wasn't moving.

He looked up. "What?"

"I need to find Stella. She's here somewhere. Minor injuries." She saw the horror come to his face. "Do you want to stay here or come with me?"

"I'll stay," he said.

CHAPTER ONE HUNDRED

LYNN FOLLOWED DI Woolley and the sarge out of the interview room, then stopped short.

They were standing in the corridor, facing each other like boxers at a weigh-in. Lynn pulled the door shut behind her. Had DI Woolley just said they should let Marc Langham go?

"No," said DS Keyes.

"I beg your pardon?" said DI Woolley.

"I said no."

DI Woolley smiled sweetly. "I told you not to arrest Marc Langham, and you ignored me. Now I'm telling you to release him. It's not a request. It's an order from a senior officer."

"And I've told you I won't be doing that. Marc Langham hasn't been arrested in connection with the assault charge. He's been arrested for murder."

"What?"

"He's been arrested legitimately, with sufficient grounds, and yes, you might be a senior officer, but I don't report to you."

"You'll need to—"

"And I haven't finished this interview," he concluded, then turned and walked back to the interview room.

DI Woolley stared after him, her mouth open.

"You coming?" he asked Lynn.

She nodded and followed him back in.

DS Keyes didn't waste any time when the interview restarted. "Mr Langham, we are in possession of the item we believe was used to strangle Kevin Downes."

He slid a sheet across the table.

"I'm producing photograph 1 of item Z3 in the list that will be made available to you on request. I'd like you to—"

"This is unacceptable," said the lawyer. "My client hasn't had sight of this."

"He's having sight of it now," said Lynn, feeling stronger.

The lawyer's brow furrowed. "No, I can't allow this to stand. I will be raising this at the very highest levels. Obviously the court. But my associates in the House of Lords will be interested to hear—"

"You're not in court now," said the sarge. "Human rights lawyer, are you?"

"Among other things," replied Bothwell-Jones.

"And you provide this sort of service to all your clients, do you? Running off to the House of Lords to complain to your friends?"

The lawyer shrugged. "To paraphrase Orwell," he said, "we all have human rights, but some of us have more human rights than others."

Lynn leaned closer to him, directing her germ-laden exhalations in his direction.

"Back to the point," said DS Keyes. "Do you recognise this?"

Marc Langham stared at the photograph.

"No." He looked like a man who'd just seen a ghost.

"We believe it's part of a saddle strap," Lynn said.

"And as your solicitor will no doubt confirm," the sarge added, "what with you being under arrest for murder and everything, we can search your property and see if this item matches any of the tack in your stables."

Marc shrugged. "I don't ride." Then smiled. "Sinead Conway does, though. Maybe you should speak to her."

"We've been trying to, Mr Langham," replied DS Keyes. "But you're the one who's here."

Marc shrugged again. "What can I say? There was a load of gear left in the stables by the previous owner. You might find a match, but it's got nothing to do with me. I've never so much as touched it. Got no interest in horses. Maybe the woman who used to own the place did it."

The sarge glanced at Lynn, who shook her head.

"The previous owner was Mrs Galloway," she said. "An octogenarian widow. I think it's unlikely."

"Maybe not her, then," Marc agreed. "Maybe the killer broke in and stole it, then used it to murder Kevin Downes."

Shit.

Lynn stared at him.

CHAPTER ONE HUNDRED ONE

STELLA WAS AWAKE. Zoe could hear her shouting from the end of the corridor and through two sets of double doors.

"Get your bloody hands off me!"

Zoe broke into a trot.

Stella sat up and argued with two nurses, a porter, and a doctor. She looked rough, but...

But that was it. She looked rough. Bandages around one hand. Her face raw. Black in places.

And she was sitting up.

"You need to stay here until you've been discharged," the doctor said.

"You're a doctor, aren't you?" Stella asked.

The woman nodded.

"Then why the hell can't you discharge me?"

"Stella." Zoe was at her side. The doctor gave her a grateful look. Zoe had seen it before, on people she'd rescued from arguments with Stella Berry. "What's the latest?"

"Apparently, I've got minor burns and a few cuts and grazes. They've had a look. There's nothing to worry about."

"That's not what I s—" the doctor began.

Stella fixed her with a glare, and she fell silent.

"I need to get to the lab, Zoe."

"No, you need to recover."

"For God's sake," Stella roared. "Not you too!"

She closed her eyes. When she opened them again, there was a fraction of a second where she looked confused, as if she didn't know where she was. Then the fire was back.

"Zoe," she said. "The gun."

"What about it?" The nurses were staring at her and Stella, their mouths hanging open.

"It's in my van. It needs to be examined. Shit!"

"What is it?" asked one of the nurses. "Are you in pain?"

"Denise," Stella said. "How... What's the latest?"

"I don't know," Zoe told her. "We're still waiting to hear."

It was almost true. They were waiting to hear. To hear how she'd recover, if she'd recover. No need to mention the rest.

Major injuries to major organs. Significant blood loss.

"The gun. It's safe. In my van. I need to analyse it."

"It's OK," Zoe told her.

"No, it's not. We need to get the bastards."

"Caroline can do it," Zoe pointed out.

"Caroline." Stella's mouth moved through the syllables slowly, as if trying them out for the first time. "Caroline." She nodded.

"Yes," said Zoe.

"I'd forgotten about Caroline," Stella admitted.

"It's all there," Zoe said. She'd taken a call from Caroline on the way over. "All the evidence that survived the explosion, including the gun, has been taken to your lab. Caroline's already looking at it."

"Caroline." Stella shook her head. "How could I forget about Caroline?"

"I think you might be in shock," a nurse said.

"I think you might be right," Stella agreed.

Stella will be OK, Zoe thought, as she headed out of the ward and towards the hospital exit. Her injuries were minor, and she was in good hands.

Denise, on the other hand... It wasn't something she could allow herself to think about.

CHAPTER ONE HUNDRED TWO

"Obviously that's possible," Aaron said. "But there were fingerprints and DNA on the murder weapon, belonging not just to the victim, but to someone else."

"To whom?" Marc asked.

Had that smile flickered?

"We don't know yet," Aaron admitted. "But you've been arrested for murder, and we've got your prints and DNA. We'll be comparing them with what we've found on the evidence. And since, as you say, you never so much as touched the tack in your stables, you won't be worried about a match, right?"

Marc turned to his lawyer. "Is that right?"

"Is what right?"

"They can do this? With my prints and DNA?"

"Yes, yes," replied Bothwell-Jones. "But I wouldn't worry about that."

"I'm not worried." There was defensiveness in Marc's voice. "Look, let's rewind a bit. When I said I'd never so much as touched it, perhaps I was exaggerating. I mean, I probably moved it, checked what was there, you know the sort of thing."

"Of course." Aaron turned to Lynn and nodded.

"I'm producing item Z5 on the evidence list." She reached down and placed a clear sealed bag on the table.

Inside was a mobile phone.

"Have you seen this phone before?" she asked.

Marc looked puzzled for a moment, then nodded. "I mean, I can't tell for sure, but I think so, yes. It belongs to my former fiancée."

"You mean Sara Miller," Aaron said.

"Your friend Sara Miller," replied Marc. "Yes. Her."

Lynn took over again. "A text was sent from this phone to the victim, arranging to meet him close to the location in which he was subsequently murdered. Sara Miller tells us she didn't send that text, and that you had her phone at the time."

"What?" Marc looked bewildered.

"Is this true, Mr—" Aaron began.

"She said what?" Marc cried.

Aaron nodded to Lynn.

"Sara Miller tells us she didn't send that text," she repeated. "And that you had her phone at the time."

"That bitch." The bewilderment had gone, replaced with a cold, hard arrogance.

"Are you denying her claims?" Lynn asked, but Marc didn't seem to be listening.

"I can't believe she'd turn against me."

"What do you mean?" Aaron asked.

"After all I did for her."

"Just to clarify," said Lynn, "are you referring to—"

"And that she'd turn against me for that piece of shit!

That waste of space! It was bad enough that she'd been sleeping with the animal, but I taught her a lesson."

"I'm sorry, Mr Langham, but can—"

"I cut the bitch out of my life. And then I cut the loser out of everyone else's. I'd have thought she'd have learned that lesson by now."

Lynn stared at Marc, mute with surprise. The lawyer's smile had a fixed quality, his eyes darting around the room as if looking for a way out.

"You 'cut the loser out of everyone else's'?" Lynn said. "Do you mind clarifying what you mean by that?"

"Fine." Marc shook his head, leaning forward, all but slumping onto the table. "You fucking people," he said. "You don't understand that some of us are simply more important than you. We contribute more. We're worth more to the world. And when you let us down..."

There was a short silence.

"Mr Langham," Aaron said. "Are you confessing to the murder of Kevin Downes?"

Langham looked down at the table for a long moment, at his own hands, then back up again.

"Sara was mine," he said. "She had no right to go near that loser. He certainly had no right to go anywhere near her."

"And you—"

"Yes," said Marc. "I killed him."

CHAPTER ONE HUNDRED THREE

AN HOUR TO GO.

Nina looked around the room. It was half past one in the morning, and the team had assembled. The boss, Tom, the sarge, back from Elterwater with an arrest, a confession, and a murder charge under his belt, Harriett Barnes, and DI Whaley.

Everyone except DS Gaskill. Denise.

Everyone except her.

And all they could do was wait.

Nina looked down at her desk, felt the grey edges of things close in, and shut her eyes.

"Anything?" said someone.

She looked up. She wasn't sure who'd spoken, but the clock on her screen showed three minutes past two. She checked her phone.

She'd fallen asleep, and no one had said a thing.

"No," someone else said. The boss. "Nothing."

At the desk opposite, Harriett Barnes looked as tired as

Nina felt. Tom sat beside Harriett, white-faced. DI Whaley looked like he'd just heard the worst news of his life.

Only the boss looked normal. More serious than usual, maybe. But not ill. Not like the rest of them.

Nina stretched, stood up, walked one lap of the team room, and sat down again. As she passed Harriett, she took another look and saw the DC wasn't tired after all.

She'd been crying.

Denise Gaskill. A colleague. Maybe a friend. Who the hell knew?

And Denise wasn't the first. Harriett had been through it in the months she'd been here. Roddy Chen, her partner. He'd nearly died, too. They'd all been through it, all come close to something terrible. But they'd had each other's backs.

Who had Harriett's back?

Nina stood up again. She walked over to Harriett and rested a hand on her shoulder. Harriett looked up questioningly.

"It'll be OK." Nina's voice cracked. "It has to be OK."

But all they could do was wait.

Wait for news from the hospital.

Wait for news from the technical services team, who were decoding the file Ryan Tobin had sent the boss. She'd shown Nina the message.

Your man Aaron's done well. Here's the emails. Jenson & Marley. The whole server.

Jenson & Marley was Carter's front company. The one that took the money he received for the women he trafficked. Its email server could be a goldmine.

Only the files were encrypted, and right now they had other things on their minds.

Waiting for news from Caroline, who was processing the

gun and what was left of the car, and would have to find something in the next twenty-three minutes.

Either that, or they'd have to let Streeting go, and it would all be for nothing.

Nina heard Harriett stifle a sob. Tom reached out to her, looking as exhausted as Nina was.

It was like... Nina tried to find something to compare it to. Not a funeral. At a funeral you had some sort of closure, you moved on, you mourned but you celebrated, too.

It was just shit. All the sombre, none of the morbid humour.

She felt her eyes fall shut again, and didn't do anything to stop them. Then, suddenly, it was five minutes later and someone had just said her name, and everyone was looking at her.

"What?" she said.

"Your phone," Tom told her.

She looked at her desk. Her phone was ringing. The caller's number clear on the screen.

Caroline Deane.

CHAPTER ONE HUNDRED FOUR

ZOE HAD NEVER SEEN Ralph Streeting look so pleased with himself.

"Can we get this over with?" Trevor Singleton said. "It's rather late."

He offered a forlorn smile. Zoe turned to Carl, who shrugged, started the recording, and kicked things off.

Ten minutes until their extension ran out, and Streeting was free.

"Where's the other one?" Streeting said. "What's Zoe Finch doing here? She's not PSD."

"We found your Jeep," Carl said.

Zoe saw the tension in him, the way he held his neck, his body. The way he held himself back from lunging across the table and throttling the man opposite him.

Then she turned to look at Streeting. His expression had changed. The smile was gone, his mouth open slightly, in shock or horror.

She hoped it was both.

"There was an accident," Carl continued.

Trevor Singleton looked up from his notes, interested.

"What happened?" Singleton asked. "Not that we accept that any vehicle you claim to have found has any connection whatsoever with my client."

"It blew up," Carl said. "We lost a lot of evidence."

The smile was back.

"I do hope no one was hurt," Streeting said.

He didn't know. He couldn't know. But he'd said those words in the voice of someone who did. Zoe saw Carl's jaw throbbing.

"There was a bomb in the Jeep," he said.

"As I've pointed out, this vehicle has no connection with my client," the lawyer said.

Carl ignored him.

"Does she even need to be here?" Streeting tilted his head towards Zoe.

She smiled at him and enjoyed the look of confusion that briefly replaced his resting sneer.

"Aren't you concerned that the bomb that destroyed your Jeep might have been intended for you?" she asked.

Streeting shrugged.

"Unlikely." He smiled again, but the smile was fixed.

The explosives experts would be looking at it, but Zoe had a good enough idea of what had happened. The buzzing noise hadn't been interference from a remote radio trigger. If it had been, then why wait until the gun was clear of the car before detonating?

The buzz had come from an altitude sensor rigged to the bomb. It had gone off because the Jeep had moved. And if Streeting had been the one moving it, he'd be in pieces right now, and Denise Gaskill would be having a good night's sleep at home.

Something Ralph Streeting was no doubt looking forward to himself.

"Anyway," Carl said, "I mentioned that we lost a lot of evidence."

"Yes," Streeting said. "Shame, that. I'd have liked some actual evidence to work with when I take over the Bobby Silver investigation again, but you lot just can't seem to hang onto anything."

"I didn't say we'd lost all the evidence," Carl continued.

"I'm sorry?"

"We managed to preserve this. I'm producing images marked Q and P, representing photographs of the item referred to as Firearm 1 in the list we'll provide in due course, and a printout from IDENT1 and NDAD, the databases for—"

"I know what they fucking are, Whaley," Streeting said.

They'd reached Zoe's line.

"In that case, DI Streeting," she said, "you won't be surprised when I tell you that as a result of the forensic analysis of this weapon, and following consultation with the Crown Prosecution Service, you are being charged in connection with the murder of Roberta Silver, known as Bobby Silver, on January the twenty-fifth of this year."

It had been a terrible day. One of the worst of Zoe's career. But the sight of Ralph Streeting looking like he'd been punched in the stomach meant at least it could end on a high.

CHAPTER ONE HUNDRED FIVE

It hadn't ended on a high. It hadn't ended at all.

Back in the team room, there'd been no inclination to celebrate, not with Denise hanging on by a thread. And no time for celebration, either, with the charge to process and the first batch of emails coming through from technical services.

Zoe had sent the team home after half an hour. They needed sleep. Whatever the future held, they'd need to be fit and awake to face it.

At home, lying on her back, staring into the dark, trying not to wake Carl, she picked up her phone.

She couldn't sleep. Not after everything. It was a wonder Carl could.

"Still awake, then?" he said.

She sighed. "Thought I'd take a look at these emails."

She checked her messages first. Still no news on Denise. Then she pulled up the file and began to go through it.

"Bloody hell," she said after less than thirty seconds.

"What is it?"

The first exchange she'd found was between Myron Carter and Dean Somerville. Zoe frowned, thought through the timings, and nodded. Ryan had left Jenson & Marley before the deal with Somerville was agreed. But it looked like the negotiations had been going on for a while.

It was nearly five in the morning, and there was no way she could go through all of this now. She scrolled quickly through the set of emails.

"Bloody hell," she said again.

Carl sat up. "Seriously. What is it?"

"Listen to this. 'I think we can agree on a price per unit.' That's Carter to Somerville. Then Somerville gives him a thumbs up. Carter goes for the hard sell. 'Romanian and Hungarian units are currently cheaper than Ukrainian and Russian, due to comparative ease of supply, but these things can change quickly. It'll make more sense for you to take what we can give you while the prices are low.'"

There was a short silence.

"He could just pretend he was talking about cars or cigarettes or something," Carl said.

"He can try. It won't fly. Not with what we know about Somerville's business. What he actually bought, in the end. I think this could be it, Carl."

"Be what?"

"Enough to bring Carter in." She lay down, smiling. Then the phone in her hand started to ring, and she answered without thinking.

"Hello?"

She heard breathing, fast, panicked, and knew whose voice she was about to hear before the woman spoke.

"They've found me," said Olivia Bagsby. "There's someone here. I don't know what to do."

Zoe sat up. "Can you see someone?"

"Yes. There's a man standing outside. By the door."

"Is there another way out?"

"No. Oh, God. He was here earlier. I saw him through the window. I thought he was just walking past. Now he's just standing there. Oh, Christ!"

The last two words came out as a moan, something filled with such fear it was barely human.

"What is it, Olivia? What's happened?" Zoe's heart raced.

"He's seen me. He's... He's moving. Right up to the door. He's saying something."

"What's he saying?"

There was a short silence.

"What?" said Olivia, but Zoe knew she wasn't talking to her.

And then she was.

"He says he knows you."

"Me?"

"He said, 'I'm a friend of DI Finch.' He says Carter's people are on to me. Oh God. He's one of them, isn't he?"

"A friend of mine?" Zoe shook her head to clear the confusion. "Put your phone on speaker. I want to hear his voice. And ask him what his name is."

She waited.

"I have DI Finch on the phone," she heard, the sound now echoing through a larger space. A hallway, she guessed. "She says to say who you are."

It had been obvious for so long. It was inevitable.

"Just like you, Olivia," the man said, "I have to live under an assumed identity these days. It wouldn't be wise for me to shout my real name out for everyone to hear."

Zoe's mouth hung open. How had David Randle found her?

"What should I do?" said Olivia.

"Let me think," Zoe told her.

Had Randle been working for Carter all along?

He'd pushed her for information about Olivia. She'd told him about Glasgow. The last time Olivia had called, there had been a seagull. A train. Zoe had told Randle about that, too.

He'd been playing her from the start.

She glanced to her side and saw Carl, sitting up too, staring at her phone.

"Is that..." he said.

She nodded. "Olivia Bagsby."

"David Randle."

So he'd heard.

"You've been talking to him," he added.

She nodded, and then Olivia started talking again, fast, frantic.

"There are cars now," she said. "Two of them just drove past, then turned and drove back again. And your friend is banging on the door. What should I do?"

No time to think it through.

"Go with him," Zoe said. "Do what he says. Keep the line open. Talk when you can."

She waited and listened and said nothing, while she heard the sound of a door opening, voices conferring quietly, urgently. More movement. Footsteps, moving fast. Running. Panting. Stopping. Another door opening, or closing.

And then an explosion.

No. Not an explosion. She'd heard the sound of an explosion earlier. This wasn't that. It was loud, sharp, but...

"Olivia?" she said.

There was no reply, just the sound of an engine starting up, moving off at speed.

"Olivia? David? What's going on?"

Silence, again. She turned to Carl and saw something like horror in his eyes.

Maybe a minute later, a voice came on the line, hoarse with pain.

"Zoe?"

"David? What's going on? What have you done to Olivia?"

"What I've done is get her out of her flat seconds before Carter's people got to her. Oh, and you're welcome."

"Let me speak to her."

"She's driving. I shouldn't let her—"

"Shut up, David."

To Zoe's immense relief, the next voice she heard was Olivia Bagsby's.

"It's true," she said. "I don't know who this man is, but he got me out. We're in his car. Heading north."

"Why are you driving?"

"Well, I can't bloody drive," Zoe heard. Randle's voice again.

"Why not?" she asked.

"Why not? Christ almighty, Zoe."

Then Olivia.

"He's been shot, Zoe. He can't drive because he's been shot."

We hope you enjoyed reading *The Wood*. The story continues in a short story, *The Pool*, which is available from book retailers or for FREE as ebook and audio from rachelmclean.com/pool.

Happy reading! Rachel and Joel.

READ A NOVELLA, THE POOL

When a group of walkers and wild swimmers finds one of their number drowned in a remote Cumbria beauty spot, it looks like little more than an unfortunate accident.

But appearances can be deceptive, and DI Zoe Finch and her team are soon sifting through the seemingly innocent lives of the dead man's family and fellow walkers, and bringing a host of buried secrets to light.

Is there a connection with a notorious local Harman? Are gambling debts involved? Or is someone not who they're pretending to be?

As the days lengthen and summer finally looms, Zoe and her team will have their work cut out finding the true and unmasking a killer.

The Pool is available from book retailers or for FREE in ebook and audio from rachelmclean.com/pool.

READ THE CUMBRIA CRIME SERIES

The Harbour

The Mine

The Cairn

The Barn

The Lake

The Wood

The Port

...and more to come

Buy from book retailers or via the Rachel McLean website.

ALSO BY RACHEL MCLEAN

The DI Zoe Finch Series – buy from book retailers or via the Rachel McLean website.

Deadly Wishes

Deadly Choices

Deadly Desires

Deadly Terror

Deadly Reprisal

Deadly Fallout

Deadly Christmas

Deadly Origins, the FREE Zoe Finch prequel

The Dorset Crime Series – buy from book retailers or via the Rachel McLean website.

The Corfe Castle Murders

The Clifftop Murders

The Island Murders

The Monument Murders

The Millionaire Murders

The Fossil Beach Murders

The Blue Pool Murders

The Lighthouse Murders

The Ghost Village Murders

The Poole Harbour Murders

The Chesil Beach Murders

...and more to com

The McBride & Tanner Series – buy from book retailers or via the Rachel McLean website.

Blood and Money

Death and Poetry

Power and Treachery

Secrets and History

The London Cosy Mystery Series by Rachel McLean and Millie Ravensworth – buy from book retailers or via the Rachel McLean website.

Death at Westminster

Death in the West End

Death at Tower Bridge

Death on the Thames

Death at St Paul's Cathedral

Death at Abbey Road

The Lyme Regis Women's Swimming Club series by Rachel McLean and Millie Ravensworth – buy from book retailers or via the Rachel McLean website.

The Lyme Regis Women's Swimming Club

A Brush with Death

The Mystery of the Runaway Reindeer

...and more to come

ALSO BY JOEL HAMES

The Sam Williams Series – Buy now in ebook, paperback and audiobook

Dead North

No One Will Hear

The Cold Years

The Art of Staying Dead

Victims, a Sam Williams novella

Caged, a Sam Williams short